In the distant backdrop, sirens wail, growing louder with each passing second. All eyes are drawn to the approaching vehicles, slowly snaking their way around the bend, their flashing lights casting an eerie glow. Curiosity seizes everyone, bringing them to an abrupt standstill.

Three police cars come to a screeching halt in front of the majestic 23-story building. The bustling activity in the grand foyer, reminiscent of a luxurious resort, suddenly fades to silence as the reception desk is manned. Detective Lam steps forward, addressing the nervous receptionist, Alina, with a sense of urgency, "Selamat Petang. I need to go to Tengku Bean's house on floor 21."

Alina's voice trembles as she responds, "Hello Sir, Sure, please turn right, and the elevators are on the left. You will require this access card, swipe it in the lift to gain access to the floor." She hands him a small white card, marked with "Pier8 Klang."

The six police officers, clad in their sombre black uniforms, radios attached to their jackets, step into the elevators. The cold and unsettling voices emanating from their microphones add to the tension. In an instant, they ascend, disappearing, heading up to Tengku Beans' penthouse apartment.

The elevator doors open, revealing a lavish interior with thick red and grey carpets underfoot. Warm white walls line the short passage, adorned with shimmering lights that cast dancing shadows. The delicate fragrance of lavender and vanilla fills the air, as the officers approach the thick walnut veneered door, brass-like handles beckoning them forward. A firm press of the doorbell announces their presence.

Awaiting them inside is Alicia, Tengku Beans' beautiful wife, radiating elegance in her sleek black pants and satin pink blouse, adorned with a grey, black, and pink scarf wrapped gracefully around her neck. Despite her apparent distress, her natural beauty shines through. A small smile graces her face as she directs Detective Lam and his team into her home.

The entrance exudes tasteful decor, reflecting Alicia's classy demeanour. As they proceed to the lounge, Tengku Beans' sons greet them, Akanji and Kyrie. Akanji, 17, and completing grade 12, and Kyrie, fifteen and in grade 10, both attend the British international school nearby. Rising to greet the detective, they extend their hands in a welcoming gesture. The air is thick with worry, and the family's distress is palpable.

Alicia reveals that Tengku Beans has been missing since the previous day, an uncharacteristic absence for him. He has not answered his phone, and his assistant, Amy, confirmed that he left the office the day before and hasn't returned.

The suspense and intrigue deepen as the mystery surrounding Tengku Beans' disappearance unfolds. As Detective Lam delves deeper into the enigma, the stakes grow higher, and the family's concerns intensify. Little do they know that the path ahead holds more twists and turns, leading them into a world of action, suspense, and danger.

Chapter 2

Three months before Tengku Bean's mysterious disappearance, the family gathered for breakfast in the lavish dining area. Tengku, the patriarch, sat at the head of the table, flanked by his loving wife, Alicia, on his right, and their spirited sons, Akanji and Kyrie, on his left. The table was a feast for the senses, adorned with an array of delectable delights - golden fried eggs, sizzling sausages, warm toast, buttery croissants, and more.

As the morning sun streamed through the windows, Akanji couldn't contain his excitement. He pleaded with his dad to allow him and his friends to embark on a thrilling weekend adventure to KLCC. Their plans included visiting the majestic Petronas Towers and indulging in a shopping spree at the Pavilion shopping centre. The anticipation of the weekend's escapades filled the air with a buoyant energy.

Tengku couldn't help but be amused by Akanji's passionate appeals. He relished in the jovial banter and laughter that filled the room as Akanji playfully tried to win his case. Lost in the joyous moment, they lost track of time until a lady cleared the table. The sudden realization that the day was already in full swing spurred everyone into action, and they rushed to gather their belongings and head out.

With Tengku bound for his office, Alicia on her way to run errands, and the boys off to school, the house quickly emptied, leaving behind a quiet hush and remnants of the morning feast.

In the sleek elevator, sweet classical music enveloped them, soothing their spirits as they descended to the parking level. Alicia gracefully glided to her Land Rover Evogue, while

Tengku and the boys settled into the luxurious comfort of the Porsche Cayenne. Their paths diverged as they reached the school, where Akanji and Kyrie were led through the gates to their educational pursuits, while Tengku continued on to his bustling office.

Tok and Beans Shipping Sdn Bhd, an empire under Tengku's helm, thrived at the renowned Port Klang, the tenth largest port in the world. Nestled on the western shores of Selangor, this bustling port had been operational since 1901, and Tengku's shipping enterprise was at its heart.

Tok and Beans boasted a thriving export business, sending fruits and vegetables to various corners of the globe - from Europe and Egypt to Turkey and Asia. With 150 dedicated staff members and a sprawling warehouse adjacent to their offices, the company's success seemed unstoppable. Tengku's vision and hard work had paved the way for a decade of exponential growth and prosperity.

Arriving at his office, Tengku was warmly greeted by Amy, the loyal and slightly over-weight receptionist. Her glasses perched at the mid-point of her nose, she exuded a pleasant charm in her navy-blue trousers, crisp white shirt, and matching jacket. "Selamat Pagi Tengku!" she exclaimed; her excitement palpable.

"Selamat Pagi, Amy," Tengku replied with a smile, settling into his high-backed black and white leather chair behind his empire-like black and white marble desk. As Amy brought his coffee and messages, she could not help but inquire about his morning.

"It was great," Tengku replied, a glimmer of joy in his eyes. "I had lots of fun with Akanji this morning."

But amidst the cheerfulness, a dark cloud loomed over Tengku's serenity. His eyes fell upon a particular message that enraged him. It was from Daniel, an old high school friend who had taken advantage of Tengku's generosity in the past. Tengku had provided funding for Daniel's business venture, only to see him squander it on a lavish lifestyle.

Now, Daniel had the audacity to demand more money, threatening dire consequences if Tengku did not comply. The crude message read, 'Hey Beans, give me what you owe me, or you will regret it!'

Tengku's gaze shifted to the view outside his office window, where the serene waters of Port Klang seemed to hold secrets of their own. The honking of ships' horns echoed like a haunting symphony, and the containers stacked high resembled imposing walls guarding untold stories.

As the shadows grew longer and uncertainty lingered in the air, little did Tengku know that the message from Daniel would be the first step into a web of intrigue and mystery that would shake the very foundations of his world. Unseen forces were at play, and the fate of Tok and Beans Shipping would hang in the balance.

Chapter 3

Tengku, seething with frustration and annoyance, decided to escape the confines of his office and head to the bustling warehouse. He strode purposefully, meeting his devoted staff with warm greetings. The bond between him and the team was undeniable; he was not just the boss but a hands-on leader. Unafraid to get his hands dirty, Tengku would skilfully operate the forklift, pack pallets, and immerse himself in the heart of the warehouse operations. His motto was clear: hard work builds character, and he practiced what he preached.

The warehouse buzzed with efficiency, and Tengku could not help but admire how Charles and Edward, the two head foremen, treated the space like their own kingdom. Loyalty was the bedrock of their relationship with Tengku, and it translated into a sense of family among all the staff members.

As Charles called out to him, Tengku knew there was something important on his mind. "Hey Boss! Do you have a moment?" Charles' voice rang out above the bustling warehouse floor.

"Sure, what's up?" responded Tengku, always attentive to his team's needs.

Charles explained, "There was this guy, Tristan, who showed up yesterday and this morning. He is looking for a job. I told him he needed to speak to you."

Considering the idea of hiring a new pair of hands, Tengku inquired, "What can he do, and do we need the extra help?"

"We can always use an extra pair of hands. Tristan seems rough around the edges but quiet. He mentioned he has been

6

out of work for six months and is desperate to support his family," Charles explained, shedding light on Tristan's situation.

"Let me meet with him tomorrow, and we'll take it from there. Did he leave a resume?" Tengku asked, knowing the importance of reviewing qualifications.

Heading back to his office, Tengku felt a sense of calm washing over him. The walk had served as a valuable respite, allowing him to gather his thoughts amidst the demanding business environment. However, his tranquillity was short-lived when he heard someone urgently shouting his name.

"Tengku, Tengku!!!!" came the loud cry, snapping him back to the present.

Turning around, Tengku saw a dishevelled man in his thirties rushing toward him. Tristan, as he introduced himself, appeared worn out, his clothing showing signs of hardship and struggles. Yet, there was an undeniable determination in his eyes.

"Hello, Tengku, my name is Tristan, and I really need a job," he stated with a mixture of anxiety and hope.

Recognizing the name from earlier conversations, Tengku replied, "Oh, hello, Tristan. I heard about you just a few minutes ago."

Tristan seemed anxious, and Tengku wanted to put him at ease. "Follow me, I'm headed to the office, and I'll take a look at your resume," he offered, leading the way.

Inside the office, Tristan's nerves were evident, but Tengku's warm and welcoming demeanour helped ease the tension.

"Amy, Charles handed you a resume. May I have it for Tristan? Bring it to my office," Tengku requested politely.

"Sure thing, boss," Amy replied, bringing the resume promptly.

Reviewing the document, Tengku learned about Tristan's job loss six months ago due to a struggling shipping company at Port Dickson. The man had a family to support, and his desperation was palpable.

Touched by his story, Tengku believed in the power of second chances. With a genuine smile, he extended his hand to Tristan and declared, "Well, today is your lucky day, Tristan. You are hired. We will review your performance in two weeks and see how it's going. In the meantime, welcome to Tok and Beans Shipping. Welcome to our family."

Tristan's eyes lit up with gratitude and excitement. Eager to make a fresh start, he hurriedly made his way to the warehouse, ready to embrace his new opportunity.

Upon meeting Charles, Tristan opened up about his hobbies, sharing the poignant connection he felt with his late father through fishing. Charles playfully suggested they go fishing together someday, evoking laughter as they continued their walk through the bustling warehouse. The spirit of camaraderie was alive, and new beginnings were on the horizon.

Chapter 4

As the weekend dawned, Akanji could barely contain his excitement, eagerly anticipating the thrilling adventure he had planned with his friends. He carefully packed his bag, ensuring he had everything needed for their escapades. They had ambitious plans to explore KLCC, visit the majestic Petronas Towers, and indulge in a shopping spree at the luxurious Pavilion shopping centre. The anticipation of their weekend extravaganza filled the air with a contagious energy, setting the stage for unforgettable memories.

With Akanji away for the weekend, Kyrie saw the perfect opportunity to spend quality time with his buddies. They had one mission in mind - to watch the highly anticipated Fortnite event together. The thrill of competitive gaming, the camaraderie among friends, and the joy of being fully immersed in their shared passion made this weekend a special one for Kyrie and his pals.

Meanwhile, Alicia saw the empty nest as a chance to immerse herself in her true passion - interior designing and decorating. Her home office was her creative sanctuary, drenched in the warm embrace of sunlight. The vibrant rays seemed to infuse her with a creative edge, igniting a spark of inspiration. Alicia's talent for transforming dull spaces into exquisite works of art had earned her admiration among friends and family. What started as a mere hobby soon blossomed into a sought-after service, and she found herself being approached by people eager to have her unique touch grace their personal spaces.

As she sipped her cup of coffee, the world outside her window came alive. She watched people bustling about, each with their own dreams, aspirations, and challenges. The sights and sounds of life unfolding before her eyes fuelled her sense of gratitude for the beautiful life she had built with her family.

Alicia and Tengku Beans shared a love story that was both unexpected and enchanting. It all began with a serendipitous encounter in the Gardens by the Bay in Singapore. A simple coffee-spilling incident led to a conversation that felt like destiny had intervened. From that moment, their lives became intertwined, and they journeyed through life's ups and downs together, hand in hand.

As her phone rang, Alicia was pulled back from her reverie, greeted by her husband's warm voice. Tengku suggested going out for a delightful seafood meal to celebrate their weekend together. Alicia's heart swelled with love for her husband, and she eagerly agreed to meet him in an hour.

The View Seafood Terrace, nestled on the waterfront, provided a perfect setting for their romantic dinner. They dined with a breathtaking view of fishing boats and fishermen, as the ocean breeze enveloped them in its salty embrace. They indulged in grilled king-size prawns, golden fried chips, and spicy rice, accompanied by refreshing virgin mojitos. Each moment was a celebration of their love, their journey, and the joy of simply being together.

Indeed, it was a weekend filled with adventures, cherished friendships, and the pursuit of passions. Each family member had found their own slice of happiness, creating a beautiful tapestry of love, unity, and contentment.

Little did they know that the calm and joy they were experiencing would soon be disrupted by unforeseen events that would challenge their very foundations. Unseen forces were at play, and a storm was brewing on the horizon, threatening to shatter the tranquillity they held so dear. As the weekend came to a close, a sense of suspense hung in the air, foreshadowing the uncertain path that lay ahead for the Beans family.

Chapter 5

As the days passed, Tristan's excitement grew, fuelled by the success of his cunning plan. He relished the feeling of being a step ahead, even if it meant playing a dangerous game. This job, he thought, would be the gateway to his ultimate goal - the riches and power he had always dreamed of.

Late at night, he carefully strategized the next steps in his operation. His connection with Sadiki in Egypt was crucial, and he knew that any slip-up could lead to catastrophic consequences. With a deep sense of determination, he made contact with Sadiki, reassuring him that everything was set for the first small shipment.

Tristan devised a routine to cover his tracks. He frequented the remote fishing area near Port Klang, befriending the local fishermen to blend in and divert any suspicions. He wanted to be invisible to anyone who might wonder about his true intentions.

The crucial day arrived, and as darkness fell, Tristan seized the opportunity. He skilfully sneaked into the warehouse through the unguarded emergency door. The semi-automatic rifles were strategically packed beneath a shipment of bananas, a perfect cover for their illicit journey. He felt an adrenaline rush, a sense of satisfaction, as he completed the mission, knowing he had outsmarted everyone around him.

In the shadows of the bustling Port Authority, there was a man named Sam, a figure often overlooked in the midst of the busy harbour operations. He was an unassuming character, with a thinning hairline and a weary expression etched onto his face. What set him apart was not his appearance, but rather the heavy burden he carried on his shoulders - the health of his gravely ill wife.

Sam's life had taken a cruel twist when his wife's health deteriorated rapidly. Medical bills piled up, and despite his best efforts, the mounting expenses drained him of every last cent. He was a man cornered by fate; his desperation palpable in every action he took.

It was during this bleak time that he crossed paths with Tristan, a man who could smell vulnerability from a mile away. Tristan recognized Sam's vulnerability, the profound need for cash to provide for his ailing wife. And he capitalized on it, ruthlessly exploiting Sam's desperate situation to further his own illicit agenda.

Sam became Tristan's puppet, dancing to the tune of extortion and coercion. Whatever Tristan demanded, Sam carried out without hesitation, driven by the haunting fear of losing his wife, the love of his life, to a merciless illness.

Back at his apartment, he sent the coded message to Sadiki, indicating the imminent arrival of the shipment, and received the thumbs-up response. The plan was in motion, and Tristan's ambition seemed to know no bounds.

However, amidst the excitement, an unexpected encounter shook him to the core. In the port parking lot, he witnessed a heated confrontation between Tengku, and an unfamiliar face named Daniel. Tristan was unaware that Tengku knew Daniel from high school, a man driven by envy and greed. Fear and anxiety washed over him as he realized that Daniel's presence here was no coincidence.

Daniel's threats were escalating, and Tristan knew he had to act quickly to protect his elaborate scheme. He had to ensure that his carefully laid-out plan wouldn't unravel before he could claim his prize. With his heart pounding, Tristan wondered how much he was willing to risk achieving his dreams. The stakes were higher than ever, and his every move had to be precise. The fate of his future hung in the balance, and he was about to play a dangerous game of survival.

In the shadows of the night, the clock was ticking, and the suspense in the air was palpable. What would Tristan do next to secure his ambitions and survive the dangerous web he had woven? The answer would determine the course of his life and the lives of those entangled in his web of deceit.

Chapter 6

Two days had passed since the successful dry run, and Sadiki's message confirmed that the Long Greens were on their way. Excitement and tension filled the air as Tristan prepared for the next shipment of illicit weapons. He managed to procure an even larger arsenal of firearms, including semi-automatic rifles, multi-barrelled pistols, and fully automatic machine pistols. During the evenings, under the shroud of darkness, he would sneak back into the warehouse to securely pack the deadly cargo, sending the shipment numbers to both Sadiki and Sam without raising suspicion.

Despite his devious activities, Tristan kept up appearances during the day, maintaining the facade of a struggling family man. His upcoming two-week review had him on edge; he needed to keep his job to ensure the plan's success. Charles informed him that the review was set for that afternoon, and Tristan nervously headed to Tengku's office at the appointed time.

With humility, Tristan greeted Tengku, assuring him that he was enjoying his work and was grateful for the opportunity. The review went smoothly, and Tengku expressed his gratitude for Tristan's assistance during the altercation with Daniel. The job was secured, and Tristan felt relieved to be part of the Tok and Beans Family.

As the day came to a close, the warehouse staff found themselves engulfed in a sudden and fierce storm. Heavy rain lashed down, delaying their departure. Tristan's agitation grew as he worried about making his evening weapons run. He concocted a story about his wife being unwell to mask his true intentions, and the others understood his need to leave early.

Finally, the storm subsided, and everyone rushed to their cars. Tristan stayed behind, eager to pack the weapons for the next day's shipment. Unbeknownst to him, he was not alone. Jack, curious about the noise he heard, stayed back to investigate. He saw a shadowy figure repacking boxes but could not discern the man's face due to the dim lighting. Suspicion arose in Jack's mind, and he decided to keep his discovery to himself until he had solid evidence.

As Tristan was about to leave, he heard the front warehouse doors lock, making him uncertain if his presence had been detected. The air was thick with intrigue, and the events that unfolded next would plunge everyone into a web of secrecy, deceit, and danger, leaving no one unscathed. Little did they know that their lives were about to take an unexpected and treacherous turn, one that would test their loyalty, courage, and integrity in ways they could never have imagined.

As Tristan drove away from the warehouse, he couldn't shake the feeling that he was being watched. His heart pounded in his chest as he tried to dismiss the thought, attributing it to his nerves and the eerie atmosphere of the stormy night. Little did he know that Jack had seen more than just shadows in the warehouse. Jack's instincts told him that something was off, and he was determined to uncover the truth. The next day, as the sun rose over the city, a series of events would set off a chain reaction that would lead them all down a perilous path, and the lines between right and wrong would blur beyond recognition. The secrets hidden within the walls of the warehouse were about to unravel, revealing a tangled web of betrayal and deceit that would keep everyone entangled in suspense, wondering who could be trusted and who would be left swimming exposed when the tide had dissipated.

Chapter 7

As the sun set over Port Klang, casting long shadows across the shipping yard, a sense of foreboding settled over the area. Tristan couldn't shake the feeling that he was being watched as he left the warehouse, his heart pounding in his chest. The weight of his illicit actions bore heavily on his conscience as he drove away, the darkness of the night amplifying his anxiety.

Back at the Beans' residence, Alicia noticed Tengku's troubled expression. Her intuition told her that something was amiss, and she gently asked, "Tengku, is everything alright?"

Tengku hesitated for a moment, then decided to confide in Alicia. He shared the message from Daniel and the growing suspicion that something nefarious might be happening in their shipping business. Alicia listened attentively, her concern growing as she realized the potential danger their family might be facing.

"We need to get to the bottom of this, Tengku. We'll face it together," Alicia assured him, her voice filled with determination.

Tengku nodded, grateful for Alicia's unwavering support. With her by his side, he felt stronger, ready to confront the ominous forces that seemed to be closing in around them.

Unbeknownst to Tristan, Jack, the sharp-eyed warehouse worker, had indeed seen a mysterious figure late at night, repacking boxes with an air of secrecy. Jack's curiosity was piqued, and he knew he had to find out more. The next day, he decided to discreetly investigate further, determined to uncover the truth behind the enigmatic presence he had observed.

As the stormy night wore on, Tengku couldn't shake the nagging feeling that something was amiss. He meticulously went over financial records, searching for any clues that might shed light on the threatening message from Daniel.

Meanwhile, the ominous clouds above mirrored the growing uncertainty that loomed over the Beans family. Each member felt the gravity of the situation, and they knew that they needed to be cautious and united in their efforts to uncover the truth.

Tristan, on the other hand, felt the walls closing in around him. The thrill of his illegal activities was fading, replaced by the fear of being caught. He knew that he had to act swiftly and carefully to protect himself and those he cared about.

The stage was set for a high-stakes game of cat and mouse, where secrets and lies intertwined, and danger lurked around every corner. The Beans family found themselves entangled in a web of intrigue, unsure of who they could trust.

As night fell, the city's secrets came alive, and the fate of Tok and Beans Shipping Sdn Bhd hung in the balance. With each passing moment, the mystery deepened, and the suspense grew, leaving the Beans family to grapple with the unknown and the looming threat that was closing in on them.

And so, the night held its secrets, and the Beans family braced themselves for the challenges that lay ahead. Little did they know that the path they were about to embark on would test their bonds, challenge their courage, and lead them to revelations that could shatter their world. As the darkness enveloped the city, Jack's watchful eyes remained vigilant, ready to uncover the truth lurking in the shadows.

Chapter 8

The morning sun streamed through the curtains as Tengku rose from a restless night's sleep, his mind still preoccupied with the events of the previous day. Alicia greeted him in the kitchen with a gentle kiss on the forehead, noticing the fatigue in his eyes. Concerned for her husband, she suggested that he meet with Daniel to resolve the issue and put an end to his anger. Tengku appreciated the advice, realizing that a face-to-face conversation might be the best way to resolve things. Without delay, he messaged Daniel to meet for a coffee at the waterfront coffee shop.

An hour later, Daniel arrived, and as they sat facing each other, Tengku listened intently to Daniel's plea. He learned of Daniel's financial struggles and his desire to start a business to secure a steady income. Empathy washed over Tengku as he understood the root of Daniel's anger. In a moment of generosity, Tengku offered not only his assistance with the company but also a small loan. However, to ensure the money was used wisely, he proposed setting up the business in a trust. Although Daniel was initially reluctant, he realized this was the chance he needed to turn his life around.

With their agreement in place, Tengku and Daniel planned to meet at the lawyer's office within two days to finalize the necessary documents. Tengku felt a sense of relief that things were heading in the right direction with Daniel. Daniel also felt a sense of excitement as he was about to embark on his newfound opportunity.

Meanwhile, back at the warehouse, Jack couldn't shake the memory of the figure he had seen the previous night. His instincts told him that the warehouse held secrets that could unravel the very fabric of Tok and Beans Shipping Sdn Bhd. He discreetly questioned the workers, trying to gather any information that might lead to an answer. Hours passed without any significant leads, and Jack began to wonder if he had imagined the whole thing. However, he couldn't let go of the nagging feeling that something was amiss.

Tristan, on the other hand, was wary of Jack's presence and recent inquiries. When he bumped into Jack in the warehouse canteen, he felt a hint of suspicion in Jack's eyes. Quickly fabricating a story about receiving a distressing message that left him in a foul mood, Tristan hoped to distract Jack from any further probing. But deep down, he knew he needed to be cautious.

As the day unfolded, Tengku shared the positive outcome of his meeting with Daniel, bringing a sense of relief to both him and Alicia. Their spirits lifted, and they felt the burden of the past few days starting to ease.

In the evening, Tristan made an effort to approach Jack and apologize for his earlier behaviour, attributing it to a personal matter that had left him on edge. Jack accepted the apology, but the doubt still lingered in his mind.

As the night settled, a sense of calm washed over everyone. Tengku and Alicia found comfort in each other's presence, hoping that this newfound peace would last. Little did they know that amidst the tranquil facade, secrets and mysteries were beginning to intertwine, setting the stage for what would unfold in the days to come. The warehouse held secrets of its own, as did the bustling port of Klang. Unseen forces were at play, and a chain of events had been set in motion. Deep within the heart of the port, a clandestine network operated in the shadows, unbeknownst to Tengku and his family. Smuggling operations, arms deals, and treacherous alliances were concealed behind the veneer of legitimate businesses.

As the days passed, Tengku's shipping empire continued to thrive, seemingly untouched by the underbelly of illicit activities. But destiny had a way of weaving intricate patterns, bringing together lives that were seemingly disconnected.

Chapter 9

Daniel and Tengku met at Jason Chow and Associates law offices. They were ready to complete all the necessary legal documents. Things started working out for Daniel, and his focus on getting his business going was his focal point. Tengku felt a sense of relief that things were finally settling down. After the documents were signed, Daniel felt calmness engulfing him and his excitement was tangible.

At the warehouse, Jack had planned to leave last so he could put his suspicions to rest. He went on with his day as normal, and as closing time approached, the staff started leaving one-by-one to head home or enjoy their evening plans. Jack hid in the little maintenance room where all the cleaning supplies were stored. The room was crowded, and the smell of bleach and detergents made his eyes burn, but he waited patiently. As the warehouse fell into silence, he felt safe to exit the room and investigate. The darkness crept in, and the only light was from the dim lampposts outside, casting eerie shadows on the warehouse floor. The once-familiar space now seemed unfamiliar and unknown to Jack.

The waiting continued, and just as Jack was about to give up, he heard noises outside the warehouse. Startled, his heart pounded in his chest, deafening his ears. Doubts crept in as he wondered if this investigation was worth it. But he knew he had no choice but to continue. Peering through a small crack in the boxes, he hid, hoping to remain invisible to the intruder he anticipated. Tick tock, tick tock, time continued, but no one entered.

Suddenly, the door creaked open, and a figure cautiously stepped inside. Jack strained to see who it was, but the dim light obscured their face. As he moved closer to get a better look, he accidentally knocked over some empty boxes, startling the intruder, who quickly fled the scene. Jack watched them disappear into the night, leaving him with more questions than answers.

Determined to uncover the truth, Jack decided to create a diversion. He knew there were stray cats in the area, so he grabbed one and left it in the warehouse. This would make the intruder think that the noise was caused by a wandering feline. Jack planned to return for further investigation. Hoping that this diversion would work and ensure that the intruder was none the wiser.

Meanwhile, Tristan arrived at his apartment, still uneasy about the night's events. He messaged Sadiki, explaining that the shipment wasn't completed and that he would have to delay it by a day. Worried about Sadiki's reaction, Tristan hoped he could calm the client down and ensure the next shipment went smoothly. Sadiki was not too happy with the shipment being delayed. He cautioned Tristan about another delay, and this did not bode well for their relationship if delays continued. But deep down, he couldn't shake the feeling that someone was onto him.

As the night wore on, each character was left with their thoughts and suspicions, all unknowingly connected by the threads of intrigue that were slowly pulling them closer together. The enigmatic puzzle they found themselves entangled in was far from being solved, and the next chapter of this investigation was about to be exposed. With time and patience, the truth was close.

Chapter 10

As the early Friday morning sunlight streamed into their home, casting a warm glow on the walls, the Bean family buzzed with anticipation and excitement. The past week had been relentless, filled with the lingering stress of their recent trials and tribulations. Tengku, ever the family man, sensed the toll it had taken on them all.

Sitting down with Alicia, he gently suggested, "You know, my love, I think we could all use a little break. A weekend getaway as a family, perhaps? It might just be what we need to recharge our spirits."

Alicia's eyes lit up with enthusiasm at his proposal. It was as if he had read her mind. The idea was a breath of fresh air, a glimmer of hope amid the chaos of their recent experiences. Instantly, their home filled with an electric energy, as the prospect of the upcoming adventure became a topic of joyful conversation, their spirits lifted by the mere thought of it.

Tengku's suggestion was like a spark that ignited their enthusiasm. "Why not head to KLCC, Kuala Lumpur City Centre, for the weekend?" he proposed with a grin. The idea of exploring the bustling heart of Kuala Lumpur was met with unanimous approval. The promise of exciting city adventures brought an even more vibrant energy to their preparations.

After making the necessary arrangements, including letting the staff off for the weekend and making reservations at the luxurious Four Seasons Hotel, they were ready to hit the road. With the Porsche Cayenne packed and spirits high, the Bean family embarked on their journey to KLCC. The drive took about an hour and a half, but they were not deterred. The prospect of exploring the vibrant city kept their energy levels up.

They arrived at the Four Seasons Hotel which is adjacent to the Majestic Petronas Twin Towers. The car pulled up in front of the entrance and the attentive staff were ready to welcome the Bean family to the hotel. They were ushered into the foyer of this beautifully decorated hotel. The perfumed scented foyer was reminiscent of a vacation on a luxury island. They checked into the three-bedroom suite and without wasting time, they headed out again. They had not eaten all morning and by this time they were extremely excited to head to one of the amazing eateries in KL.

Traffic in the city was always outrageous so they opted to walk or take public transport. It was the most efficient way getting around the city. Being close to the Towers, they decided to eat at Suria shopping mall. The mall in interlinked with the Towers and there was a massive array of different foods to choose from. BBQ nights had just opened up and the fragrance of their food made them salivate. They chose to have beef kebabs, with chicken tikka, grilled fish and some naan and rice. They loved spicy food, and this hit the mark.

After completing the meal, they decided that it would be fun to go to the indoor theme park. The Theme Park was in the heart of the bustling Bukit Bintang. This time they chose to take the monorail from where they were to Berjaya Time Square. The monorail stopped at the mall, so they walked in immediately and headed to the Indoor Theme Park. The family enjoyed the rides, but the rollercoaster was their favourite. The laughter and the noise from the rides were exhilarating. When they completed all the rides the Bean family decided to walk around a bit. They wanted to see the progress of the magnificent Merdeka Tower. The second tallest building in the world. This skyscraper was seen from all over the city. It was built with the design of the Prime Minister raising his arm in the air for Malaysia's independence. The accuracy was truly captured in his stunning building. Tengku asked his family if it would be okay with his family if he visited his brother at Tun Razak Exchange, better known as TRX or Exchange 106. The 106 was to state how many floors were in the building. This was the financial hub in Kuala Lumpur. The family were happy about that because they knew they could head to their favourite sushi restaurant after the visit. They hailed a grab and were on their way to TRX. A few minutes later they arrived and as they stepped out of the grab they were welcomed by this financial metropolis. The buildings looked like something out of a futuristic movie. Money exuded through this area. Tengku was on the phone with his brother, who decided to meet them downstairs and take them up to his office. Tengku Farhan was into investment portfolios. His office was in the main building of TRX. A moment later, he walked towards the family. Tengku Han was a splitting image of his brother. He was eleven months younger than Beans, but they could have passed as twins. People would get confused between the two brothers.

After a warm embrace, they were on their way to the office that was located on sixty second floor. The views from the office were so amazing. You could see as far as Genting Highlands and Batu caves from that height. While the adults were catching up, Akanji and Kyrie were taking selfies at every angle they could find. Shortly after the visit the family headed to the station which was below TRX main building. The station was also spectacular and extremely classy. The train was just one stop away from their favourite sushi restaurant that was located at MyTown mall. They arrived at the mall where more locals than tourists visited and sat at Sushi Jiro. Before long, the sushi plates were stacked up as if it were a miniature version of the twin towers. By this time evening set in and they felt a bit tired from their day. They grabbed a cab and went back to the hotel. They all showered and rested for a bit. Alicia was excited to see the symphony of light at KLCC park. The boys were not in the mood, so Tengku and Alicia took a romantic stroll to the park. They arrived a few minutes before the show. The show was on the lake with the water dancing to the sound of music and lights. The place was filled with people admiring this vision and the arena filled with others videoing and taking pictures of this beauty This is what they needed to recharge their batteries and bond as a family.

The next day, they went for breakfast to the hotel's restaurant and enjoyed some traditional food such as roti Canai, nasi lemak and nasi goreng. While eating they were deciding what they wanted to do for the day, looked like the boys won on this one and they were going to Sunway Lagoon. This time they took their own car as it was a bit of a distance from the hotel. Sunway Lagoon was a full day of excitement in the sun and the water was simply perfect. As late afternoon set in, they left the waterpark and got a meal at Sunway Pyramid that is adjacent to Sunway Lagoon. As evening came in, they headed back to the hotel. Knowing this was the last evening at KLCC, they didn't want to miss out, so they went to Bukit Bintang. Extremely crowded with people moving back and forth, live music filling the streets with fun, and enjoyment and cars stuck in traffic. They headed to the Pavilion Shopping Centre, or rather known as Pavi as locals would say, and did a bit of shopping.

As the weekend came to an end, the Bean family checked out of the hotel, cherishing the memories they created together. The drive back home was filled with reflection and contentment. Home, their little haven, awaited them with warmth and comfort.

The weekend had been an absolute delight, and the family felt recharged and bonded. As they settled back into their routine, they knew that the memories of their KLCC adventure would stay with them forever, reminding them of the love and joy they shared as a family. Little did they know that more thrilling and unexpected experiences were yet to come, waiting just around the corner.

Chapter 11

Sitting on his fishing boat, Tristan knew that he had to start thinking of ways to close the loop of being caught with his illicit arms. Still unaware of who the person was that suspected him, he had to come up with a plan to push the evidence over to someone else. He sat there thinking of who the perfect candidate could be and would have the mind to pull this off. His arrogance made him feel a lot superior to others, and he believed that no one could execute the plan with the precision he could. Pride and entitlement consumed him, blinding him to the dangers that lay ahead.

After a while of contemplating, he thought that the only person he could come up with was Daniel. Daniel seemed to have some beef with Tengku, and the confrontation in front of the warehouse could corroborate the fact that he was out to get Tengku. This was the right person to take the fall. Daniel's impulsive nature and temper clouded his judgment, making him an ideal candidate for Tristan's scheme. All he needed was to get familiar with Daniel and plant some evidence on him to make it appear as if Daniel was behind the illicit activities.

Excited that he came up with a solution, Tristan knew that it was only a temporary fix because he still needed to smuggle his weapons. This job was his only way to move the product out undetected, and he couldn't afford to slip up. He knew he had to find out who suspected him and discredit the snitch before they had the chance to expose the secrets of that fateful night.

Tristan knew that the evening was going to be busy as he had to make sure the next shipment was ready and had to go off without a hitch. Sadiki's ominous words still echoed in his mind, reminding him of the dangerous game he was playing. Headed back to the shore, he prepared himself for his evening rendezvous at the warehouse. He scanned the surroundings, cautious of any potential threats, before proceeding inside to deal with the shipment.

With adrenaline pumping through his veins and the rush of fear and excitement, he completed his task quickly and hurried out as discreetly as he could. Sadiki received the message, and Tristan breathed a sigh of relief, knowing that the operation was back on track.

The evening was still young, and Tristan decided to do some reconnaissance on Daniel. He wanted to get more familiar with his nemesis. He discovered that Tengku and Daniel went to school together and were once close during their university years. However, information was scarce on the internet, so he knew he had to be more creative and dig deeper through alternative methods. He was determined to find out what had caused the tension between them, unaware that Daniel and Tengku had already called a truce and their friendship was on the mend. This new mission became his obsession, and he couldn't rest until he uncovered the truth.

Tristan, so consumed by his plotting and deceit, did not realize that he hadn't eaten all day, and his stomach was now growling with hunger. He decided to grab something to eat and headed to Coconut Flower Restaurant, a few minutes' walk away from his place. He ordered himself a Seafood Tom Yam soup and a tea, finding solace in the quiet ambiance of the restaurant. For Tristan, being around too many people was bothersome, and he preferred solitude. He disliked being questioned and felt that people needed to mind their own business. His life was a labyrinth of mystery and secrets, and he was determined to keep it that way. Little did he know that as he delved deeper into his schemes, he was inching closer to the edge of the abyss that could swallow him whole.

Chapter 12

As Tristan delved deeper into his plan to frame Daniel for his illicit activities, an insatiable obsession consumed him. His thirst for information about Tengku's old friend turned foe, Daniel, grew stronger with each passing day. Operating in the shadows, Tristan discreetly asked around, seeking any fragment of Daniel's past, motives, or connections that could serve his sinister agenda.

Unbeknownst to Tristan, his furtive inquiries attracted the attention of an unexpected observer. A mysterious figure lurked in the shadows, diligently following Tristan's every move. This enigmatic presence added an intriguing layer of complexity to the unfolding narrative, leaving readers on the edge of their seats, pondering who this unknown person might be and what their intentions were.

As Tristan ventured further into his web of deception, he failed to realize the danger of his actions. The evidence he planned to plant on Daniel may not be as foolproof as he presumed, and he might be steering himself toward a perilous trap.

The enigmatic stalker, ever watchful, left cryptic clues and messages in Tristan's path, heightening his paranoia and suspicion. Anonymous warnings reached Tristan, unsettling him with the knowledge that someone was keenly observing his every move. Distrust grew within him, casting a shadow over his interactions with others, leaving him uncertain about whom he could trust.

Tristan's carefully constructed plans began to unravel under the pressure of his newfound adversary. With each step he took, the mysterious figure seemed to anticipate his moves, deepening Tristan's sense of vulnerability. An unnerving connection between this enigmatic presence and his past started to haunt him, adding to the complexity of the unfolding events.

Amidst the chaos, Tristan found himself confronting not only external threats but his own inner demons. Long-buried secrets from his troubled past resurfaced, forcing him to confront the repercussions of his choices. It became apparent that he could not outrun the consequences of his actions forever, and the decisions he made in the present would determine his fate.

Unexpectedly, Tristan's troubled past came back to haunt him when an ex-co-worker, Choi, surfaced after being laid off from his previous employment. Choi possessed information that could expose Tristan's dark secrets, leaving him no choice but to let Choi in on his dangerous dealings.

That evening, when a loud thump echoed at his door, Tristan's heart raced with fear. As he cautiously peered through the peephole, he was taken aback to find Choi, a face from the past, staring back at him. Tristan couldn't shake the eerie feeling that Choi knew more than he let on, as if he had a way of seeing through the door.

Reluctantly, Tristan invited Choi in, and they sat down at the dining table, the air tense with an air of authority emanating from Choi. He had a proposition for Tristan - he wanted in on whatever secretive dealings Tristan was involved in, and he wasn't taking no for an answer.

Seeing an opportunity to use Choi to his advantage, Tristan deviously agreed to a tentative partnership. He would have Choi tail Daniel, gathering information and reporting back to him daily. In return, Tristan would reward Choi with cash for any valuable intel he uncovered.

With this new arrangement in place, Tristan began to feel a glimmer of hope. He could now concentrate on more pressing matters, reassured that Choi's presence might prove beneficial. But little did he know that this pact would only add another layer of unpredictability to his already perilous world, leaving him to question whether Choi could be trusted or if he was just another pawn in this dangerous game.

As the stakes grew higher and the web of deceit tightened, Tristan found himself teetering on the precipice of a treacherous abyss, unsure of who was friend or foe, and the clock was ticking relentlessly towards a dramatic climax.

Chapter 13

The new day had dawned and Choi, who had no other place to stay, spent the night at Tristan's apartment. He came looking for Tristan without a plan or focus. He needed a payout and that was the easiest way. Choi left rather early as he wanted to get a head start on Daniels life and routine. Daniel resided at Maple Residence which was a classy and very modern condominium. The security was very tight so Choi could not enter without notifying the person you needed to visit.

Choi stood across the road and waited to see when Daniel was ready to leave. He had an excellent view of the pedestrian walkway as well as the car park. This ensured that he would not miss the chance to follow him. About an hour later, he sees a Mercedes C class, leaving and Daniel is driving, he was headed towards the waterfront.

Daniel had opened his Real Estate business at the waterfront. He felt that the beauty of the waterfront would attract the right kind of clientele he was after. The commission he would earn on high-end Apartments and homes were greater in a place that attracted people with lots of money.

Before heading to his office, he stopped by the coffee shop on the corner of the building. They made an excellent cappuccino and salmon and creamed cheese bagels. He took the snacks to his office so that his staff as well as him could enjoy while catching up on what was happening within the business and the updates on what was on the market and who was brokering which sale. Daniel had employed four staff members, all of them were commission earners so they were hungry for business. In a short space of time, he managed to get settled in the new offices and have staff working for him. He also had many properties in his portfolio. Daniel was grateful for the opportunity he had, and he was enjoying his new venture.

The entire day was spent in the office with people going in and out of his offices. As the day drew to a close, the staff started to leave one-by-one. Daniel was the last to leave. He locked up and headed towards the brightly lit waterfront where music played at every corner. The tantalizing fragrances of grilled meats and seafood filled the air. People crowding the area and deciding where they wanted to spend the next few hours of their evening. Laughter and talking through the walkways made the evening welcoming. The warmth of the night was what drew people out to get together and socialize. Daniel was spoilt for choice as to what to consume. Malaysia was well known for the different western and local foods. Malaysian people loved their food and Daniel was definitely no exception.

He settled for a delicious well done wagyu beef fillet and a baked potato with creamed cheese and corn. The portions were rather large and bode a challenge to complete. He washed it down with a caramel and toffee infused bubble tea. He was so stuffed that he did not feel like getting up to leave as yet so he sat there and scrolled through his social media accounts to see what was interesting.

A short while later, he paid the bill and proceeded to his car. Leaving into the direction of his home, and within 15 minutes he pulled into the parking garage and was not seen for the rest of the evening.

Choi followed him all day and found that Daniel had no excitement in his life. He nonetheless continued this for the week. He had a feeling that Tristan may have put him on this so Choi would not find out more about the smuggling business. Although this was so boring, Choi still reported back to Tristan about Daniels day. For Tristan this was still good news because if he needed to do plant evidence or create a diversion, the dreadful boring routine of Daniels would work.

For Daniel, this lifestyle was working. He was happy with being in this mundane pattern as it gave him time to reflect on what he did wrong previously and his determination to be successful on his own terms is what drove him. Tengku being empathetic to him and giving him that second chance helped him and gave him a sense of security. He did not want to squander this amazing opportunity. He wanted to prove to all but mainly to himself that could be make it and earn his place in society as an independent businessman.

Chapter 14

Tengku had been engrossed in his day at the office. The pace was relentless, with new clients pouring in and the business expanding rapidly. It was a whirlwind of documents and contracts, but he relished every moment. The sheer intensity of it all made him feel like he was truly accomplishing something remarkable.

A knock at his office door broke his concentration. Amy, his loyal secretary, stood there amidst the organized chaos of his workspace. "Tengku, Charles needs to speak with you at the warehouse," she informed him with a sense of urgency.

Tengku, always hands-on with his operations, wasn't taken aback by the request. Trips to the warehouse were not uncommon, usually to ensure everything ran smoothly. After a few hours glued to his desk, he saw this as an opportunity to stretch his legs and take a well-deserved break. Determined to see what needed attention, he decided to head down to the warehouse.

Charles sat in his compact office, diligently attending to the pile of delivery documents and port clearances scattered across his desk. When Tengku Beans approached, he rapped lightly on the door before entering. Charles greeted his boss with an eager smile and gestured for him to take a seat. They exchanged a firm handshake before settling down.

As Tengku stepped into Charles' office, an air of tension enveloped them. Their conversation quickly delved into serious matters, with both of them scrutinizing a multitude of documents and delving deep into discussions regarding the intricacies of their operations.

As Tristan stealthily passed by the office, he couldn't help but notice the impromptu meeting taking place inside. In his mind, the walls were closing in, and the grim expressions on Tengku and Charles's faces made it abundantly clear that something was amiss within Tengku's business empire.

Their heads turned slightly, reacting to the sound of approaching footsteps, but it wasn't their coffee arriving as they expected. Instead, their eyes seemed to lock onto Tristan for a moment, sending a shiver down his spine. Quickly, they returned to their conversation, but Tristan couldn't shake the feeling that they were discussing him and his clandestine activities. He loitered nearby, eavesdropping in a desperate attempt to gather more information, preparing himself for the impending storm.

Charles and Tengku pored over an avalanche of documents strewn across the desk, their expressions growing tenser by the second. In Tristan's mind, a tightening noose symbolized his predicament, and his heart pounded so loudly that it drowned out the ambient noise.

Then, finally, the office door swung open, and Tristan strained to hear Charles utter the words that confirmed his worst fears - Tengku and Charles were heading to the Port Authority at 4 PM. For Tristan, this was the nail in the coffin. He had been discovered, and the consequences for his illicit activities were about to catch up with him. Panic flooded his thoughts as he realized that Charles might have been the one who had noticed his suspicious activities in the warehouse, or worse yet, someone else might have exposed him.

With no clear plan or escape route, Tristan knew that time was running out. The impending meeting had arrived, and Charles and Tengku departed for the Port Authority with an air of grim determination. They had requested additional cargo slots due to the escalating business, a matter of urgency since perishable goods had a limited shelf life. The Port Authority agreed to address their request and assured them of a prompt response within a day, foreseeing no major issues.

An hour later, the two men returned to the warehouse, their expressions more relaxed this time. Tristan's desperation grew as he pondered the mystery of their meeting. He needed to discover what had transpired and how much time he had left to evade the impending disaster. With stealthy determination, he positioned himself near the office door, straining to eavesdrop on their conversation, but it seemed he might already be too late. All he caught were their words about waiting for confirmation from the Port Authority before taking further action.

Tristan recognized that he needed to engage in casual conversation with Charles to uncover the details of their confidential meeting. As the day at the warehouse drew to a close and colleagues began departing, it was the ideal time for casual interactions. Tristan seized the opportunity, casually remarking that he had seen the boss earlier that day and wondered if the boss frequented the warehouse regularly.

Charles, aware that delicate matters were best discussed in person with the boss, confirmed that Tengku did visit the warehouse when necessary. He explained that sometimes the boss wanted to ensure that the staff were content and that everything ran smoothly. Tristan, keen to maintain his façade, praised the boss, expressing admiration for his exceptional qualities as an employer.

Charles then divulged that they required additional cargo slots, and only the boss possessed the influence to secure them. Tristan felt a wave of relief wash over him, convinced that his secret remained safe, and no one suspected his involvement in any wrongdoing.

Filled with confidence, Tristan exited the warehouse and made plans to meet Choi for an early dinner at a nearby restaurant. In Tristan's perspective, everything remained secure, and there were no imminent concerns. The two men savoured their meal before returning to their apartment. The night was pleasantly warm, and the serenity of the evening provided Tristan with a comforting sense of relief.

Chapter 15

Frustration gnawed at Jack as he realized his investigation was stalling. Determined to up his game, he turned to the vast realm of the internet in search of discreet espionage techniques. After diligent research, he stumbled upon a potential solution: a nanny cam. This concealed camera promised to be his perfect tool. It allowed him to livestream video footage directly to his mobile phone, all without the need to physically approach the person he was surveilling.

Jack was eager to implement this new strategy in his quest to uncover the mysterious intruder haunting the warehouse. He embarked on a mission to find the most inconspicuous nanny cam on the market, one that could seamlessly blend into its surroundings while covertly recording every move without raising any suspicion.

His determination to crack the case and identify the nighttime trespasser pushed him to be even smarter and more strategic. Jack, armed with the nanny cam, covertly planted it in an unassuming corner of the warehouse, ensuring it remained hidden from anyone's view. This method allowed him to maintain vigilant surveillance over the area without giving potential suspects any reason to be wary.

The days passed, and Jack's patience was tested as he kept a vigilant eye on the live video feed from his phone. The daylight hours at the warehouse remained uneventful, and there were no apparent anomalies. Yet, Jack understood the importance of persistence and knew that the most significant developments often unfolded after dark.

Then, one fateful night, while stationed in the dimly lit maintenance room, his heart raced as movement flickered across the screen. A shadowy figure stealthily entered the warehouse through the back entrance, and a surge of adrenaline coursed through him. This was the moment he had been waiting for. Jack remained glued to the live feed, observing the intruder navigate the shadows with apparent disregard for any surveillance.

As the illegal arms were swiftly concealed within boxes, meticulously disguised to evade detection, a shocking revelation struck Jack with the force of a sledgehammer – the trespasser was Tristan, the last person he ever expected to be entangled in such a perilous operation.

Silently, Jack watched the damning evidence unfold before him, unaware of a slight delay in the video feed loading on his phone. Unbeknownst to him, a faint beam of light escaped from beneath the maintenance room door. Stealthily, Tristan closed in on the maintenance room, carefully turning the doorknob to reveal a scene that could alter the course of their lives.

In a desperate bid to salvage the dire situation, Tristan had to act quickly and decisively. His trembling hands reached for a roll of shrink wrap used to secure boxes on pallets, and with the nimbleness of a man accustomed to evading the law, he lunged at Jack from behind. Fear gripped Jack's heart as he realized the gravity of his predicament; he had not anticipated getting caught.

With quivering fingers and terror in his eyes, Jack complied with Tristan's menacing command to delete the incriminating video footage. Slowly, he navigated the menu and clicked on the trashcan icon, erasing the damning evidence in a desperate attempt to placate his captor. However, unbeknownst to both of them, the nanny cam still retained a memory card that stored the footage separately.

Tristan's ruthless demand continued as he ordered Jack to power off his mobile phone and hurl it deep into the recesses of the warehouse. Jack, consumed by fear for his life, obeyed without hesitation. His heart pounded as he hoped against hope that Tristan might show a modicum of mercy. But deep down, he knew that hope was a fleeting sentiment.

In an unrelenting grip of desperation, Tristan unspooled the shrink wrap and coiled it around Jack's face, depriving him of the precious air that sustained life. The seconds ticked by relentlessly, and within moments, Jack's struggle ceased. The life was mercilessly extinguished from his body, leaving behind a lifeless shell – a grim testament to the unyielding ruthlessness that lurked in the heart of Tristan.

With chilling determination, Tristan continued his macabre task. He procured more shrink wrap, and with methodical precision, he enshrouded Jack's lifeless body. This macabre cocoon would serve a dual purpose – concealing the gruesome truth from prying eyes and facilitating its clandestine disposal.

With the burden now concealed from view, Tristan carried it with eerie calmness to his pickup truck, sliding it onto the back seat. He covered the wrapped package with a nondescript blanket, ensuring that the world outside remained oblivious to the grim cargo hidden within.

Returning to the warehouse, Tristan conducted a thorough inspection, leaving nothing to chance. He meticulously eradicated any traces of the grim encounter, leaving no room for suspicion. The mobile phone was intentionally left behind, a deliberate ploy to divert any potential searches for Jack away from the warehouse – a calculated move designed to ensure that his nefarious activities remained undetected.

In a grim ballet of concealment and disposal, Tristan swiftly left the now pristine crime scene behind. His mind was set on ensuring that no trace of his heinous act would ever come to light.

Driving with a single-minded determination, he knew that the body's disposal had to be carried out with the utmost discretion. An idea crystallized in his mind - his fishing boat, anchored at Wah Sempoh, offered the perfect solution. It was a resource he had kept in reserve for a situation just like this.

On the way to the boat, he made a calculated stop at a construction site. Concealing his identity with a cap and gloves, he selected several bricks, loading them discreetly into the back of his truck. These innocuous objects would play a pivotal role in his gruesome plan.

Arriving at the boat's location, he scanned his surroundings, ensuring that no prying eyes were watching. With eerie calmness, he transferred the concealed body to the boat, strategically placing the bricks alongside it. The next phase was crucial – he set out to sea, as if he were merely embarking on a routine fishing trip. In the boat's seclusion, he further weighted the lifeless form with the bricks, ensuring it would descend into the abyss of the ocean floor.

In mere moments, Jack was swallowed by the inky depths, his existence erased as he vanished into the silent abyss. Tristan returned to shore, securing the boat as if nothing had transpired. As he headed home, he bore the chilling knowledge of a secret that would forever remain hidden beneath the waves.

Chapter 16

The following day dawned with an eerie sense of normalcy at the warehouse. Tristan, having meticulously cleaned away any evidence of his crime, returned as if nothing had occurred. His demeanor was one of calculated indifference, and he made a conscious effort to deflect any suspicion.

Throughout the day, snippets of conversation from his colleagues swirled around the workplace, inquiring about Jack's conspicuous absence. Charles, still unaware of the horrifying truth, assumed that Jack might have fallen ill and needed a day off. This excuse seemed plausible enough, and it temporarily dispelled any unease among the staff.

Unbeknownst to everyone, a hidden camera perched discreetly on a metal beam above them, silently recording their every move. It was strategically placed and expertly concealed, only detectable to someone who knew precisely where to look. The camera was an ever-watchful eye, capturing the warehouse's activities clandestinely.

As the day progressed, Tristan's confidence grew like a malignant tumour. He began to believe that his crime had gone unnoticed, and the sense of relief washed over him like a chilling wave. His heart swelled with satisfaction, and a cunning smile crept onto his lips. It was as though a fresh chapter of his life had begun, free from the shadows that had haunted him for the past few days. There was no need for a contingency plan anymore; he was once again in control.

However, his fleeting relief was disrupted when he met Choi for dinner that evening. Tristan informed Choi that his services were no longer required to tail Daniel. This abrupt decision did not sit well with Choi, who relied on the income. Frustrated and desperate, he threatened to expose Tristan's secrets to Tengku if he wasn't compensated.

Tristan found himself entangled in yet another predicament. With a weary sigh, he realized he had to find a way to pacify Choi. After a heavy silence, he hatched a plan – to recommend Choi for Jack's vacant position at the warehouse. It was a risky gambit, and Tristan knew he had to proceed with caution to avoid arousing suspicion.

He decided to give Choi some time off and promised to explore the possibility of securing him a job at the warehouse. This delay would mitigate any suspicion, as it would seem that Tristan had no prior knowledge of Jack's disappearance. Tristan believed that Choi's limited intelligence would prevent him from questioning the situation too deeply. This arrangement would not only appease Choi but also position him as a useful pawn in Tristan's unfolding schemes.

The next morning, Tristan observed the warehouse's atmosphere tensing up as Jack failed to make an appearance. Charles, puzzled by Jack's uncharacteristic absence, questioned his colleagues, and attempted to contact him. With no success, he decided to give it another day before reaching out to Jack's parents, who resided in Penang.

Tristan, overhearing the murmurs about contacting Jack's family, decided to intervene. Using a burner phone, he posed as Jack's father, sending a message to Charles to explain that Jack had returned to Penang to care for his parents and could no longer work at Tok and Beans. Charles, albeit disappointed, informed the staff that Jack would not be returning and that they would start the process of hiring a replacement.

Tristan seized the opportunity and approached Charles about recommending a friend to fill the vacant position. Charles, relieved to forgo the hassle of advertising the job, agreed to meet with Choi the following day.

With his schemes aligning, Tristan returned home to brief Choi about the interview. After meticulous preparation, Choi was ready, and Tristan was confident that he would ace the meeting. The following day, they arrived early at the warehouse, and Charles, impressed with Choi's credentials, readily hired him for the logistics role. Tristan's intricate web of manipulation and deceit continued to expand.

Chapter 17

Tengku and Daniel arranged to meet at the latter's real estate office to discuss the progress of Daniel's business. Both were looking forward to the meeting. Ever since they resolved their past conflicts, Daniel had been working tirelessly to ensure the success of his venture. When Tengku arrived at the office, he was immediately impressed by the vibrant and welcoming atmosphere. The glass entrance displayed enticing advertisements of properties for sale or rent, attracting the attention of passersby. Daniel's office had become a hub of activity with walk-in clients and scheduled appointments keeping the staff busy.

With an air of excitement, Tengku greeted his old friend and spent some time reviewing the business's books and getting updates on its performance. Over lunch, Tengku admired Daniel's passion and dedication, finally seeing him thrive in what he loved. Their meeting stretched for a few hours, and as Tengku headed to pick up his children from school, he felt a sense of contentment for Daniel's progress.

At the school gate, Tengku surprised his boys, Kyrie and Akanji, who were delighted to have some quality time with their father. The trio headed to the mall, where Kyrie sought to enhance his gaming setup with a new monitor, keyboard, and mouse, while Akanji indulged in designer clothing from luxury brands. Tengku couldn't help but laugh at his son's expensive taste, reminding him not to make it a habit. The day continued with laughter and bonding as they shopped and shared stories.

Tengku couldn't resist buying a new clutch bag from the Chanel store for Alicia, his wife. He knew she wouldn't splurge on herself, but he enjoyed surprising her with thoughtful gifts. After their shopping spree, the family shared a meal at the mall's food court. The evening at home was filled with warmth and love as Alicia had prepared a delicious meal for the family. Even though they were already full from their mall treats, they admired the feast she had prepared and saved it for later.

As the evening settled in, Kyrie set up his new gaming additions, and Akanji tried on his new clothing, taking selfies to share his excitement. The Beans family always cherished their time together, and they had an unspoken bond that kept them close and supportive of each other. With a sense of peace and harmony, they enjoyed another magical evening in their home.

As the evening progressed, the Beans family gathered in the living room, each sharing highlights from their day. Kyrie eagerly showed off his upgraded gaming setup, boasting about the improved graphics and smoother gameplay he was experiencing. Akanji, on the other hand, flaunted his new designer outfits, playfully modelling them for the family, who couldn't help but applaud his fashion choices.

Amidst the joyous chatter, Tengku couldn't help but feel immense pride and gratitude for his family. They were his pillars of strength, always supporting him in both good and challenging times. Alicia, sitting beside him, beamed with a mother's love, her eyes filled with adoration as she watched her sons animatedly share their experiences. Tengku couldn't have asked for a more loving and supportive wife and a closer-knit family.

As the evening wore on, the family decided to watch a movie together. They settled on an action-packed thriller that captivated their attention, drawing them into a world of suspense and adventure. Throughout the movie, laughter and gasps filled the room as they shared the experience of the characters' trials and triumphs.

After the movie ended, the family gathered in the kitchen to enjoy Alicia's deliciously prepared dinner. The table was adorned with an array of delectable dishes, each a testament to Alicia's culinary skills. They savoured each bite while continuing their light-hearted conversations and sharing plans for the upcoming weekend.

As the night grew late, the boys reluctantly retreated to their rooms, exhausted yet content with the memorable day they had spent with their father. Tengku and Alicia lingered a while longer in the living room, cherishing the quiet moments together.

"I'm so proud of you," Tengku said, gazing into Alicia's eyes. "You've created a warm and loving home for our family, and I can't thank you enough for everything you do."

Alicia smiled, feeling the depth of Tengku's affection. "And I'm proud of you too," she replied. "You've always been such a dedicated and caring father, and our boys are lucky to have you as their role model."

With hearts full of love and gratitude, they embraced, cherishing the bond that had grown stronger over the years. They knew that their journey together would continue to be filled with challenges and triumphs, but they were confident that as a family, they could overcome anything life threw their way.

As they headed to bed, Tengku and Alicia were grateful for the simple joys of everyday life—the laughter of their children, the warmth of their home, and the love they shared.

In the darkness of their room, they held each other close, finding solace and comfort in the presence of the one they cherished most.

The night passed peacefully, and as the first rays of dawn peeked through the curtains, the Beans family began a new day, united in love and ready to face whatever adventures life had in store for them.

Chapter 18

Tristan had a lot on his plate, and he needed to maintain control. The next day, Charles felt the effects of a late night as he sluggishly made his way to the warehouse. He greeted his colleagues, trying his best to appear unaffected by his tiredness. A strong cup of coffee from the canteen was essential to kickstart his day, and he joined his buddies for a quick chat before getting to work.

As he settled at his desk, Charles noticed an urgent message from the Port Authority regarding a potential discrepancy with one of their containers. Worried, he immediately called Tengku and informed him about the situation. Tengku agreed to meet him at the Port Authority promptly.

Meanwhile, Sam, the corrupt Port official, was running late for his responsibilities. Concerned that someone else might discover the issue with Tok and Beans' shipment to Egypt, he called Tristan for help. Tristan, annoyed by the unexpected call, knew he had to act fast to protect his operations. He sneaked out of the warehouse to meet Sam at the Port Authority.

Tristan asked Sam to manipulate the scales temporarily to avoid suspicion. Sam successfully tampered with the temperature control on the scales, making it unable to provide accurate readings. Satisfied that they had a temporary solution, Tristan returned to the warehouse unnoticed.

Shortly after Tristan's return, Tengku and Charles arrived at the Port Authority with the shipment files. They knew their reputation was impeccable, and they were determined to maintain a good relationship with the Port. The supervisor assured them that the issue seemed to be an error and not a deliberate act. The problem was traced to an overheated scale, and they agreed to rectify it. Tengku and Charles left the Port Authority reassured that their good name remained intact.

Tristan updated Sadiki on the situation and informed him that the next shipment would be delayed by a day. Sadiki understood and remained calm, trusting Tristan's ability to handle any challenges that arose.

The pressure on Tristan was mounting, but he managed to keep his secrets hidden and everything under control. With Choi, Sam, and Sadiki on his side, he felt confident in resuming his arms trade. Though exhausted, he knew he had to remain alert and prepared for anything that came his way. He had worked hard to rebuild his position of power, and he was not about to let it slip away.

As the days passed, Tristan kept a close eye on all the moving parts of his illicit trade. He knew that any misstep could lead to disastrous consequences. The warehouse continued its usual activities, with shipments coming and going, and Charles diligently overseeing the operations. The incident at the Port Authority had been successfully covered up, thanks to Sam's manipulations and Tristan's quick thinking.

Tristan felt a strange mix of relief and anxiety. On one hand, he was glad that his plan had worked, and suspicions had been diverted. On the other hand, the pressure to maintain the charade weighed heavily on him. He couldn't afford any slip-ups or careless mistakes. Each day, he woke up with a knot in his stomach, uncertain about what new challenges might arise.

He spent his evenings strategizing and reviewing every detail of his operation. He had to stay two steps ahead of everyone else, including those who were closest to him. With Choi now working at the warehouse, Tristan had a valuable ally on the inside, but he also had to be cautious not to reveal too much to him. Trust was a precious commodity, and Tristan knew better than to put all his cards on the table.

However, beneath the surface, tensions simmered. Sadiki, the mysterious arms dealer, occasionally reached out to Tristan with new demands and requirements. The arms trade was a dangerous game, and Tristan knew he had to keep playing it if he wanted to keep himself and his family safe.

As time went on, the stakes grew higher, and the risks became even greater. Tristan felt the weight of the criminal underworld on his shoulders, but he couldn't turn back now. He was in too deep, and there was no way out. He had to keep moving forward, navigating the treacherous waters of deception and intrigue.

Despite the danger, Tristan couldn't deny the thrill he felt. He was addicted to the adrenaline rush, the feeling of power and control. It was a double-edged sword, one that could both elevate him to new heights and bring him crashing down.

Chapter 19

In the enchanting coastal city of Penang, Malaysia, nestled under cerulean skies and along sandy shores, Jack and his family had woven the fabric of their lives. It was here that their roots ran deep, anchored by familial bonds, traditions, and love. Jack, driven by aspirations of prosperity, had ventured to Port Klang in pursuit of brighter economic prospects. His decision to leave behind the embrace of his family was not without sacrifice. It was a sacrifice he willingly embraced, for he sought to send home the fruits of his labour, a lifeline to their dreams.

Yet, for all the geographical separation, the ties that bound him to his family remained unyielding. The rhythms of their lives had danced in harmony, bridging the distance with daily conversations, laughter, and shared dreams. Every ring of the phone had been a bridge connecting two worlds, and every call had been a testament to their enduring love.

In recent days, however, an eerie stillness had settled upon the family home. It was as if the vibrant symphony of their lives had been muted, replaced by a disconcerting silence. What had once been an atmosphere of warmth and joviality now bore an unspoken tension, a gnawing unease that defied explanation.

The absence of Jack's customary calls and updates had become an unspoken worry. Perhaps, the initial thoughts whispered in their hearts, he was engulfed by the demands of work, his time hijacked by responsibilities. But days had turned into a week, and their anxieties could no longer be placated by hopeful speculations.

Behind their reassuring smiles hid the gnawing apprehension that refused to be ignored. It was in the missing calls and unanswered voicemails that they found the undeniable proof – something was amiss.

Desperate to soothe their mounting worry, Jack's parents turned to Mueez, Jack's close friend who had embarked on his own journey to Port Dickson in pursuit of a better future. Mueez had been a lifeline to Jack in this new chapter of his life, a friend who had shared dreams, hopes, and the challenges of a distant city.

As Mueez contemplated the drive to Port Klang, uneasiness coiled in his stomach, vying with hope for dominance. He clung to the belief that there would be a simple explanation, that perhaps Jack's phone was misplaced, or he had been caught in an unexpected situation. Yet, an unshakable feeling, like a shadow cast by an unseen specter, lingered in his heart.

The journey to Jack's apartment was laden with anticipation and trepidation. Each mile traversed brought him closer to the unknown, and every second spent on the road seemed to amplify the gravity of the situation. He hoped for clarity, yet feared what revelations lay ahead.

Arriving at the apartment building, Mueez ascended the stairs, each step laden with a mixture of anticipation and trepidation. He stood before Jack's door, his knuckles rapping with a blend of hope and dread. The silence that greeted him was a heavy omen, echoing with ominous weight. He dialled Jack's number, only to be met with the cold emptiness of voicemail.

A restless night passed for Mueez, who stayed in a nearby homestay. The morning sun brought little solace to his troubled mind as he embarked on another journey to Jack's apartment. The neighbour's curt reception from the previous day was replaced with understanding, offering a modicum of comfort to Mueez's frayed nerves.

Yet again, Jack's apartment remained locked in an unsettling quietude. A creeping realization washed over Mueez – something was deeply wrong. The neighbour offered his spare key, unwittingly unlocking a door to an unsettling revelation.

Stepping into Jack's apartment was like stepping into a time capsule. The unattended dishes, the untouched surfaces – they all painted a stark picture of absence, a sudden departure that defied explanation. The realization settled heavily within him – Jack had been absent from his own life for days.

The next logical step led Mueez to Jack's workplace, Tok and Beans. The drive was punctuated by his racing thoughts and his heart pounding against his ribs. His mind played out various scenarios, each one more dire than the last. The dread weighed heavily on his shoulders as he crossed the threshold into the building, a place where normalcy was expected to unravel.

Approaching Charles's office, Mueez's hand hovered over the doorknob, his hesitation a testament to the gravity of his mission. The creaking door seemed to echo the unease that gripped him. Stepping inside, he found himself facing Charles – a beacon of familiarity in the midst of his turmoil.

Charles's eyes met Mueez's, and their silent exchange conveyed a sense of urgency. Mueez's voice wavered as he cautiously unraveled the mystery of Jack's vanishing act. Charles absorbed the words, his expression mirroring the gravity of the situation. Days ago, Jack had disappeared from work, leaving behind a void that no one dared to question.

The dreaded call beckoned. Mueez knew that Jack's parents needed to know, that they needed to mobilize forces to locate their son. The burden of informing them weighed heavily on Mueez.

Suspense lingered in the air, wrapping around every word, every breath, as the investigation into Jack's sudden disappearance plunged further into an abyss of uncertainty.

Chapter 20

Mueez's phone trembled in his hand as he dialled Jack's father's number. The anticipation hung heavy in the air, and when the call connected, neither of them could bring themselves to speak immediately. A sense of foreboding settled between them, a silent acknowledgment that the news might not be good.

Finally, Mueez found his voice, his tone heavy with worry. He explained how he had searched for Jack, how he had visited Jack's workplace and received the message about Penang. But the words seemed hollow, offering no real answers. Jack's father listened, his heart sinking with every passing second of silence.

Tears welled in his eyes as he absorbed the reality that his son was missing, possibly in danger. He struggled to hold back the flood of emotions threatening to overwhelm him. The phone call ended with a heavy sigh, both parties left with a gnawing sense of uncertainty.

Jacks' parents wasted no time. With a sense of urgency that only desperation can fuel, they hastily packed their belongings and rushed to the bus terminal. Fear clung to them like a shadow, and the bus ride felt like an eternity of anxious anticipation.

Inside the bus, memories of Jack filled their thoughts. A radiant, happy boy who had grown into a responsible young man with dreams and plans for the future. They clung to those memories, hoping that they would guide them through this nightmare.

The bus finally arrived in Port Klang, and Mueez was there to greet them. The tension in the air was palpable, a heavy cloak of uncertainty that wrapped around them. After a brief exchange of words, they piled into Mueez's car, the journey to Jack's apartment marked by a tense silence.

Arriving at the apartment, a chilling stillness seemed to hang in the air. Mueez watched as Jack's parents stepped through the door, their faces a mix of hope and dread. The apartment itself seemed to hold its breath, frozen in a state of suspended animation.

They walked through the rooms, their footsteps echoing in the emptiness. The untouched belongings, the unwashed dishes—it all felt like a cruel reminder of Jack's absence. Mueez could see the pain etched into their expressions, the longing for answers that seemed to slip further away with every passing moment.

Determined to find help, they headed to the police station. The atmosphere within was heavy with a mix of frustration and desperation. They navigated through the bureaucratic process, their patience stretched thin as time seemed to stand still.

Hours passed, and finally, they found themselves in front of Detective Lam, a beacon of hope in the darkness. With a mix of weariness and resolve, they recounted their ordeal. Jack's father's voice wavered as he described his son, the bright light of their lives, now inexplicably missing.

Detective Lam listened attentively; his experience etched into the lines on his face. He asked probing questions, trying to piece together the puzzle of Jack's disappearance. His inquiries delved into every corner of Jack's life, probing for any hidden shadows.

As Mueez and Jack's parents left the police station, a mixture of emotions swirled within them. The promise of the investigation offered a glimmer of hope, but the weight of uncertainty still bore down on their hearts. Mueez extended his support, offering his homestay as a temporary refuge, a place to gather strength for the challenges that lay ahead.

Exhausted and emotionally drained, they accepted his offer and settled into their temporary lodgings. Sleep came fitfully, their minds haunted by the question that loomed large: Where was Jack, and what had befallen him? The coming days held the promise of answers, but the journey ahead was shrouded in shadows.

Chapter 21

The following morning dawned with a renewed sense of purpose. Mueez had already coordinated with Detective Lam, and together they assembled outside Jack's apartment building. The early morning light cast long shadows, adding to the eerie atmosphere that hung over the scene.

As they entered the apartment, a sense of urgency filled the air. Detective Lam's team meticulously combed through every inch of the space, their gloved hands carefully examining each object. Jack's parents watched with bated breath, their hearts racing as they hoped for any sign that might lead them to their son.

Every sound seemed amplified—a drawer being opened, a muffled conversation—as they waited for the breakthrough they so desperately needed. Detective Lam's experience and intuition guided the search, his sharp eyes catching even the smallest detail.

Hours passed, and the apartment seemed to surrender no significant clues. The anxiety in the room was palpable, and as time ticked away, hope began to wane. Jack's parents exchanged worried glances, their thoughts racing with fears of the unknown.

Detective Lam's voice finally broke the silence. He motioned to a corner of the room, where something caught his attention—a small piece of paper wedged between the edge of the bed and the wall. With gloved hands, he delicately retrieved it, carefully unfolding it.

The till slip, now a pivotal piece of evidence, raised more questions than answers. It was a puzzle piece that didn't quite fit, and as they continued to investigate, they hoped that it might eventually lead them down a path that would reveal Jack's whereabouts and the enigmatic circumstances surrounding his disappearance.

They checked the note, but it turned out to be a till slip from an electronics store. It seemed that just two days before Jack's disappearance, he had purchased a nanny cam. Confusion and surprise clouded their faces as they exchanged puzzled glances.

As the investigation continued, the questions multiplied. Why would Jack buy a nanny cam right before disappearing? What did he intend to use it for? The answers remained frustratingly out of reach, adding to the mounting unease that hung in the air.

Jack's parents clung to each other, their emotions a mixture of worry and determination. Mueez's presence offered a sense of comfort, a reminder that they were not navigating this unsettling journey alone.

With each passing moment, the apartment seemed to hold its secrets tighter, resisting their attempts to uncover the truth. Detective Lam's resolve remained unshaken, his commitment to solving this mystery unwavering.

The room was heavy with tension as they tried to decipher the implications of this discovery. Detective Lam's team resumed their search with renewed vigour, focusing their attention on uncovering any other potential clues that might shed light on Jack's intentions.

Back at Mueez's homestay, the trio gathered around the table, their thoughts consumed by the mystery surrounding Jack's disappearance. Jack's parents clung to each other, their faces etched with worry and exhaustion. Mueez offered words of comfort and encouragement, reminding them that they were not alone in this ordeal.

The hours stretched into the evening, and as darkness settled over the city, the sense of urgency only grew stronger. Detective Lam's promise to uncover the truth offered a glimmer of hope, but it also underscored the gravity of the situation.

Amid the shadows of uncertainty, they clung to their resolve. Jack's parents, Mueez, and Detective Lam formed an unlikely alliance, bound by the common goal of bringing Jack back home and discovering the truth behind his baffling disappearance.

Chapter 22

The morning sun cast a warm glow over Port Klang as Detective Lam, Jack's parents, and Mueez gathered outside the bustling Tok and Beans warehouse. The air was filled with a mix of determination and anxiety, knowing that they were stepping closer to potentially unravelling the mystery surrounding Jack's disappearance.

As they walked through the doors of the warehouse, the usual hum of activity greeted them. Employees bustled around, loading, and unloading crates of goods, seemingly absorbed in their tasks. Charles's office was located on the upper floor, overlooking the warehouse floor. It was a small but neat space, filled with paperwork and the lingering scent of coffee.

Detective Lam led the way, his authoritative presence drawing the attention of those they passed. Charles looked up from his desk as they entered, surprise registering on his face. He greeted them politely, a touch of confusion in his voice.

"Good morning. How can I assist you all today?" Charles inquired, his gaze shifting from one person to another.

Detective Lam introduced himself and explained that they were investigating Jack's disappearance. Jack's parents looked at Charles with a mix of hope and concern, their eyes searching for any sign of knowledge or guilt.

"We've been going through all the possible angles in Jack's life," Detective Lam said. "We're here to ask you a few questions, Mr. Charles, in the hope that it might shed some light on his whereabouts."

Charles nodded, a slight furrow appearing on his brow. "Of course, I'll do whatever I can to help. But I must admit, I'm just as baffled as you are by Jack's sudden disappearance."

The conversation that followed was a mixture of inquiries about Jack's behaviour at work, his relationships with colleagues, and any changes in his demeanour leading up to his disappearance. Charles answered each question with a genuine sense of concern, reiterating his fondness for Jack as a member of the team.

As the discussion continued, Detective Lam's experienced eyes caught something—a fleeting hesitation in Charles's tone when asked about Jack's recent behaviour. Sensing an opening, he pressed further.

"Mr. Charles, we've learned that Jack had been engaging in online discussions related to digital privacy and surveillance. Does that ring a bell?"

Charles's eyes flickered with surprise; his reaction not lost on Detective Lam. He hesitated for a moment before replying, "Yes, I was aware that Jack had an interest in those topics. He often talked about it with some colleagues during breaks."

"Did he ever mention any specific online forums or individuals he interacted with?" Detective Lam asked, his gaze unwavering.

Charles's gaze shifted slightly, and Mueez exchanged a knowing glance with Detective Lam. There was a hint of discomfort in Charles's demeanour, and they both sensed that there might be more to this story.

"He did mention some online discussions, but I'm not sure about the details," Charles replied, his voice a touch unsteady. "Honestly, I never delved into it much. It seemed like a hobby."

Detective Lam thanked Charles for his cooperation and exchanged a look with Jack's parents and Mueez. The encounter had revealed a subtle undercurrent of tension, suggesting that Charles might be withholding something. As they left the warehouse, Detective Lam vowed to dig deeper into Jack's online activities and the potential connections they might hold to his disappearance.

Outside the warehouse, the sunlight felt almost blinding after the dim interior. Jack's parents looked at Detective Lam with renewed hope, their hearts clinging to the possibility of answers. Mueez's determination burned brighter as well, knowing that they were inching closer to the truth, no matter how elusive it seemed.

The investigation had taken another twist, uncovering layers of complexity that extended beyond what they initially anticipated. As they walked away from the warehouse, the questions continued to pile up, and the urgency to find Jack and unveil the secrets that had engulfed his life grew stronger than ever before.

Chapter 23

Detective Lam carefully examined the till slip from the electronic store, his brows furrowing as he considered the implications of Jack's purchase of a nanny cam. He turned to Jack's parents and Mueez, his expression grave.

"It seems like Jack had purchased a nanny cam just days before his disappearance," Detective Lam remarked, his voice carrying a mix of concern and curiosity. "This could be an important lead. Perhaps he intended to capture something on camera."

Jack's parents exchanged worried glances; their hearts heavy with the unknown possibilities. Mueez leaned in; his eyes fixed on the till slip. "Do you think he was suspicious of something or someone?" he asked, his voice barely above a whisper.

Detective Lam nodded thoughtfully. "It's a possibility. Sometimes people buy these devices to monitor their surroundings discreetly."

Mueez's mind was racing, thinking of every possible scenario. "Maybe he caught something on camera that led to his disappearance," he mused aloud.

Detective Lam turned his attention to Mueez. "It's a good theory. We should explore this further. But to understand why he purchased it and what he intended to capture; we might need to retrace his steps."

With a renewed sense of purpose, the group agreed to visit the electronic store where Jack had bought the nanny cam. They hoped that the store clerk might remember Jack and provide them with some valuable information.

Arriving at the store, the fluorescent lights hummed overhead as Detective Lam approached the counter. The store clerk, a young woman with purple streaks in her hair, looked up from her paperwork.

"Good morning," Detective Lam greeted with a small smile. "We're looking into a missing person's case, and we believe that one of your customers, Jack, might have purchased a nanny cam from here recently."

The store clerk paused, her fingers stilling over the paper. She furrowed her brows, clearly trying to recall any memory of the purchase. "Jack... Jack," she repeated softly. Then, her face brightened with recognition. "Oh yeah, I remember him now. He was a really nice guy."

Detective Lam leaned in slightly. "Did he mention anything specific about the nanny cam? Or perhaps something that he wanted to capture on camera?"

The store clerk tapped her chin thoughtfully. "Well, he did ask a few questions about how to set it up properly," she recalled. "I remember him mentioning something about keeping an eye on his apartment while he was away. He seemed a bit concerned about something."

Mueez exchanged a glance with Jack's parents, their concern deepening. "Do you remember when exactly he purchased the nanny cam?" Mueez inquired.

The store clerk tapped on the keyboard of the cash register. "Let me check the records," she said, her fingers dancing across the keys. After a moment, she nodded. "He bought it two days before he went missing."

Detective Lam thanked the store clerk for her assistance, his mind already racing with the new information. "Thank you for your help. If you remember anything else or if you think of anything that could be relevant, please don't hesitate to contact us."

As they left the store, the group fell into a hushed discussion. The idea that Jack was concerned enough to purchase a nanny cam weighed heavily on their minds. What had he been worried about? What did he intend to capture?

Detective Lam turned to Jack's parents; his expression determined. "We're starting to piece things together," he said. "It's becoming clear that there's more to this than meets the eye. We'll find out what happened to Jack."

As they left the store, they were filled with a mix of anticipation and dread. Each step they took was a step closer to unravelling the mystery of Jack's disappearance. And they were determined to uncover the truth, no matter how unsettling it might be.

Chapter 24

The mystery surrounding Jack's disappearance continued to baffle Detective Lam, casting a shadow of confusion over his investigative efforts. The revelation of the nanny cam had opened up a new avenue of inquiry, but its absence from Jack's apartment only deepened the enigma. With the packaging nowhere in sight, it was clear that Jack had used the device elsewhere—a fact that raised more questions than it answered.

Detective Lam knew that they needed to gather more information about Jack's daily routines and activities. Every detail mattered now, and they had to piece together his life one fragment at a time. With a renewed sense of purpose, Detective Lam, Jack's parents, and Mueez embarked on a mission to uncover the truth.

They began their journey by scouring the neighbourhood around Jack's apartment. Every alley, every corner, held the possibility of a clue that could shed light on his last moments. They inquired at food stalls, hoping that someone might remember seeing Jack and provide a hint about his whereabouts.

Though they found a few vendors who recognized him, their hopes of discovering any concrete information were dashed. The food stalls didn't have video recordings, and Jack's interactions with the vendors seemed to be brief and routine—nothing that could explain his sudden disappearance.

The search then led them to restaurants and eateries in the area. Jack's parents and Mueez accompanied Detective Lam as they visited each establishment, hoping to find surveillance footage that would provide a glimpse into Jack's life. Their hearts raced with anticipation as they approached each place, their eyes scanning for any sign that Jack had been there.

But luck remained elusive. Video recordings were either non-existent or had already been overwritten due to time. The frustration in the group's collective sighs was palpable, yet they refused to give up.

"We have to keep trying," Detective Lam insisted, his voice firm. "We need to understand his routine, his interactions, anything that could lead us to him."

Through their persistent efforts, they managed to construct a rough timeline of Jack's daily activities. Colleagues at work provided valuable insights into his routine there. He was known for his punctuality and dedication. He interacted with his colleagues in a friendly manner, yet he seemed to maintain a certain distance from them. Tristan's name emerged, but he appeared to be a new addition to the workplace and had minimal interactions with Jack.

Detective Lam's determination remained unshaken. He continued to dig deeper, exploring every angle of Jack's life. Yet, despite their best efforts, the evidence seemed to lead them in circles. Tristan's involvement appeared limited, and the absence of any conclusive evidence of foul play added to the complexity of the case.

Tristan, in the meantime, carried on with his work as if nothing had changed. He maintained a semblance of normalcy, his interactions with colleagues and superiors seemingly unremarkable. His calm demeanour and unassuming presence cast a veil of innocence over him, shielding his true intentions from prying eyes.

As the investigation continued, Detective Lam couldn't shake off the feeling that there was a deeper layer to this case—a hidden truth that remained just out of reach. The missing nanny cam hinted at a secret purpose, one that might hold the key to Jack's disappearance. But unravelling that purpose required unravelling the intricate threads of Jack's life, a task that grew more complex with every passing day.

The tension and suspense in the investigation intensified, drawing each character deeper into the enigma surrounding Jack's vanishing. Detective Lam, Jack's parents, Mueez, and even Tristan were locked in a battle against time and the unknown. With every revelation and setback, the shadows of uncertainty deepened, leaving them to wonder if they would ever uncover the truth that lay hidden beneath the surface.

Chapter 25

As the investigation delved deeper into Jack's disappearance, Detective Lam and his team found themselves grasping at threads of information, hoping for a breakthrough. The mystery surrounding the nanny cam and its absence from Jack's apartment only added to the intrigue. They needed a solid lead, something that would help them piece together the puzzle.

With the anticipation building, they decided to employ cell phone triangulation to shed light on Jack's whereabouts. It was a painstaking process, but they hoped it might provide a glimpse into his last movements. Armed with a warrant, they approached Jack's cell phone provider, seeking access to his records and the crucial data they needed.

Days went by as they waited for the cell phone records to be handed over. The tension in the air was almost palpable, each passing moment seeming to stretch their patience. Then, finally, the awaited information arrived. Jack's last known location was pinpointed to the warehouse, and the timestamp indicated that it was late in the evening on the day he disappeared.

This revelation deepened the mystery. Why was Jack at the warehouse that evening? What had he been doing there? Detective Lam's mind raced with possibilities. He knew they had to visit the warehouse and speak to those who were there that evening, especially Tristan, who had only recently joined the team.

Their visit to the warehouse was met with a mixture of tension and curiosity. The bustling environment seemed starkly different from the eerie atmosphere of Jack's apartment. They approached Tristan and his colleagues, explaining their purpose and inquiring about the events of that evening.

Tristan's demeanour was calm, his answers seemingly straightforward. He stated that he and Jack weren't particularly close due to their recent acquaintance, and he had no knowledge of Jack's activities on the night he disappeared. The other colleagues echoed similar sentiments, mentioning that they were all occupied with their respective tasks and hadn't noticed anything unusual.

Detective Lam's instincts nagged at him, sensing that there might be more beneath the surface. He probed further, asking about the warehouse's security measures, its layout, and if anyone had noticed any unfamiliar faces that evening. The responses were expectedly vague, but Detective Lam wasn't discouraged. He knew that sometimes the smallest details held the key to unlocking the truth.

As they left the warehouse, Detective Lam's mind was racing. The warehouse had a life of its own, a bustling hub of activity during the day and an eerie emptiness during the night. He couldn't shake off the feeling that there was something vital they were missing, some detail that had yet to be uncovered.

Back at their base, Detective Lam reviewed the information they had gathered so far. The cell phone records placed Jack at the warehouse, but why? What was he doing there late in the evening? And where was the nanny cam? It was as if Jack had left a trail of questions behind him, each one leading to another enigma.

With determination burning in his eyes, Detective Lam knew that he needed to continue digging, to follow every lead and uncover every clue. He was resolved to solve this mystery, to bring clarity to Jack's disappearance, and to provide his family with the answers they so desperately sought. The investigation was far from over, and Detective Lam was determined to uncover the truth, no matter how deep it was hidden.

Chapter 26

A tense week had slipped by since the investigation into Jack's unsettling disappearance had begun. The passing days seemed to blur together for Mueez, who reluctantly returned to his work at Port Dickson after offering his unwavering support to Jack's distressed parents. Though the responsibilities of his job demanded his presence, Mueez's mind remained consumed by thoughts of his missing friend.

Mueez maintained his promise to Jack's parents, staying in regular contact with them and ensuring that Detective Lam was kept informed of any developments that might arise. He conveyed to the detective his willingness to assist in any way he could, even while being miles away.

As the evening settled in, Mueez found himself back on the road to Port Dickson. The miles stretched out ahead of him, a journey that now felt far longer and more somber than usual. He carried with him a heavy heart, his concern for Jack's safety gnawing at his every thought. The lack of progress in the investigation weighed heavily on him, and he longed for a breakthrough that would bring them closer to understanding Jack's fate.

The departure of Mueez left Jack's parents in a renewed state of desolation. The warmth and reassurance Mueez had provided seemed to fade with his leaving, leaving an emptiness that seemed to surround them once again. Their hope had been briefly rekindled by Mueez's presence, and now they faced the reality of their son's absence once more.

Detective Lam, understanding the emotional toll this uncertainty was taking on Jack's parents, made an effort to maintain a close connection with them. He paid them visits at the homestay, ensuring they were aware that he was dedicated to finding answers. In one such visit, he offered them an option that would allow them to be physically closer to their missing son: relocating to Jack's apartment.

The suggestion struck a chord with Jack's parents. They felt a strong need to be in the place that their son had called home, surrounded by his belongings and the remnants of his life. With Detective Lam's assistance, they packed their belongings and made the emotional move to Jack's apartment. The familiar surroundings seemed to offer a sense of solace, even if the questions surrounding Jack's disappearance still loomed large.

As night settled in, the apartment took on a different aura. Every sound seemed magnified, and the shadows held an air of mystery. The parents found themselves going through Jack's belongings, each item a connection to their son. Photographs, trinkets, and memories stirred up a mix of emotions—joy, sorrow, and an underlying determination to uncover the truth.

In the midst of this, Detective Lam made his presence felt. He joined them in the apartment, offering his unwavering support and a promise to pursue every lead. The weight of their collective worry seemed to bear down on them, a reminder that time was of the essence. Jack's parents yearned for answers, and Detective Lam was resolute in his commitment to finding them.

As the night wore on, the apartment held its secrets close, offering no easy answers. But within its walls, a sense of unity was forged between Jack's parents and Detective Lam. They were bound by a shared purpose—to unravel the mystery and bring Jack back, whatever it took. And so, in the midst of uncertainty, they braced themselves for the challenges ahead, determined to uncover the truth and bring Jack home.

Chapter 27

The bustling warehouse had turned into a scene of chaos and confusion. The morning's operations, once brisk and organized, were now marred by an unexpected disaster. Tristan observed from the sidelines, his heart racing as he tried to mask his internal turmoil. His eyes darted between his colleagues, knowing that suspicion would eventually fall upon someone. The weapons strewn across the floor were an ominous reminder of the dangerous world they were all entangled in.

As the staff gathered in the canteen, tension hung heavy in the air. Whispers filled the room like a low hum, each employee trying to make sense of the situation while casting wary glances at one another. Tristan and Choi exchanged guarded looks, understanding the gravity of what had just transpired. Choi's mind raced, suspecting Tristan's involvement but unable to confirm it.

In another corner of the canteen, Tengku and Charles were the focal points of the ongoing investigation. Questions swirled around them, fueled by the shocking discovery of illegal weapons hidden within the warehouse's legitimate cargo. Tengku's mind raced through the implications of this incident on his company's reputation and his own personal standing. He knew he had to cooperate fully with the authorities to clear his name.

Detective Lam took charge of the situation, his sharp gaze sweeping over the assembled staff. He began with Tengku and Charles, probing into their knowledge of the incident, their business practices, and any potential rivals who might seek to sabotage them. The gravity of the situation was palpable, each question cutting through the room like a knife. Tengku's frustration at the intrusion into his business affairs mixed with his determination to uncover the truth.

The police interviews spread to the rest of the staff, their anxiety evident in their body language and stammering responses. The fear of losing their jobs battled with the fear of being implicated in something far more dangerous. It was a harrowing experience as each individual faced the piercing scrutiny of Detective Lam's investigation.

Tristan maintained a façade of shock, answering questions with a mix of surprise and concern. He avoided making eye contact with anyone, knowing that his composure was being closely watched. The weight of his own secrets pressed down on him, threatening to suffocate him.

Choi, on the other hand, kept his gaze level and composed. He offered information to the police about the shipment procedures and the general workflow of the warehouse, carefully omitting any knowledge of the illicit arms trade he suspected Tristan was involved in.

The canteen remained a hushed space, every whispered conversation contributing to the sense of unease. Colleagues who had once been friendly now regarded each other with suspicion, wondering who among them could be responsible for introducing such danger into their workplace.

As the hours ticked by, Detective Lam meticulously gathered information, piecing together the fragments of the puzzle. The weight of the investigation bore heavily on everyone's shoulders, its outcome uncertain and the implications far-reaching. The veil of suspicion had descended, casting shadows of doubt over every individual involved. The truth remained elusive, hidden beneath layers of deception, just waiting to be uncovered.

Chapter 28

Detective Lam's office was a dimly lit room with a large table at its centre. The air was charged with tension as Tengku sat across from Detective Lam, his eyes narrowing as he tried to gauge the intention behind each question.

Detective Lam leaned forward, his gaze unwavering. "Mr. Tengku, thank you for coming in today. I understand that Tok and Beans has been operating for quite a while now. Can you tell me how long exactly?"

Tengku adjusted in his seat, his voice steady. "Yes, Detective. Tok and Beans has been operating for around twelve years."

Detective Lam made a note on his pad. "And during this time, where are your main distribution points for your products."

Tengku cleared his throat, his fingers tapping slightly on the table. "Our main distribution points are primarily in Asia, Turkey, Egypt and South Africa."

Detective Lam nodded. "I see. Now, we'll need access to your company's financial records. We want to ensure that everything aligns properly. Can you provide us with those documents?"

Tengku leaned forward, producing a folder from his briefcase. "Certainly, Detective. I've prepared all the necessary financial documents for your review."

Detective Lam took the folder, his eyes scanning its contents. "Thank you. Now, moving on, we also need to examine your client files. This includes anyone who might have engaged in any arms dealings. Can you provide us with that information?"

Tengku nodded. "Of course, Detective. Our client files are well-organized. I've compiled them here as well." He handed over another folder.

Detective Lam accepted it, adding it to the stack of documents. "Good. Now, Mr. Tengku, have you encountered any threats or enemies in your line of work?"

Tengku's brow furrowed, his eyes reflecting sincerity. "No, Detective. We've always operated with integrity. While there are always challenges in the business world, I can't think of anyone who'd hold a grudge against us to the point of becoming an enemy."

Detective Lam paused, his fingers tapping rhythmically on the table. "Mr. Tengku, I understand this might be a sensitive topic, but we need to address it. Have you had any involvement in any illegal arms dealings?"

Tengku's eyes widened in surprise, his voice firm. "Absolutely not, Detective. Tok and Beans is a legitimate company. We follow the law in all our operations."

Detective Lam nodded, making a final note. "Thank you, Mr. Tengku, for your cooperation. Now, before we conclude, let me bring something to your attention. We've been investigating the disappearance of one of your employees, Jack. He's been missing for over a week."

Tengku's expression shifted from calm to perplexed. "Jack? Missing?" He seemed genuinely taken aback.

Detective Lam leaned in, his voice softening slightly. "Yes, Mr. Tengku. Jack's sudden disappearance is a matter of concern. You mentioned you weren't aware?"

Tengku's brows furrowed deeply. "No, Detective. I was not aware of this at all. Jack has always been punctual and reliable. I find this very surprising."

Detective Lam observed Tengku's reaction closely. "Thank you for your honesty, Mr. Tengku. We will continue our investigation and keep you informed."

As Tengku left the office, the weight of uncertainty lingered in the air. Detective Lam's mind was a whirlwind of possibilities. The link between the weapons discovery and Jack's disappearance was becoming clearer, but the puzzle was far from solved.

As Tengku exited the room, Detective Lam's gaze remained fixed on the closed door for a moment, his mind racing. The pieces of the puzzle were starting to align, but there were still gaps that needed filling. The connection between the weapons and Jack's disappearance couldn't be ignored, and the thought of it sent a shiver down his spine.

Leaning back in his chair, Detective Lam clasped his hands behind his head, lost in thought. The warehouse was at the centre of this mystery, and he couldn't shake the feeling that Charles held more information than he was revealing. The role of a foreman often meant a deep understanding of the daily operations, a knowledge that might not be entirely innocent.

With a determined expression, Detective Lam reached for his phone and dialled a number. He needed answers, and he was prepared to dig deeper to uncover the truth. As the phone rang on the other end, he contemplated his approach to the upcoming interview with Charles. He knew that every word, every expression, would be crucial.

"Charles," Detective Lam's voice was firm as the call connected, "we need to have a more detailed conversation about what happened in the warehouse. Tomorrow, if possible."

On the other end of the line, Charles hesitated briefly before responding. "Detective, I've already told you everything I know. But if you think there's more to discuss, I'll be there."

Detective Lam's eyes narrowed slightly. Charles's response was cautious, and the detective sensed that there might be more beneath the surface. "I appreciate your cooperation, Charles. Let's meet tomorrow at 10 AM at the station. We need to get to the bottom of this."

Ending the call, Detective Lam's mind was a whirlwind of thoughts and theories. The case was becoming more complex with each turn, and he was determined to uncover the hidden truths that lay beneath the surface. As he stood up from his desk, he gathered the folders and documents from Tengku's interview, ready to delve into them in search of any clues.

With a sense of purpose, Detective Lam locked his office and walked down the corridor. The faint buzz of fluorescent lights accompanied his steps, creating an eerie atmosphere that mirrored the uncertainty of the case. Jack's disappearance, the illegal weapons, the enigmatic link between the two—it was a web that he was determined to unravel.

As he exited the police station, Detective Lam took a deep breath of the evening air, his mind already focused on the next day. The pieces were falling into place, and the momentum was building. The truth was out there, waiting to be discovered, and he was committed to finding it—no matter how deep he had to dig.

Chapter 29

The next morning, Charles stepped into the police station, a sense of apprehension lingering in the air. He was about to face Detective Lam for an interview, and he knew he had to be prepared for whatever questions were coming his way.

Seated across from Detective Lam in a dimly lit room, Charles felt the weight of the impending conversation settle on his shoulders. Detective Lam began with straightforward questions, probing into Charles' history at Tok and Beans, the responsibilities he managed, and his familiarity with the recently discovered weapons cache.

As the dialogue progressed, Detective Lam delved into the intricacies of the warehouse operations. He questioned Charles about the duration the goods remained within the facility, the meticulous processes they underwent, and the chain of custody from arrival to departure. Charles explained the checks and balances, detailing how multiple employees handled various stages of the products' journey, ensuring their accuracy and security.

Detective Lam's keen inquiries pressed further, exploring the workflow intricacies. Charles described the final stage of the process, involving the goods being left overnight before being transferred to the Port Authority for weighing and final documentation checks before containerization and shipping.

Satisfied with the operational rundown, Detective Lam shifted the focus to the staff. He asked about the employees, any history of conflicts or disturbances among them. Charles emphasized that the team was cohesive, without any notable issues. The air in the room remained tense as the detective inquired about the possibility of reviewing employee files to conduct background checks.

Charles acknowledged the request and assured Detective Lam that the company would cooperate fully. He understood that the investigation needed to be thorough, considering the seriousness of the situation. Throughout the conversation, he maintained his composure, answering each question openly and honestly.

As the interview continued, the dialogue began to shift subtly. Detective Lam's questions probed deeper into Charles' personal knowledge of the company's operations. He inquired about specific shipments, clients, and timelines, seeking to gauge Charles' familiarity with every facet of the business.

Charles found himself navigating a delicate balance between providing accurate information and ensuring he didn't reveal too much. Detective Lam's line of questioning hinted at a potential interconnection between Jack's disappearance, the arms trade, and the seemingly legitimate Tok and Beans operations.

Detective Lam's inquiries turned more pointed, probing potential blind spots within the warehouse's security and operational procedures. Charles explained the security measures in place, but Detective Lam's questions hinted at gaps that Charles hadn't previously considered.

The interview concluded with Detective Lam expressing his gratitude for Charles' cooperation. Charles left the police station with a whirlwind of thoughts swirling in his mind. Detective Lam's questions had opened up new avenues of doubt and suspicion that Charles couldn't ignore. As he returned to Tok and Beans, he realized that the layers of the mystery were deeper than he could have ever imagined.

In the coming days, Charles knew he had to tread carefully, not only to protect the reputation of the company but to unravel the truth that seemed to lie hidden beneath the surface of their seemingly normal business operations. The interview had left him with a lingering sense of unease, a feeling that the answers they sought might be closer than anyone had anticipated.

Chapter 30

Detective Lam, accompanied by his team of investigators, set up their workspace in a quiet corner of the police station, surrounded by files and documents of the warehouse employees. Their mission was clear: to dig into the backgrounds of each employee, uncover any potential connections, and bring to light any anomalies that might shed light on Jack's disappearance and the mysterious arms dealings.

As they sifted through the files, the atmosphere was tense with anticipation. Detective Lam had gathered his best team for this intricate task, and each investigator was assigned a specific employee's profile to delve into. The room was alive with the hum of phone calls and keyboard clicks, as they dialled previous employers and cross-referenced information.

Hours passed in silence; the investigators absorbed in their work. Detective Lam took a moment to review his own findings. He examined the employee records meticulously, searching for patterns, gaps, or any unusual circumstances. He was looking for connections between these individuals that could provide a breakthrough in the case.

After thorough research, the team gathered to discuss their findings. Each investigator presented their insights on the four employees who had raised suspicions. Detective Lam listened attentively as they discussed details, backgrounds, and potential motives. It was clear that they were dealing with a complex web of possibilities.

Choi's name came up frequently during their discussion. His recent arrival at Tok and Beans, coupled with the timing of Jack's disappearance, made him a prominent person of interest. Detective Lam decided to prioritize interviewing Choi, hoping that his involvement might unravel the larger picture.

The next day, Detective Lam and his team visited Tok and Beans once again. They requested to speak with Choi, who looked visibly nervous as he was called into the questioning room. Detective Lam's experience in reading body language kicked in immediately, as he observed Choi's fidgety behaviour and the anxious glances, he cast around the room.

Detective Lam, a master of the psychological chess match that was an interrogation, continued the interview by crafting an atmosphere of camaraderie. He wanted Choi to lower his guard, to feel a false sense of security that would encourage him to spill his secrets. The detective delved into Choi's life, his past, and his role at Tok and Beans, all while maintaining a façade of casual conversation. He let Choi's guard drop, little by little, like an expert angler playing a stubborn fish.

As they continued to chat, the atmosphere shifted subtly, as if a sudden change in weather had been announced. The moment the topic of Jack's disappearance emerged; Choi's demeanor transformed. The casual smiles were replaced by nervous twitches and sweat glistened on his brow. Detective Lam, sharp as ever, sensed the shift and zeroed in on it. He started to ask probing questions about Choi's relationship with Jack and his understanding of the inner workings of the warehouse. Choi's responses grew increasingly evasive, mirroring the growing tension in the room.

Detective Lam recognized this as the perfect moment to introduce the revelation – the cache of weapons discovered in the warehouse. Choi's reaction was a masterpiece of human expression. His eyes widened involuntarily, pupils dilating like a hunted animal. A bead of sweat traced a path down his temple, and his throat seemed to constrict as he swallowed hard. Detective Lam leaned forward, his voice as sharp as a scalpel, and inquired about Choi's role in the weapons operation and his knowledge about Jack's sudden vanishing act.

Choi's eyes darted, like a cornered rat seeking an escape route. His lips quivered, betraying his anxiety, and finally, the dam broke. He confessed, his voice barely audible, that he had been coerced into being a pawn in this dangerous game. He revealed that a more formidable figure within the operation had manipulated him, effectively puppeteering his actions. The name Tristan hung in the air like a malevolent ghost, and it sent shivers down the spines of everyone present. This unexpected revelation injected a potent dose of intrigue into an already complex case.

Detective Lam continued to dig deeper, probing into the arms dealings, the identities of those higher up the chain, and the reasons behind this elaborate scheme. Choi's revelations opened doors to new lines of investigation, connections that had previously remained concealed.

As the interview concluded, Detective Lam knew that they were now on the cusp of unravelling the complex tapestry of crime that had woven its way into the seemingly innocuous world of Tok and Beans. The information Choi had provided was the key to unlocking a deeper understanding of the arms deals, the missing Jack, and the shadowy figures orchestrating this web of deceit.

With Choi's confession, the investigation had taken a significant leap forward. The challenge that lay ahead was deciphering the intricate connections, tracing the arms dealings, and untangling the truth from the web of lies. Detective Lam and his team were determined to unravel the mysteries, even if it meant delving into the darkest corners of the city's underworld.

As they left the questioning room, Detective Lam's mind was already racing with plans for the next steps. He knew that with each layer they peeled back, a new layer of intrigue would be exposed, bringing them closer to the heart of the darkness that had enshrouded Tok and Beans.

Chapter 31

Detective Lam was well aware that dealing with Tristan required a different approach. The young man was a master of deception, making a straightforward confrontation futile. The need for irrefutable evidence was clear, and this realization had Detective Lam devising a clever strategy to corner Tristan into incriminating himself.

On the day of the interview, Tristan arrived at the police station, exuding an air of controlled confidence. He was no novice at masking his emotions; he knew how to navigate through tension without revealing his true thoughts. Guided into the dimly lit interrogation room, he took his seat, the flickering fluorescent light casting an eerie ambiance that perfectly matched the charged atmosphere. Detective Lam, joined by his team, decided to observe Tristan's demeanour silently for a while before initiating the conversation.

Tristan, conscious of being under scrutiny, appeared outwardly concerned, yet internally he was crafting his responses with care. The anticipation in the room was palpable, heightened by the muted flickers of the light overhead. When Detective Lam finally entered the room, Tristan greeted him with a restrained smile, his eyes betraying none of the thoughts that churned within.

The questioning began with innocuous inquiries about Tristan's role at Tok and Beans. He answered confidently, providing details that he had carefully rehearsed. The detective moved on to explore Tristan's past, asking about his reasons for leaving his previous job. With practiced ease, Tristan wove a tale of company downsizing and retrenchment—a fabricated story that Detective Lam keenly noted, though he chose not to reveal his suspicions just yet.

The interrogation shifted focus to weapons, and Tristan feigned innocence, pretending that the subject matter was utterly foreign to him. Detective Lam maintained a calm demeanour, allowing Tristan to believe he was in control. The detective's experience told him that Tristan's composure was a facade, and that behind the calm exterior lay a web of lies waiting to be unravelled.

As the conversation delved deeper into Tristan's role at Tok and Beans, his knowledge of the company, and his relationship with Choi, the tension in the room became almost tangible. The detectives, seasoned professionals, expertly probed for inconsistencies, but Tristan's answers remained infuriatingly poised. The detective sought to determine how Tristan was introduced to Tok and Beans, hoping for a hint of vulnerability in his narrative. The subject of Choi was broached, and Tristan recounted their interactions as though he was disclosing the most casual acquaintance.

The dialogue eventually circled back to Jack. Tristan's responses painted a picture of someone who barely knew the missing man, attributing Jack's popularity to a general camaraderie that had little impact on him. The detective, while maintaining his cool demeanour, couldn't shake off the feeling that Tristan was a master manipulator, skilled at bending truths to his advantage.

Detective Lam understood that this interview was just one step in a complex game. By allowing Tristan to think he had evaded suspicion, the detective hoped to lull him into a false sense of security. He concluded the interview, letting Tristan leave with an air of confidence. Tristan's exit painted a portrait of a triumphant young man, convinced he had successfully misled the investigators.

Unbeknownst to Tristan, the room held a profound sense of tension, anticipation, and an unspoken determination. Detective Lam's gaze lingered on the closed door as he reviewed the interview mentally. He knew that the battle was far from over; the intricate web of deceit surrounding arms deals, the missing Jack, and Tok and Beans concealed more layers than met the eye. Detective Lam's commitment to unravelling the truth burned brighter than ever. With each step forward, the intricate puzzle unravelled, revealing a tapestry of deception that they were determined to expose, no matter how long it took.

Chapter 32

In the midst of the ongoing investigation, Detective Lam found himself immersed in a web of concealed motives and interconnected plots, all with Jack at the centre. The truth was complex, and Detective Lam felt a responsibility to keep Jack's parents informed, to assure them that their son was not forgotten and that the relentless search for answers was continuing.

Seated at a table in Jack's apartment, Detective Lam maintained a composed demeanour as Jack's mother graciously fetched him a drink. The atmosphere was sombre yet charged with anticipation. With a heavy heart, he began to unravel the intricacies of the investigation to Jack's parents, outlining the leads they had uncovered. Each lead, he emphasized, was a puzzle piece that required careful examination and irrefutable evidence to form a complete picture.

As he spoke, Detective Lam observed the emotions that flickered across the faces of Jack's parents – a mixture of hope, anxiety, and a desire for closure. He recognized the toll that uncertainty was taking on them, but he also knew the importance of thoroughness in the pursuit of justice. The progress might seem slow, he acknowledged, but it was imperative to leave no stone unturned.

Jack's parents listened intently, nodding occasionally as Detective Lam elaborated on the strategies being employed to uncover the truth. They understood the necessity of patience, yet their lives were intertwined with their son's, and they had responsibilities to attend to – a reality that Detective Lam empathized with deeply.

Amidst the gravity of the situation, Detective Lam urged them to return home. Jack's father had a job to uphold, and their residence in the village demanded their attention, especially the care of their cherished paddy field. Detective Lam assured them that he would maintain regular communication, providing updates that would keep them engaged with the investigation's progress. It was not just a matter of practicality; it was about giving them something else to focus on, a glimmer of hope amid the uncertainty that had consumed them.

In this poignant moment, as Detective Lam's words hung in the air, he recognized the weight of the responsibility he bore. The trust Jack's parents had placed in him was immense, and he was determined to see this through for their sake, for Jack's sake. As they concluded the meeting, Detective Lam extended a reassuring hand to Jack's parents, a silent promise that their collective effort would not waver.

With that, the parents left Jack's apartment, their hearts a blend of emotions, but perhaps a shade lighter than before. Detective Lam remained seated, a maelstrom of thoughts and emotions within him. The road ahead was challenging, yet he was resolute – Jack's story was not just a case to solve; it was a story of resilience, secrets, and a quest for justice that would not be deterred.

Chapter 33

In the midst of the tumultuous events surrounding Tok and Beans, the very heartbeat of the business had been stilled. The arms deals and Jack's disappearance had cast a chilling shadow over the once-bustling establishment. Tengku, burdened by the looming financial strain, recognized the urgency of resuming operations. He turned to Charles, expressing concern over the halted shipments and the potential loss of valuable clients.

An idea struck Charles – perhaps a conversation with Detective Lam could shed light on the way forward. Tengku, willing to explore any avenue that would rescue his business, contacted the detective. A meeting was arranged, and Tengku found himself at the police station, seated across from Detective Lam. As they exchanged greetings, Tengku's mind swirled with a mix of apprehension and hope.

The conversation began, Detective Lam acknowledging the complexities of the investigation. While he couldn't divulge specific details due to its ongoing nature, he revealed their progress and the pursuit of leads. Tengku's heart surged – a glimmer of optimism amidst the darkness. Detective Lam proposed an intriguing strategy: Tengku could continue normal business operations, a move that would ideally keep the culprit off-guard. It was a tactical approach that could potentially lead them closer to the truth.

Relief washed over Tengku; he saw a chance to restore his business and to gain valuable insight into the enigma that had infiltrated Tok and Beans. Detective Lam emphasized the necessity of bolstering security measures. A suggestion was made to install CCTV cameras, a silent sentinel that would vigilantly watch over the warehouse. Tengku wholeheartedly agreed, envisioning a safeguard against any further treachery.

With renewed purpose, Tengku returned to the warehouse that evening. The space, once bustling with activity, lay vacant – an eerie emptiness that mirrored the void left by Jack's absence. Armed with instructions from Detective Lam, Tengku oversaw the installation of the CCTV cameras. The dimly lit warehouse transformed as each camera took its place, their lenses promising to capture the truth that had eluded them thus far.

The process carried a sense of catharsis for Tengku. The cameras became his guardians, a silent testament to his commitment to the business and to uncovering the sinister secrets that had woven their way into its fabric. In the stillness of the night, as the last camera was adjusted, Tengku felt a flicker of optimism. Perhaps this measure would reveal the hidden adversary, expose the shadows that threatened to engulf them all.

Morning arrived, bringing with it a renewed sense of purpose. As employees trickled into the warehouse, Tengku gathered them for an impromptu meeting. A palpable tension filled the air, a mixture of uncertainty and hope. With a steady voice, Tengku addressed the room, announcing that operations were set to resume. A collective sigh of relief swept through the crowd, and a spark of determination ignited in their eyes.

Tengku shared a carefully crafted narrative – one that painted the arms discovery as an external act, an attempt to sabotage their integrity. He concealed the true nature of the investigation, his words designed to maintain a façade of normalcy. Only he and Detective Lam knew the truth, understood the complexities of the web they were weaving.

As the day unfolded, work buzzed back to life within the warehouse. Machinery hummed, conversations resumed, and crates were moved. But beneath the veneer of normalcy lay a subtle tension, a shared secret that bound Tengku and Detective Lam in their pursuit of justice. With each passing moment, the warehouse's unassuming cameras stood vigilant, awaiting the pivotal moment that would shatter the veil of deception and bring to light the tangled truth that lay beneath.

Chapter 34

The business's temporary halt had energized the warehouse staff, invigorated by the break. Crates were meticulously checked, each pallet reweighed before being loaded onto trucks. The stakes were high, job security was on their minds, and they were prepared to go the extra mile to safeguard their employment.

However, amidst this renewed vigour, Tristan found himself facing an unexpected visitor. That evening, as he returned home, he spotted a stout man with a beard and thick mop of curly hair waiting in the parking lot. A sense of urgency pushed Tristan to join the man, leaving his belongings behind as he climbed into the car. They drove into the obscurity of the night until the road itself faded into invisibility. Eventually, they reached a deserted construction site, a suitable setting for a clandestine meeting.

The silence that had accompanied their drive was broken by Tristan's voice, a mix of surprise and concern. "Hey Sadiki, why didn't you tell me you were coming here?"

Sadiki's response was blunt, "Getting hold of you isn't easy."

Attempting to project confidence, Tristan tried to reassure Sadiki. "I've managed to overcome the road bumps. With the factory running again, we'll find a way to continue smoothly."

Sadiki's tone remained stern. "A little too late. Since you've started operations here in Port Klang, we've encountered several issues. This isn't how we conduct business."

As Tristan struggled to convince Sadiki, fear pushing him to devise a solution, he proposed a plan. He suggested involving Sam, someone at the Port Authority, to intercept the boxes and include them in the shipment seamlessly, ensuring Tok and Beans remained oblivious. This proposal seemed to strike a chord with Sadiki, who delivered a stern warning, leaving Tristan with no doubts about the gravity of the situation.

Eventually, an uneasy agreement was reached, and Tristan was dropped off at his apartment. The weight of the meeting's intensity lingered as he retreated to his apartment. There, he immediately dialled Sam on his second phone, outlining the plan's details. Sam wasn't thrilled about the idea, but he acknowledged its necessity in avoiding further problems.

Understanding that timing was crucial, Tristan resolved to reach Sam the following morning before the regular business hours. He delivered the illicit crates to Sam, who seamlessly incorporated them into the container bound for Alexandria. The timing worked out perfectly, with the ship departing before any suspicions were raised. A wave of relief washed over Tristan as he realized he had fulfilled his commitment to Sadiki.

In the days that followed, the warehouse buzzed with activity, the staff working tirelessly to ensure the business got back on track. Unbeknownst to most, a concealed operation had taken place, involving Tristan, Sam, and a shipment veiled in secrecy. As the machinery of commerce resumed its hum, the web of intrigue continued to expand, stretching into unexpected corners of the operation. And while the façade of normalcy resumed at Tok and Beans, the undercurrents of criminal activities simmered, threatening to unravel even the most carefully woven threads.

Tristan's heart raced as he sank into the solitude of his apartment. The gravity of what he had just done weighed heavily on his mind. His alliance with Sadiki was a double-edged sword. On one hand, it bought him some semblance of security, a temporary reprieve from the wrath he had seen lurking in Sadiki's eyes. On the other hand, it tethered him even more tightly to a world of danger and deceit.

As the night settled in, Tristan's thoughts raced like a wild river. The success of the recent covert shipment brought him both relief and apprehension. The scheme had worked, the contraband had slipped through the cracks of legality, and the illusion of normalcy had been maintained. Yet, Tristan's conscience nagged at him. The business that had once been about providing quality products to customers had now become a labyrinth of subterfuge.

The sound of rain tapping on the windows mirrored Tristan's turbulent emotions. He realized that every move he made was driving him further down a treacherous path, one that would ultimately lead to his downfall. He had been living on the edge of two worlds—the legitimate facade of Tok and Beans and the underbelly of illicit arms dealing. The thin line that separated them was rapidly blurring.

Tristan understood that his involvement with Sadiki was a pact with the devil. There was no turning back now. His attempt to outwit the authorities by involving Sam had only ensnared him in a complex web of criminality. And with every shipment that left the warehouse, the stakes grew higher. The weapons traded were more than just merchandise; they were instruments of destruction and chaos.

His gaze shifted to his reflection in the window. The man staring back at him was a far cry from the young, ambitious professional he used to be. He was now a cog in a dangerous machinery that he could no longer control. The relentless pursuit of wealth and power had led him down a path he could scarcely comprehend. The thrill of deception had given way to the burden of guilt.

As dawn broke, Tristan found himself staring at his phone, contemplating his next move. He was now trapped between the authorities and the criminal syndicate, both vying for control over his actions. The more he delved into the depths of deception, the more entangled he became. He realized that he had to find a way to break free from this dangerous dance before it consumed him entirely.

The rain had subsided, leaving a dampness that seemed to seep into Tristan's very bones. The world outside continued its oblivious rhythm, unaware of the turmoil within his heart. He knew that he had to find a way to untangle himself from the webs he had woven. The road ahead was uncertain, fraught with peril and uncertainty. But if he was to salvage any semblance of his former self, he had to make a choice— whether to continue down the dark path he had chosen or to find a glimmer of redemption in a world that had lost its innocence.

Tristan's fingers hovered over his phone, his heart heavy with the weight of his decisions. The choices he made in the coming days would determine not only his fate but also the destiny of Tok and Beans, the unsuspecting entity that had unwittingly become a pawn in a deadly game of shadows. And as he wrestled with his inner demons, the clock continued to tick, counting down to a reckoning that would change everything.

Chapter 35

Tengku and Detective Lam delved into the surveillance footage with a renewed sense of purpose. Their collaboration had evolved into a careful dance of strategy and observation. Tengku's presence within the warehouse had sparked curiosity and apprehension among the employees, creating a tense yet vital atmosphere.

Detective Lam agreed with Tengku's idea to unsettle the culprit. He knew that their plan required precision and subtlety. The stakes were high, and any misstep could alert the guilty party and drive them deeper into hiding. With a shared understanding, they began to orchestrate a sequence of events to provoke a reaction.

The next day, Tengku's calculated foray into the warehouse marked a shift in their strategy. His interactions with the staff were a combination of casual banter and astute observations. He wanted to gauge the reactions, to discern the nuances that might reveal the hidden truth.

As he conversed with the employees, Tengku's presence seemed to draw a mix of emotions. While most welcomed the opportunity to chat with the owner, a select few exhibited telltale signs of unease. Their fleeting glances and hesitant responses didn't escape Tengku's notice.

Surprisingly, Tengku found himself enjoying these conversations. The warehouse, once a distant part of his business, was now an integral aspect of his quest for answers. Yet, among the friendly exchanges, Tengku was searching for the chink in the armour, the one response that might betray the guilt of the saboteur.

For some employees, their interaction with Tengku served as an alibi, a moment in time that would later be scrutinized. Detective Lam monitored the proceedings from the surveillance room, his experienced eye observing the staff's body language, detecting shifts in demeanour that might hint at deeper truths.

Among the interviews, Tristan's behaviour was particularly intriguing. His attempts to maintain a composed exterior were evident, but Detective Lam's trained gaze spotted the micro-expressions, the fleeting changes in facial expressions that signalled anxiety and discomfort. A crucial piece of the puzzle might lie within Tristan's actions, perhaps hidden beneath the veneer of confidence he projected.

The turning point came when the footage captured Tristan sending a message on his phone. Suspicion ignited as Tengku and Detective Lam considered the possibility that this message might hold the key to unravelling the web of deception. Their instincts told them that this message was no ordinary communication—it was a breadcrumb, a trail leading to the heart of the mystery.

Piece by piece, they dissected the footage, observing Tristan's expressions as he typed the message. His gaze shifted; his fingers tapped with a sense of urgency. This wasn't just a casual exchange; it bore the weight of something pivotal. But the frustrating truth remained: the surveillance camera couldn't provide them with the message's content.

Determined to decipher this cryptic clue, Tengku and Detective Lam intensified their efforts. They reached out to their tech team, exploring the possibility of retrieving deleted messages or tracing the recipient. The clock was ticking, and every moment that passed brought them closer to the brink of exposure.

As the investigation progressed, their partnership deepened. Tengku's determination to reclaim his company's integrity and Detective Lam's relentless pursuit of justice fused into a formidable alliance. The warehouse, once a battleground of shadows, now held the promise of unearthing the truth.

The discovery of Tristan's message marked a pivotal juncture in their quest. It wasn't just a text—it was a breadcrumb, a slender thread leading to the labyrinthine heart of the mystery. The path forward was uncertain, fraught with challenges, but Tengku and Detective Lam were determined to follow it to the very end, driven by the promise of revealing the truth and unravelling the sinister plot that had woven its web around Tok and Beans.

Chapter 36

As Detective Lam and Tengku continued to investigate the mysterious arms dealings at Tok and Beans, they realized that they needed to start connecting the dots. The various pieces of evidence they had gathered so far seemed disjointed, but they were convinced that there was a hidden pattern waiting to be revealed.

Late into the night, Detective Lam meticulously spread-out documents, photos, and notes on the investigation board. He and Tengku stood before it, studying the array of information, hoping to uncover the underlying connections that would lead them to the heart of the criminal operation.

Tengku pointed at a photograph on the board. "Look at this, Detective. That's Tristan messaging someone, but the message content isn't clear on the footage. We need to find out who he was communicating with."

Detective Lam nodded; his expression determined. "Agreed. Let's try to trace the recipient of that message. It might lead us to a key player in this network."

They began to brainstorm ways to uncover the recipient's identity. Tengku suggested looking into phone records, tracking IP addresses, and cross-referencing known associates. Detective Lam knew that every lead, no matter how small, could potentially crack the case wide open.

A breakthrough came when they discovered that the recipient's number was linked to a burner phone. This was a common tactic used by criminals to maintain anonymity. Detective Lam requested assistance from tech experts to trace the location of the burner phone and monitor its activity.

Days turned into nights as they tirelessly pursued leads and connected threads of information. They realized that the arms dealings were not just a local operation but had international ties. The suspects had cleverly established layers of secrecy, making it challenging to trace the flow of weapons and money.

One evening, while reviewing financial records, Tengku's eyes widened. "Detective, I think I've found something. There's a series of transactions that seem irregular. They're coded, but they might be our key to unravelling the bigger picture."

Detective Lam leaned in to examine the records. "Good catch, Tengku. These transactions might hold the answers we need. Let's dig deeper into these codes and see if we can decipher their meaning."

They spent hours deciphering the coded transactions, trying to uncover the money trail and how it connected different individuals. As they painstakingly decoded each entry, they realized that they were dealing with a complex web of financial exchanges, shell companies, and intermediaries.

In a moment of clarity, Detective Lam connected one of the decoded transactions to a recent shipment. "Tengku, this transaction corresponds to the date of the last shipment. It seems like the money exchange and the arms delivery are intricately linked."

Tengku's eyes widened. "This means that the money is being funnelled through these coded transactions to fund the arms deals. It's a clever way to obscure the source."

"Exactly," Detective Lam affirmed. "And we need to find out who's orchestrating these transactions and who's on the receiving end."

As they pieced together the puzzle, they realized that they were closing in on a significant breakthrough. The coded transactions held the key to not only identifying the mastermind behind the arms dealings but also exposing the entire network.

"We're getting closer, Tengku," Detective Lam said, a mix of exhaustion and excitement in his voice. "We're about to uncover the heart of this operation. Once we have the mastermind, we can bring down the entire network."

Tengku nodded, a renewed determination in his eyes. "Let's continue connecting the dots, Detective. We're on the verge of exposing the truth and bringing justice to everyone affected by this."

And so, as the night grew darker, Detective Lam and Tengku immersed themselves in decoding the financial puzzle. With each code broken, they inched closer to the revelation that would not only crack the case but also reveal the extent of the deceit that had infiltrated Tok and Beans.

Chapter 37

Detective Lam and Tengku found themselves in an apartment at the homestay, a space they had commandeered for their research. In this cocoon of focused work, they could delve deeper into the heart of the complex international arms smuggling operation that had entwined itself with Tok and Beans. The urgency of the situation pushed them to uncover every shred of information they could.

As the realization of the grave situation deepened, Detective Lam's resolve grew stronger. He understood that the stakes were higher than he had initially thought. It was no longer just about solving Jack's disappearance; it was about dismantling a network that had infiltrated a seemingly innocent shipping business.

With the focus now shifting to Tristan's connections, Detective Lam recognized Choi as a potential source of valuable information. He arranged a clandestine meeting with Choi at a discreet food stall, away from prying eyes and unwanted ears. Disguised in casual clothing, Detective Lam tried to put Choi at ease, making him comfortable enough to share what he knew.

Choi, though fearful of being connected to any investigations, wrestled with his conscience, and began to recount his observations. Over the course of their conversation, he hesitantly revealed that he had overheard Tristan mentioning the name "Sadiki." Although he couldn't recall the context or whether it was significant, it was the first tangible lead they had received.

As the conversation continued, Choi's memory jogged further. He recounted snippets of conversations he had come across during his time at the warehouse. Words like "shipment," "arrangement," and "deal" had been casually dropped in Tristan's talks. Though Choi couldn't put together the entire puzzle, these fragments painted a disturbing picture. Detective Lam understood that this was a critical break in their investigation, a breadcrumb trail that might lead them closer to the mastermind behind the arms smuggling operation.

After parting ways with Choi, Detective Lam rushed back to the homestay to share the newfound information with Tengku. They both recognized the name "Sadiki" as a potential key to unravelling the operation. It was clear that Sadiki was a person of interest, someone who held the threads that connected this complex web of criminal activity. But who was Sadiki? And how did he fit into the puzzle?

As the evening sun dipped below the horizon, casting long shadows across the city, Detective Lam buried himself in research. The name "Sadiki" echoed in his mind, and he scoured databases, sifted through records, and connected dots, desperate to unearth any trace of this mysterious figure. Hours passed, and his determination intensified, fuelled by the weight of the responsibility he felt toward Jack, Tengku, and all those who had become unwitting players in this dangerous game.

Somewhere in the depth of his research, Detective Lam found a faint link. A name similar to "Sadiki" appeared in a confidential report detailing an arms smuggling network with international connections. It was just a glimmer, a thread to pull at, but it was a thread that had the potential to unravel the entire operation.

As midnight approached, Detective Lam leaned back in his chair, staring at the screen. The journey was far from over, but a spark of hope ignited within him. The investigation was gaining momentum, the puzzle pieces were starting to fit, and he knew that the darkness that had cloaked Tok and Beans would soon be exposed to the harsh light of truth.

The stage was set for the next phase of their pursuit. Detective Lam and Tengku would follow the trail of Sadiki, tracing it to its source, and hopefully, to the answers they desperately sought. In the midst of the uncertainty, one thing was clear: they were determined to unearth every secret, expose every lie, and bring justice to the victims of this intricate web of crime.

Chapter 38

The name "Sadiki" hung in the air like a cryptic riddle, a puzzle piece that could hold the key to unlocking the enigma surrounding Tok and Beans' involvement in an international arms smuggling operation. Detective Lam and Tengku were now in a race against time to unearth the truth behind this shadowy figure.

Late into the night, Detective Lam delved deeper into his investigation. His search led him to a series of classified documents from various countries, all mentioning Sadiki, a criminal mastermind with a notorious reputation. Sadiki was a name that sent shivers down the spines of law enforcement agencies across the globe. His crimes ranged from arms trafficking to money laundering, leaving a trail of chaos and destruction in his wake.

But what made Sadiki particularly dangerous was the fact that no one knew what he looked like. Despite being wanted in multiple countries, he managed to evade capture by never revealing his face. His reputation for meticulous planning, cunning strategy, and ruthless execution had earned him the moniker "The Phantom Criminal." With his true identity shrouded in secrecy, he operated as an enigma, an unseen force orchestrating criminal enterprises from the shadows.

The last known connection to Sadiki led to Greece, where he had reportedly been involved in a major arms deal that had sent shockwaves through law enforcement agencies worldwide. But even in Greece, his presence was ephemeral, leaving no tangible leads to pursue. His associates spoke of him in hushed tones, conveying a mixture of fear and reverence for the man who could make or break their criminal endeavours.

Detective Lam knew that unravelling Sadiki's web of influence required more than just local resources. It demanded an international effort. As dawn approached, he contacted INTERPOL, requesting their assistance in piecing together the puzzle of Sadiki's criminal network. Tengku's and Jack's safety were now intertwined with this dangerous criminal's machinations, and every moment counted.

The sun rose on a new day, casting light on the tangled threads of this intricate investigation. Detective Lam shared his findings with Tengku, the gravity of the situation etched onto their faces. Sadiki was not merely a faceless criminal; he was a force that had penetrated the darkest corners of the underworld.

As they waited for INTERPOL's response, the anticipation was palpable. Detective Lam couldn't shake the feeling that they were on the cusp of a breakthrough, that the information they needed to piece together the puzzle lay just beyond their grasp. Tengku, driven by a mix of desperation and determination, vowed to do whatever it took to bring down the criminal empire that had infiltrated his business.

Days turned into nights as they poured over intelligence reports, analysed data, and followed every lead. Each thread they pulled led them deeper into the intricate web that Sadiki had spun. As they delved into the history of his criminal activities, a chilling profile emerged—a man of intellect and ambition, fuelled by power and greed. But beneath the surface, he remained a mystery, a phantom figure whose true face remained hidden.

And then, the long-awaited response from INTERPOL arrived. The message contained fragments of information, bits and pieces of Sadiki's known associates and past dealings. It was like trying to assemble a shattered mirror, with each shard reflecting a different facet of his criminal empire. While they didn't yet have a complete picture, it was a start—a spark that ignited their pursuit.

The pieces were falling into place. Sadiki, the enigmatic criminal mastermind, had left a trail of chaos across the globe, and now, that trail led straight to Tok and Beans. With determination burning in their hearts, Detective Lam and Tengku prepared to follow that trail, to face the danger head-on, and to unmask the phantom behind the operation.

The journey ahead was fraught with danger, uncertainty, and relentless pursuit. As they braced themselves for what lay ahead, they knew that uncovering Sadiki's identity was not just about solving a case—it was about dismantling a criminal empire and restoring justice to those who had been ensnared in its deadly grasp. The clock was ticking, and the countdown to the truth had begun.

Chapter 39

The investigation was reaching a crucial juncture. Detective Lam and Tengku had taken up temporary residence at a discreet homestay, a haven where they could meticulously unravel the strands of the arms smuggling network without prying eyes or distractions.

Armed with the shipment records obtained from the Port Authority, they huddled in the dimly lit living room, surrounded by stacks of papers, laptops, and maps. It was in this sanctuary of investigation that they aimed to connect the dots and expose the hidden players of Sadiki's illicit trade.

Their search for clues began with the exhaustive examination of the shipment documents. Each page held a potential breadcrumb that could lead them closer to the enigmatic figure behind the arms deals. Tengku's business acumen and Detective Lam's seasoned investigative prowess formed a formidable alliance, ensuring no stone was left unturned.

The Port Authority had been forthcoming in their cooperation, recognizing the urgency of dismantling the criminal enterprise that had infiltrated their realm. The records presented a labyrinth of names, shipments, and destinations, reflecting the sprawling extent of the operation.

As they sifted through the records, a recurring name caught their attention—Sam. This seemingly unassuming individual had emerged as a central figure, appearing repeatedly as a contact person for various transactions. Detective Lam's intuition sharpened as he realized that

Sam's presence was not a mere coincidence; he held a pivotal role within the criminal network.

The investigation, however, transcended the confines of paperwork. To fully comprehend Sam's position and motivations, Detective Lam embarked on a series of interviews with individuals who had crossed paths with him. Each conversation provided a snippet of insight, an essential puzzle piece in the complex picture they were piecing together.

Tengku's involvement was integral. His presence lent credibility to their inquiries, allowing him to engage with those who had interacted with Sam. He delved into the backgrounds and affiliations of the people who orbited around this central figure, gathering fragments of information that hinted at the web of connections.

In their pursuit, a recurring link to Tristan surfaced. The tendrils of evidence began to intertwine, painting a mosaic that spanned across borders, enterprises, and individuals. Detective Lam and Tengku realized they were dealing with an intricate tapestry of intrigue that encompassed more than they had initially anticipated.

Through Choi's hesitant cooperation, they stumbled upon a name that reverberated through the underbelly of the investigation—Sadiki. This shadowy figure was no ordinary criminal; he was a mastermind whose reputation spanned continents. Descriptions of Sadiki painted a picture of a man whose influence reached beyond the tangible, a puppeteer orchestrating criminal endeavours with calculated precision.

Sadiki's last known dealings in Greece left behind chaos and uncertainty. Authorities from various nations had pursued him relentlessly, yet he remained a ghost, his true identity concealed like a well-guarded secret. Detective Lam and Tengku understood that they were now chasing an adversary who was not just evasive, but dangerously cunning.

The revelation brought forth a renewed urgency to the investigation. What had begun as an inquiry into arms smuggling had morphed into a perilous pursuit of an enigmatic criminal whose web of connections extended far beyond their reach. As they navigated through the intricacies of the network, the stakes grew higher, and the danger more imminent.

Chapter 40

As Detective Lam and Tengku delved further into the intricate web of the arms smuggling network, their relentless pursuit of answers led them back to Sam, a pivotal figure whose involvement extended beyond the pages of the shipment records. They had to uncover the layers of his story to fully understand the extent of his connection to the criminal enterprise.

After painstaking efforts, Detective Lam managed to track down Sam's modest apartment. The setting was a stark contrast to the ominous world they were unravelling, a reminder that those ensnared by criminality often had circumstances beyond their control. Sam's apartment was a testament to simple living, worn furniture accompanied by the faint hum of a television in the background.

On the day of the scheduled interview, Sam entered the small, dimly lit interrogation room. The unease was palpable, and his gaze shifted uneasily between Detective Lam and Tengku. He looked weathered; a man burdened by secrets he could no longer keep hidden.

The initial moments were tense, the weight of silence filling the room. Detective Lam recognized the urgency of breaking through Sam's fear, his innate loyalty to a man whose influence loomed larger than justice itself.

"Sam, we know you've been involved in this operation," Detective Lam began, his voice firm yet not devoid of empathy. "We understand the pressures you might be facing."

Sam's eyes shifted, torn between his loyalty to Tristan and the increasing danger that loyalty posed to his own life and his family's well-being.

"I'm... I'm just trying to protect my family," Sam's voice trembled, revealing a vulnerability that was often concealed.

Detective Lam's expression softened. He understood that in the world of crime, motivations were complex, and the choices one made were often driven by desperation rather than malice.

"Tell us, Sam, why did you get involved in this?" Tengku's inquiry was gentle, a prompt for Sam to unburden himself.

Sam's shoulders slumped, as if the weight of his secret was too much to bear. He began to recount his story, a tale that unravelled layers of humanity beneath the criminal facade.

"I needed money," Sam admitted, his voice heavy with regret. "My wife... she's been sick for years. Medical bills, treatments... it all drained me. I couldn't afford to lose her, so when Tristan offered me an opportunity... I took it."

His words revealed a desperate man, driven to the brink by circumstances beyond his control. It wasn't wealth or power that had enticed him but the sheer desperation to provide for his ailing wife and children.

"But what about Tristan?" Detective Lam pressed gently. "Why did you keep working for him?"

Sam's eyes darkened, the fear rekindling. "Tristan isn't someone you say no to. He... he had a hold over me, over my family. I didn't want to risk their safety."

It was a chilling revelation, the power one man held over another, twisting allegiances, and forcing them into submission.

Detective Lam exchanged a meaningful glance with Tengku, the understanding between them unspoken yet resolute. They were inching closer to understanding the dynamics that fuelled this criminal enterprise, each individual a pawn in a dangerous game.

"We can offer you protection, Sam," Tengku reassured, "but you need to help us dismantle this operation. You're not alone in this."

Sam's eyes shifted from one face to another, torn between fear and the glimmer of hope that there might be a way out.

Chapter 41

Sam's gaze shifted from Detective Lam to Tengku, his internal struggle palpable. The room was thick with tension, every second a battleground of fear and desperation. Finally, with a shuddering exhale, Sam's resolve crumbled.

"I... I was in charge of the Egypt shipments," Sam confessed, his voice a mix of relief and trepidation. "Tristan made me ensure that I was always handling those shipments. That way, I could slip in the additional boxes without anyone noticing."

Detective Lam and Tengku exchanged a knowing look. It was a breakthrough they had been waiting for—a crack in the fortress of secrets that Tristan had erected around himself.

"You mean the arms shipments were going to Egypt?" Tengku's voice held a mix of shock and realization. "And you were the one orchestrating it?"

Sam nodded; his eyes fixed on the table as if he couldn't bear to meet their gaze.

"Did you ever have any direct contact with Sadiki?" Detective Lam's question was measured, probing for any additional clues that might help them connect the dots.

Sam hesitated before shaking his head. "No, I never met him. Tristan handled everything related to him. I was just following orders, afraid for my family if I didn't comply."

The name Sadiki resonated with a sense of impending danger, a figure of shadows with an air of mystery and menace. The puzzle pieces were starting to fall into place, and the bigger picture was becoming clearer.

"We need to act on this immediately," Detective Lam stated firmly, his gaze unwavering. "This is a major breakthrough, and we can't afford to waste any more time."

Tengku's phone buzzed, a message that confirmed their plan to reach out to Interpol and share the information about Sadiki's involvement. The international implications of the case were taking shape, and the investigation was entering a realm beyond their jurisdiction.

The subsequent hours were a whirlwind of coordination, calls made to ensure that their intelligence reached the right hands. Interpol was on standby, ready to initiate an investigation that stretched across borders. The name Sadiki was now in the spotlight, a dangerous mastermind who had eluded capture for far too long.

As the sun dipped below the horizon, Detective Lam and Tengku looked out from the homestay's window, a mix of hope and trepidation in their eyes. They had cracked open the case, unearthed layers of criminality that went beyond their initial understanding. But in doing so, they had also ignited a chain of events that could prove to be perilous.

Chapter 42

Detective Lam's phone buzzed, signalling an incoming call from an international number. It was the moment they had been waiting for—the response from Interpol. As he picked up the call, he felt a surge of anticipation.

"Detective Lam, this is Agent Ramirez from Interpol. We've reviewed the information you provided, and we have a plan in place," the voice on the other end was firm and businesslike.

Detective Lam exchanged a glance with Tengku, both of them aware that their efforts were finally being backed by a global force that could potentially bring down the international arms smuggling operation.

"Agent Ramirez, we're ready to cooperate fully," Detective Lam responded, his voice steady. "What's the plan?"

Agent Ramirez explained that they had gathered sufficient information to stage an operation that could lead them closer to Sadiki. The plan involved allowing another shipment to pass through, under the watchful eyes of Interpol's surveillance. This time, however, they would have specific details—the dates, the times, and the routes—making it impossible for Sadiki to evade capture.

"We'll need your expertise on the ground, Detective Lam," Agent Ramirez continued. "We'll provide you with all the necessary information to coordinate with your local resources."

As Detective Lam and Tengku listened to the plan unfold, they felt a mix of excitement and apprehension. This was the culmination of weeks of investigation, a turning point that could either bring them closer to justice or plunge them into even deeper danger.

In the days that followed, the intricacies of the operation were meticulously planned. Detective Lam and Tengku found themselves poring over maps, schedules, and logistics, working hand in hand with Interpol agents to ensure every detail was covered.

The day of the operation arrived, and a sense of heightened tension hung in the air. Detective Lam and Tengku were on edge as they awaited the shipment's arrival, knowing that each passing moment was a step closer to uncovering Sadiki's elusive whereabouts.

As the cargo containers were inspected and loaded onto the waiting ships, Detective Lam's phone buzzed with a text message. It was the signal they had been waiting for—the green light from Interpol. The operation was a go.

The hours that followed were a blur of coordination and communication. Detective Lam relayed information to the Interpol team, ensuring that every aspect of the plan was executed flawlessly. Tengku's presence was vital, his knowledge of the local environment ensuring that nothing was overlooked.

As the last container was loaded onto the ship, Detective Lam felt a surge of anticipation. This was their chance to corner Sadiki, to strip away the layers of anonymity that had shielded him from justice for so long.

As the ship set sail, bound for the port of Alexandria, Detective Lam couldn't help but marvel at the global reach of their operation. From a small warehouse in Port Klang to the bustling streets of Egypt, their pursuit of truth and justice had transcended borders.

Alexandria—an ancient city steeped in history and mystery—loomed ahead. The bustling port city was a tapestry of cultures and influences, its streets lined with bazaars and grandeur. It was a place where the past intertwined with the present, where the echoes of ancient civilizations resonated.

The sun cast a warm glow over the city's skyline as the ship docked in the port. Detective Lam and Tengku were on the edge of their seats, waiting for the crucial moment when they could move in and close in on Sadiki.

As the story continued to unfold, the chapter marked a pivotal juncture—an international operation that was about to climax in the heart of Alexandria. Detective Lam and Tengku stood at the precipice of discovery, ready to unveil the enigmatic Sadiki and expose the intricate web of crime he had woven across borders.

Chapter 43

In the heart of Alexandria, a city where history whispered through every stone and alley, Sadiki emerged from the shadows like a phantom of the underworld. He was a man of indistinct features, his appearance designed to be easily forgettable. His beard was trimmed close, and his mop of curly hair was concealed beneath a well-worn cap. It was a face you might see in a crowd and never again remember, a face that vanished into the folds of anonymity.

Yet, beneath this façade of forgettable normalcy, Sadiki concealed a presence that emanated power and danger. As he moved through the bustling streets, his steps carried an air of confidence that transcended his unremarkable appearance. People passed by without sparing him a second glance, oblivious to the chilling aura that accompanied his presence. It was an aura that sent shivers down the spines of those who had crossed his path, a sensation that hinted at the darkness lurking beneath the surface.

On certain nights, Sadiki would vanish into the obsidian canvas of Alexandria, like a shadow slipping away from the light. He would join his cronies, a cohort of like-minded individuals who, like him, reveled in the clandestine world of crime and power. They would converge at dimly lit corners of the city, their laughter echoing through the narrow alleyways as if they owned the very night itself.

With glasses raised high, they would toast to their illicit successes, to the wealth that flowed like a hidden river, and to the influence they wielded in the shadows. Their laughter, boisterous and unburdened, was a stark contrast to the hidden fears and secrets that bound them together.

These nights were a temporary escape from the treacherous world they navigated daily. The clinking of glasses, the hearty laughter, and the camaraderie were their shields against the ever-present danger that loomed. In those moments, Sadiki and his comrades felt invincible, as if the world were at their mercy.

But even in their revelry, a subtle tension lingered beneath the surface. Each man knew that they treaded on a precipice, one misstep away from a fall into the abyss. The night was theirs to conquer, but the morning brought with it the reminders of their perilous reality.

As dawn broke, Sadiki would return to his role as a shadowy puppeteer, pulling the strings that controlled the fate of many. The city would continue its oblivious rhythm, unaware of the malevolent forces that roamed its streets at night. In the heart of Alexandria, history whispered, but it also bore witness to the hidden machinations of those who dwelled in the shadows.

Sadiki's reputation preceded him—an enigmatic figure feared across continents. His name was whispered in hushed tones, a name synonymous with danger and power. He was not just an arms dealer; he was a mastermind orchestrating criminal symphonies that spanned the globe.

His personality exuded control and dominance. His eyes, concealed behind tinted glasses, held an unnerving intensity—a gaze that could penetrate your very soul. His voice was a low rumble, each word carefully chosen and delivered with calculated precision. Conversations with Sadiki were not conversations; they were calculated negotiations, manipulative interactions that left others questioning their own intentions.

As Sadiki reached the designated meeting point, a warehouse on the outskirts of Alexandria, he was met by a group of individuals who bowed their heads in his presence. These were his subordinates, the cogs in the intricate machinery he had engineered. They knew better than to meet his gaze, understanding that a glance from him could spell their doom.

The cargo containers were being unloaded, their contents destined for the black market—a trade that fuelled conflict and devastation. Sadiki watched with an air of detachment as crates were stacked, his mind focused on the grand tapestry he had woven. He was a puppeteer, manipulating destinies from the shadows.

His subordinates moved around him with an air of deference, each step cautious and measured. They were well aware that displeasing Sadiki had dire consequences—consequences they had witnessed firsthand. It was a testament to his power that even his closest associates quaked in his presence.

As he surveyed the operation, his thoughts shifted to the next phase—the distribution of weapons that would wreak havoc across borders. He was not merely an arms dealer; he was a facilitator of chaos, a conductor of destruction. And with every transaction, he amassed power that transcended national boundaries.

In the midst of this criminal empire, Sadiki revelled in his mastery. He was a puzzle shrouded in enigma, a riddle the world had yet to solve. And as he stood in the shadows of the Alexandria warehouse, a city that had witnessed the rise and fall of civilizations, he represented a modern incarnation of darkness.

Sadiki's presence sent ripples through the criminal underworld, a reminder that he was a force to be reckoned with. As he awaited the culmination of the operation, he remained an enigmatic figure—a man whose motives were hidden behind layers of deception, whose very name struck terror into the hearts of those who dared utter it.

And as the chapter drew to a close, Sadiki's figure retreated back into the shadows, leaving behind a sense of foreboding that lingered in the air. The stage was set for a confrontation that would test Detective Lam and Tengku's resolve, a confrontation that would unveil the true nature of the monster they were chasing.

Chapter 44

Agent Luis Rameiraz had always been the underdog at Interpol. He was a man of average build, with a perpetual air of fatigue and resignation. While his colleagues would eagerly vie for high-profile cases, Rameiraz often found himself handed the ones that no one else wanted. The case of Sadiki, the elusive arms dealer, was no exception.

Everyone at Interpol knew that Rameiraz would be chasing shadows with Sadiki. The man was an enigma, leaving no trace, and Rameiraz was far from the best agent in the department. Yet, despite the collective scepticism, there was a certain sense of urgency surrounding this assignment. Sadiki had managed to elude authorities across the globe for years, operating in the shadows of international crime networks.

Rameiraz's office was cluttered with stacks of files, maps with pins indicating Sadiki's suspected activities, and a whiteboard with hastily scrawled connections. He sat at his desk, staring at the maze of information before him, feeling like a mouse in an endless labyrinth.

Interpol headquarters buzzed with activity around him, agents moving with purpose, phones ringing, and computers humming. The organization's reputation hinged on their ability to capture Sadiki. The mounting pressure was palpable, as they knew this was a defining moment for them. If they could finally bring down the man who had evaded capture for so long, it would be a victory of monumental proportions.

Rameiraz's thoughts were interrupted by the arrival of his superior, Agent Martinez. Martinez was a seasoned investigator, respected and feared in equal measure. He looked at Rameiraz's cluttered desk with a mix of curiosity and concern.

"Rameiraz, how's the Sadiki case coming along?" Martinez asked, his tone neutral.

Rameiraz sighed and leaned back in his chair. "It's like trying to catch smoke, sir. Every lead evaporates before I can get a solid grip."

Martinez regarded him for a moment before pulling up a chair and sitting down. "I know this case isn't easy, Luis. But you've been given an opportunity that many agents would kill for.

Rameiraz looked puzzled. "What do you mean, sir?"

"Sadiki is a ghost, yes. But if you can unveil that ghost, it would be a triumph unlike any other. Imagine the headlines, the recognition. Interpol would forever be known as the organization that brought down the untouchable. This could change everything for us."

Rameiraz considered Martinez's words. While he had often felt like the perpetual underdog, this assignment was a chance to prove himself, to show that he could tackle the most challenging cases and succeed.

Martinez leaned in. "You have resources at your disposal, Luis. A team of analysts, technology, connections. Use them. We're here to support you."

As Martinez left his office, Rameiraz's mind raced. He realized that he had been focusing on Sadiki's mystique, his ability to remain hidden. But what if he shifted his approach? What if he concentrated on the gaps, the overlooked details? Rameiraz began to review the case from a different angle, connecting dots that he hadn't seen before.

Days turned into nights as Rameiraz, and his team meticulously dissected every scrap of information. Phone records, financial transactions, known associates—every fragment was analysed. Slowly, patterns emerged. It became clear that Sadiki's operations were linked to certain key locations.

With newfound determination, Rameiraz reached out to international contacts, sharing his insights, and collaborating with agencies that had previously brushed him off. As the connections grew stronger, Interpol's web of intelligence expanded, creating a network that spanned countries and continents.

Through sleepless nights and relentless pursuit, Rameiraz began to piece together Sadiki's intricate network. The man who had once seemed invincible was gradually becoming a figure with tangible weaknesses. Rameiraz had discovered the chinks in Sadiki's armour, the vulnerabilities that he could exploit.

As Rameiraz stood before the giant world map in his office, pins marking the intersections of Sadiki's activities, he knew that he was on the cusp of something significant. This case, which had seemed like a lost cause, was now a beacon of possibility. The triumph he had once thought unattainable was within his grasp.

With renewed determination, Agent Luis Rameiraz vowed to pursue Sadiki with all the resources at his disposal. The ghost would be unmasked, and Interpol would claim its victory—one that would resonate across the world and solidify their reputation as a force to be reckoned with.

Chapter 45

Meanwhile, on the other side of the world, Detective Lam had received the information he had been eagerly waiting for. His contact at Interpol had reached out to him with a sense of urgency. The dots had been connected, and it seemed that Sadiki, the enigmatic arms dealer, had left a trace that led straight to Alexandria.

Lam's heart raced as he absorbed the details provided by Agent Rameiraz. The shipments, the connections, the operations—they all pointed to Alexandria, a city steeped in history and intrigue. It was a bustling metropolis that stood as a crossroads of cultures, a place where ancient secrets intertwined with modern mysteries.

As Lam read through the intelligence report, he couldn't help but feel a surge of excitement. This information could be the key they needed to finally close in on Sadiki. Interpol's involvement meant that the net was closing, and they were prepared to make their move.

Lam picked up his phone and dialled Agent Rameiraz's number. The call connected, and Rameiraz's voice echoed through the line. "Detective Lam, I assume you've received the details."

Lam nodded even though Rameiraz couldn't see him. "Yes, I have. This is a game-changer, Agent Rameiraz. We're ready to cooperate fully and ensure that this operation goes smoothly."

Rameiraz's voice held a mix of gratitude and determination. "Thank you, Detective. We understand that you've been working tirelessly to bring down Sadiki. We'll need your expertise on the ground to navigate local dynamics."

Lam leaned back in his chair, his mind racing. Alexandria, a city with its labyrinthine streets and hidden corners, was where Sadiki had chosen to operate. The international spotlight was now on this historic city, as the hunt for the man who had eluded justice for so long reached its climax.

"Agent Rameiraz, I'll do everything in my power to ensure this operation succeeds," Lam said, his voice resolute. "We can't afford any missteps now."

Rameiraz's response was firm. "Agreed, Detective. We're setting the stage for a calculated strike against Sadiki. This is the moment we've been waiting for."

As Lam ended the call, he knew that the stakes were higher than ever. The city of Alexandria would become the battleground, where the forces of justice and criminality would collide. It was a fight for more than just apprehending a criminal—it was a fight for the safety and security of countless lives.

As the sun set over the city, Lam stared out the window, his mind consumed by thoughts of the impending operation. The wheels were in motion, and the hunt for Sadiki was about to escalate into a high-stakes showdown, a battle that would define the destinies of those involved.

Chapter 46

The sun hung low on the horizon over Alexandria, casting long shadows on the bustling port. In a dimly lit room filled with screens and buzzing equipment, Agent Rameiraz stood huddled with his team of agents, eyes locked on the live feeds coming from the shipyard. Every movement, every sound was carefully monitored. The anticipation was palpable; this was the culmination of weeks of painstaking work.

Detective Lam had shared the crucial information with Interpol, and the agency had meticulously designed a sting operation to ensnare Sadiki and his network. This was a delicate dance – one wrong step and the entire plan could crumble. The team was well aware of the risks, but they were committed to bringing down one of the most elusive criminals in the world.

On the other side of the world, Sadiki remained blissfully ignorant of the impending trap. He had grown confident in his operations and the anonymity he'd built around himself. The shipment from Malaysia was just another successful transaction, or so he believed. As the cargo ship glided into the port, workers bustled around, unloading crates, unaware that their every move was being closely watched.

Sam was going about his duties as well, acting as if nothing had changed. His heart raced with a mixture of fear and determination. He knew that this shipment was different – it was marked for Sadiki's capture. He had a job to do, to play the role convincingly until the decisive moment arrived.

The sun dipped beneath the horizon, casting an orange glow over the shipyard. Inside the makeshift command centre, Agent Rameiraz's voice was low and commanding as he relayed orders to his team. They had to be ready, every step choreographed, every contingency planned for.

As night settled in, the atmosphere grew tense. The cargo ship was unloaded, and the crates were placed on the dock. Hidden among the workers were undercover agents, poised to strike at a moment's notice. The trap had been set – all they needed was for Sadiki to take the bait.

Back at the homestay, Detective Lam and Tengku were glued to their screens, anxious but hopeful. This was the moment they had been working towards, a chance to finally unravel the threads of this intricate criminal web. Their collaboration with Interpol was a testament to their determination, their shared goal of justice.

In the midst of the orchestrated chaos, Sadiki's senses remained keen. His intuition had served him well so far, and something – a fleeting unease – made him scan his surroundings more carefully. The port was a labyrinth of shipping containers, shadows, and echoing sounds. He could sense the tension in the air, the undercurrent of anticipation that seemed to hum beneath the surface.

As the final crates were unloaded, a hush fell over the shipyard. Every eye was trained on the cargo, on Sadiki himself. The moment had come. In a coordinated movement that resembled a perfectly executed dance, agents closed in from all sides. The once bustling dock transformed into a quiet stage; the actors ready to play their parts.

With a quick flash of movement, the net tightened. Agents moved swiftly and silently, surrounding Sadiki and his men. The surprise was evident on their faces, the realization that they had been outmanoeuvred. Sadiki's gaze flickered from one face to another, a mix of fury and disbelief clouding his features.

Agent Rameiraz stepped forward, his voice steady and determined. "Sadiki, your time has come. You're under arrest."

As the realization dawned on Sadiki that the walls had finally closed in around him, panic flashed in his eyes. He was a man accustomed to control, a puppet master orchestrating his empire from the shadows. Now, he was caught in a web he couldn't escape.

The team moved with precision, securing Sadiki and his associates. The night air was charged with tension, a feeling of victory mixed with the weight of years of pursuit. They had captured the enigma, the criminal mastermind whose name had struck fear into the hearts of law enforcement agencies worldwide.

In the dimly lit room at the homestay, Detective Lam and Tengku watched the operation unfold through the live feed. Relief washed over them, a shared moment of triumph. The journey had been arduous, fraught with danger and uncertainty, but they had reached a pivotal moment – the capture of Sadiki.

The stage was set, the pieces aligned, and the game-changing move had been executed flawlessly. The hunt was over, but the investigation was far from finished. As they looked at the screen showing the captured Sadiki, they knew that the real work lay ahead – in piecing together the puzzle of his criminal empire and bringing his collaborators to justice.

The dawn of a new chapter had arrived, and the shadows that had loomed over their lives were finally lifting. The future was uncertain, but one thing was clear – they had brought down a criminal giant, and the ripples of their success would be felt around the world.

Chapter 47

Agent Rameiraz walked into his office at Interpol, his heart pounding with a mix of pride and accomplishment. The capture of Sadiki, the enigmatic arms smuggler who had eluded law enforcement for so long, was a victory that not only boosted his reputation but also breathed new life into the entire agency. As he stepped through the door, a wave of applause and cheers greeted him. His colleagues stood up, clapping their hands, and congratulating him on a job well done. Handshakes, pats on the back, and genuine smiles surrounded him, filling the room with an air of celebration.

"I knew you'd do it, Rameiraz!" exclaimed one of his colleagues, giving him a hearty handshake.

"You've made us all proud," another chimed in, offering a genuine smile.

The sense of camaraderie and shared success was palpable. Rameiraz felt a rush of gratitude and happiness as he accepted the congratulations. He had proven once again that even the most elusive criminals could be brought to justice with dedication, determination, and a strong team behind him.

Amid the jubilation, Rameiraz couldn't help but reflect on the journey that had led them here. The long hours, sleepless nights, and relentless pursuit of clues had finally paid off. The intelligence work, coordination with various agencies, and countless leads that were followed had culminated in Sadiki's capture. It was a moment of validation for his skills and the unwavering commitment of his team.

While the atmosphere in Interpol's office was one of triumph, Detective Lam on the other end of the line listened to Rameiraz's words with a mixture of relief and anticipation. He knew that the capture of Sadiki was a monumental achievement, yet he also understood that their work was far from over. Tristan, the link between Sadiki and their illicit operations, remained at large, and it was imperative to bring him down as well.

"That's fantastic news, Rameiraz," Detective Lam responded, his voice laced with genuine happiness. "You've made a significant breakthrough."

Rameiraz's voice exuded excitement as he continued, "We've got Sadiki in custody. It's been a long time coming, and I can't wait to see what unfolds next."

Detective Lam knew that Tristan's apprehension was the next crucial step. They needed to capitalize on Sadiki's arrest to corner Tristan and dismantle the entire operation. "This is indeed a big win for all of us. Now, we need to focus on the next phase of the operation. Tristan is still out there, and we need to make sure he doesn't slip through our fingers."

"Absolutely," Rameiraz agreed, his tone growing more serious. "We can't afford to let Tristan off the hook. With Sadiki in custody, we have a strong advantage. We'll keep him in the dark about Sadiki's arrest and use that to our advantage."

Detective Lam nodded, even though Rameiraz couldn't see him. "We'll continue to feed Tristan information that makes him think he's safe. We need him to believe that he's still in control, that he's not a suspect."

Rameiraz's voice resonated with determination. "And once we've gained his trust, we'll strike. We'll set the trap and bring him down."

The two men shared a moment of mutual understanding, their objectives aligned. Both knew that the road ahead would be challenging, filled with uncertainties and risks. But they were committed to seeing it through, to ensuring that justice prevailed.

As Rameiraz concluded the call, he couldn't help but feel a renewed sense of purpose. The capture of Sadiki was a steppingstone toward a larger goal: dismantling the criminal network and ensuring that no one could operate above the law. With Tristan still out there, the challenge remained, and he was determined to see it through.

In different corners of the world, Agent Rameiraz and Detective Lam were united by a common mission, driven by their commitment to justice. The victory over Sadiki was a testament to their skill and dedication, but it was also a reminder that the pursuit of justice was an ongoing journey, one that required resilience, collaboration, and unwavering determination.

Chapter 48

Tristan's days at Tok and Beans unfolded with an air of unsettling uncertainty. Although he remained engrossed in his work, a nagging thought kept tugging at the corners of his mind. The absence of any communication from Sadiki was troubling him deeply. It had been days since he had heard anything from the enigmatic figure, and the silence was deafening. He questioned whether he was overthinking, whether the looming apprehension was just a manifestation of his own anxiety.

Choi, his trusted associate, continued his usual demeanour, showing no signs of deviation. Tristan's intuition told him that Choi was not one to betray him, and there was no direct connection between Choi and Sadiki. This somewhat calmed his nerves, allowing him to focus on the tasks at hand. Yet, a lingering sense of unease remained, an elusive feeling that refused to be ignored.

Meanwhile, Tengku, knowing that progress was being made, decided to reach out to his brother, Tengku Han. The siblings hadn't communicated for a while, and the familiar warmth of his brother's voice was something Tengku longed for. As they conversed, Tengku Han remained unaware of the intricate developments concerning Tengku Beans' business. In a heartwarming gesture, Tengku Han planned a surprise visit for the upcoming weekend. The prospect of their reunion brought a glimmer of solace to Tengku, who knew that the support of family was a pillar of strength.

As the days passed, Tristan's unease grew into a full-blown concern. He realized that he hadn't been compensated for the last shipment, and this deviation from Sadiki's usual pattern was unsettling. Frustration mingled with worry, causing his composure to falter. He attempted to reach out to Sadiki, hoping for some semblance of an explanation, but his attempts were met with silence. The air hung heavy with unanswered questions, his mind racing to decipher the enigma before him.

The mounting tension within Tristan was mirrored by Tengku's anticipation for his brother's impending visit. The notion of reconnecting and sharing moments with family provided a much-needed respite from the chaos that had consumed their lives. Tengku yearned for the comfort of familiarity, a chance to step away from the turmoil that had surrounded them.

Little did Tristan know that his mounting concerns were entwined with the larger web of events that were unfolding. The arrest of Sadiki had set off a chain reaction, leaving Tristan isolated and vulnerable. The very foundation of his operation was trembling beneath his feet, the veil of invincibility he had crafted beginning to unravel.

As the weekend approached, a convergence of emotions swirled within both Tristan and Tengku. The former grappled with an ominous uncertainty, the latter clung to the anticipation of a brotherly reunion. Unbeknownst to them, their paths were on a collision course with the impending revelations, and the unfolding chapters of their lives were intricately bound by fate's design.

Chapter 49

The weekend brought a temporary sense of relief for the Beans family as Tengku Han's arrival injected a much-needed dose of familiarity and comfort into their lives. The atmosphere in the house lightened up, and the tension that had been weighing them down began to dissipate. It was a chance for them to experience a semblance of normalcy after the turmoil they had been through.

During this time, the brothers spent quality moments together, with Beans pouring out the whole truth to Tengku Han. As he listened to the harrowing account of their ordeal, Tengku Han sat in shocked silence, his face reflecting a mix of disbelief and horror. The gravity of the situation struck him hard, and he realized that their family had become unwittingly entangled in a dangerous web of criminal activities.

Amidst this, Sadiki, imprisoned but not defeated, managed to smuggle a phone into his jail cell and sent a threatening message to Tristan. In his fury and paranoia, Sadiki accused Tristan of betrayal, believing that he had been turned in to the authorities. The ominous words of the message left Tristan rattled, his mind racing with confusion and fear. The idea that Sadiki could still have an influence over his life, even from behind bars, was deeply unsettling.

Tristan's mind raced as he tried to piece together what had transpired. He had been under the impression that Detective Lam and Tengku were working together against Sadiki, but now he questioned everything. He became consumed by thoughts of Tengku potentially double-crossing him. Was it possible that Tengku had become aware of his involvement in the illicit operations and had secretly informed the police?

The uncertainty gnawed at him, fuelling his anger and paranoia.

Driven by a mix of fear, anger, and desperation, Tristan formulated a plan. He decided to capture Tengku and interrogate him, hoping to uncover the truth behind the recent events. He selected an abandoned construction site as the location for this sinister act, ensuring that there were no surveillance cameras, and the surroundings were desolate.

To carry out his plan, Tristan gathered supplies - non-perishable food items, rope, and duct tape - from various stores around Port Klang. He meticulously set up the construction site, creating an environment that would appear normal on the surface while concealing his sinister intentions. He watched Tengku's movements closely, waiting for the opportune moment to strike.

Tristan's opportunity came when Tengku left the warehouse to spend time with his brother at the waterfront. The bustling atmosphere of the waterfront masked his sinister presence, providing a false sense of security for both Tengku and the people around them. Tristan patiently bided his time, eyes fixed on Tengku's every move.

As Tengku eventually returned to his car, unaware of the danger lurking nearby, Tristan's heart raced with a mixture of anticipation and anxiety. The moment had arrived for him to carry out his plan and confront Tengku about his suspicions. With his heart pounding, he stepped out of the shadows, his intentions as clouded as the tension that had enveloped their lives. He hit Tengku on the head to render him unconscious. There was no way for Tengku to know what was about to happen to him. Tristan grabbed him and slipped him into his pickup truck that was covered in plastic to ensure there are no DNA traces in his car of Tengku. He searched his pockets and found his phone; Tristan threw it under Tengku's car so there would be no tracking of Tengku's whereabouts. He covered Tengku with a blanket so no one would notice the body hidden. He drove off to the construction site but stopped at his apartment to leave his phone. This was to ensure that if he was ever checked on, he would have proof that he was at home when Tengku went missing.

Chapter 50

Tengku's world spun as he fought to regain consciousness. His head throbbed from the blow he had received, and his vision slowly cleared to reveal the grim surroundings of an abandoned construction site. Panic surged through him as he struggled against the ropes that bound him, but they held firm, digging into his skin with each futile attempt.

As his memory pieced together the events leading up to this nightmare, Tengku's heart pounded in his chest. He had been kidnapped, ambushed by Tristan. He realized that his phone was missing, Tristan had tossed it away, ensuring there was no way to track him.

In the dim light, Tristan emerged from the shadows, his face twisted with malice. Tengku's breath caught in his throat as he stared at his captor, a chilling fear gripping him. He was completely at Tristan's mercy, and he had no idea what the man had in store for him.

"Tengku, you thought you could escape from me?" Tristan's voice dripped with venom; his anger palpable.

Tengku's voice trembled as he tried to reason with his captor. "Tristan, I have no idea what you're talking about. I didn't do anything to betray you."

Tristan's eyes burned with a mix of fury and disbelief. "Save your lies. I know you tipped off the police. You ruined everything!"

Tengku's mind raced, desperately trying to find a way out of this deadly situation. "Tristan, please listen to me. I had no reason to betray you. I don't know what's going on."

Tristan's face contorted in anger. "You expect me to believe that?" His voice seethed with fury, barely contained.

Tengku's heart pounded as he pleaded, "I swear, I didn't do anything. I don't even know who Sadiki is."

In a moment of explosive rage, Tristan's fist lashed out, striking Tengku hard in the stomach. Tengku doubled over, gasping for air, his face twisted in pain. But Tristan wasn't finished. With a snarl, he delivered a punishing blow to Tengku's face, blood instantly trickling from his split lip.

The room seemed to hold its breath as the violence played out, the rage and anger in Tristan's eyes burning like a wildfire. His message was clear – this was not a time for deception or half-truths.

Tristan's anger seemed to waver for a moment, a glimmer of doubt appearing in his eyes. Tengku seized the opportunity. "Tristan, think about it. If I knew you were behind everything, don't you think that I would have had you arrested already but I knew nothing."

Tristan's grip on his rage seemed to loosen slightly. Tengku pressed on, desperate to make him understand. "I didn't know anything about Sadiki or whatever you're involved in. I'm innocent."

A moment of uncertainty passed over Tristan's face, and Tengku's heart raced. "Tristan, we can figure this out together. Let's find the truth."

Tristan stepped back, his anger giving way to confusion. Tengku could see that he was beginning to question his assumptions. "Why would they target you? Why would they involve you?"

Tengku's voice shook, but he held onto the chance to escape. "I don't know, Tristan. Maybe they wanted to frame me. But I'm telling you the truth—I'm innocent."

Tristan's expression remained conflicted, and Tengku's words seemed to be making an impact. "Tristan, we can work together to uncover the real culprits. I want to clear my name as much as you want to clear yours."

Tristan hesitated, torn between his anger and the possibility that he had been wrong. "I'll consider what you've said, but don't think this changes anything. You're staying right here until I get the answers I need."

With those words, Tristan turned and walked out of the makeshift room where Tengku was imprisoned. The space was incomplete, bare bricks and cement all around, full of dust and dirt. Tengku's heart sank as he took in the grim surroundings. The cold, hard ground beneath him and the darkness that enveloped him added to his sense of helplessness. He strained against his bonds once more, but they remained unforgiving. There was just no way out of this room.

Tengku knew that his fate rested on convincing Tristan of his innocence. As he lay there in the darkness, his mind raced with thoughts of escape, of strategy, of anything that could free him from this nightmare. He had to find a way to break through the wall of anger and suspicion that Tristan had built around himself, to prove that he was not the enemy. The hours dragged on, and Tengku's determination to survive and outwit his captor burned brighter with each passing moment.

Chapter 51

As the day progressed, life continued its rhythm for everyone else, unaware of the ominous situation unfolding. Down by the waterfront, a mysterious figure emerged from the shadows, carrying bags in hand, and moving with an air of calmness. The figure approached Tengku's car and, to everyone's surprise, unlocked the doors. Who was this unexpected visitor? Whose keys were they using? And why were they here?

Beneath the car, a discarded phone caught the figure's attention. Retrieving it, the screen illuminated, revealing a photo of Tengku and his brother. It was Tengku Han's phone. Confusion swept over the figure. If Tengku Han's phone was here, where was he? It was a perplexing puzzle, and one that needed solving urgently. It became clear that Tristan had made a grave mistake in his abduction.

Quickly realizing the gravity of the situation, Tengku made a call to Detective Lam, informing him of the phone's discovery and the possibility that Tengku Han had been taken. Detective Lam's response was swift and resolute. He instructed Tengku to remain at the car park, assuring him that he would be there shortly to assess the situation firsthand.

Upon Detective Lam's arrival, he and Tengku engaged in a somber discussion, each aware of the implications of the situation. There was a consensus that Tengku Han had likely been abducted, a case of mistaken identity spurred by his resemblance to Tengku. Detective Lam urged Tengku to keep a low profile for now, in hopes that whoever had taken his brother would inadvertently keep him safe while they assessed the situation further.

Tengku's eagerness to inform his family about the situation was met with caution from Detective Lam. It was a delicate situation, and any alerting of Tengku's family could potentially jeopardize his brother's safety. The detective advised Tengku to bide his time and maintain a discreet presence, all while taking refuge at the homestay—the epicentre of their ongoing investigations.

Within the walls of the homestay, Tengku found himself ensnared in a web of tension and uncertainty. The hours dragged on, each tick of the clock a reminder of Tengku Han's absence and the mystery that shrouded his abduction. The walls of the place that was meant to provide comfort now felt like a prison of questions and worries.

As Tengku paced back and forth in the dimly lit room, he couldn't help but reflect on the gravity of the situation. His brother's life was hanging in the balance, and he was forced to stay hidden, unable to take action or comfort his anxious family. Every passing moment only fuelled his determination to uncover the truth and ensure his brother's safe return.

Chapter 52

In the distant backdrop, sirens wail, growing louder with each passing second. All eyes are drawn to the approaching vehicles, slowly snaking their way around the bend, their flashing lights casting an eerie glow. Curiosity seizes everyone, bringing them to an abrupt standstill.

Three police cars come to a screeching halt in front of the majestic 23-story building. The bustling activity in the grand foyer, reminiscent of a luxurious resort, suddenly fades to silence as the reception desk is manned. Detective Lam steps forward, addressing the nervous receptionist, Alina, with a sense of urgency, "Selamat Petang. I need to go to Tengku Bean's house on floor 21."

Alina's voice trembles as she responds, "Hello Sir, Sure, please turn right, and the elevators are on the left. You will require this access card, swipe it in the lift to gain access to the floor." She hands him a small white card, marked with "Pier8 Klang."

The six police officers, clad in their sombre black uniforms, radios attached to their jackets, step into the elevators. The cold and unsettling voices emanating from their microphones add to the tension. In an instant, they ascend, disappearing, heading up to Tengku Beans' penthouse apartment.

The elevator doors open, revealing a lavish interior with thick red and grey carpets underfoot. Warm white walls line the short passage, adorned with shimmering lights that cast dancing shadows. The delicate fragrance of lavender and vanilla fills the air, as the officers approach the thick walnut veneered door, brass-like handles beckoning them forward. A firm press of the doorbell announces their presence.

Awaiting them inside is Alicia, Tengku Beans' beautiful wife, radiating elegance in her sleek black pants and satin pink blouse, adorned with a grey, black, and pink scarf wrapped gracefully around her neck. Despite her apparent distress, her natural beauty shines through. A small smile graces her face as she directs Detective Lam and his team into her home.

The entrance exudes tasteful decor, reflecting Alicia's classy demeanour. As they proceed to the lounge, Tengku Beans' sons greet them, Akanji and Kyrie. Akanji, 17, and completing grade 12, and Kyrie, fifteen and in grade 10, both attend the British international school nearby. Rising to greet the detective, they extend their hands in a welcoming gesture. The air is thick with worry, and the family's distress is palpable.

Alicia reveals that Tengku Beans has been missing since the previous day, an uncharacteristic absence for him. He has not answered his phone, and his assistant, Amy, confirmed that he left the office the day before and hasn't returned.

The suspense and intrigue deepen as the mystery surrounding Tengku Beans' disappearance unfolds. As Detective Lam delves deeper into the enigma, the stakes grow higher, and the family's concerns intensify. Little do they know that the path ahead holds more twists and turns, leading them into a world of action, suspense, and danger.

Detective Lam was keenly aware of Tengku's whereabouts, knowing the precarious situation that had unfolded. His top priority was to ensure the safety of both Tengku and his brother, all while orchestrating an intricate web of deception. The family's concern was palpable, and Detective Lam skilfully walked a fine line—reassuring them that Tengku was in safe hands, while ingeniously maintaining an air of official investigation. This careful act was pivotal, allowing them to keep the façade of a thorough inquiry, all the while shielding Tengku's true predicament from prying eyes. Detective Lam's intricate choreography extended to the police records, carefully orchestrating a veneer of normalcy that concealed the intense covert operation unfolding beneath the surface. He alone held the secret that Tengku was unharmed, hidden from those who sought to exploit the situation for their own gain.

Chapter 53

Detective Lam and his team were relentless in their pursuit of the truth. The next day, they returned to the warehouse, the epicentre of the recent string of unsettling events. The atmosphere was thick with tension as the detectives questioned the staff, aiming to unravel the mystery that seemed to have taken hold of their workplace. The disappearance of Tengku only added to the enigma that surrounded the warehouse.

Tristan's interrogation was a pivotal moment. The detective's piercing gaze bore into him as he answered their questions, his confident demeanour contrasting with the growing unease in the room. Tristan maintained that he knew nothing about Tengku's disappearance and claimed to have been at home throughout the weekend. But the pressure intensified, and he knew he needed to shift their focus elsewhere.

With calculated precision, Tristan suggested that the detectives should look into a confrontation he had witnessed between Tengku, and a man named Daniel. He emphasized the potential threat that Daniel posed, describing a violent altercation he had supposedly witnessed. This revelation caught the detective's attention, leading them to consider Daniel as a possible lead. It was a calculated move by Tristan, and the detective decided to pursue this new angle.

Tengku, who was aware of the ongoing investigation, agreed to follow this lead, even though he was certain that his past conflict with Daniel had been resolved. Detective Lam reached out to Daniel, who displayed genuine shock and concern upon learning about Tengku's abduction. He expressed his willingness to cooperate and help in any way he could. Daniel's sincerity resonated with the detective, and he decided to visit him at his agency to gather more information.

At the agency, the tension was palpable as Daniel met with Detective Lam. He was taken aback by the seriousness of the situation and showed deep concern for his friend's safety. As Daniel answered the detective's questions, he couldn't help but feel the weight of the mystery that had unfolded. He had no idea what could have led to Tengku's disappearance, and his genuine worry for his friend's well-being was evident.

The detective left the agency, the pieces of the puzzle slowly coming together in his mind. The warehouse, the arms dealings, Tengku's disappearance, and now this unexpected connection to Daniel—all of it was part of a complex web of intrigue that seemed to stretch its tendrils into every corner. As the investigation continued, the detective was determined to find the truth, no matter how deep it led him into the shadows.

The suspense was building, and the warehouse, with its myriad secrets, stood as a haunting backdrop to the unfolding story. Detective Lam knew that he was getting closer to the heart of the matter, but the pieces of the puzzle were far from complete. As he left the agency, he knew that there was much more to uncover, and the truth seemed just out of reach.

Chapter 54

Detective Lam's day was far from over as he left the agency. Carrying a takeout meal, he made his way to where Tengku was being kept hidden. It was crucial to keep Tengku informed about the ongoing investigation and to ensure his well-being away from the public eye. As he entered the secure location, he shared the developments of his interview with Daniel. The detective reassured Tengku that Daniel seemed genuinely unaware of the recent troubles plaguing Tengku and his company. Tengku's safety was paramount, and Detective Lam was committed to finding him as soon as possible. He also mentioned that Daniel had expressed his concern and intended to visit Tengku's family to offer his support.

Tengku appreciated Daniel's concern and recognized that Daniel wasn't a threat. With Detective Lam's guidance, Tengku decided that focusing on the investigation into Tristan was the most practical course of action. The web of events seemed to revolve around Tristan's involvement, and Tengku believed that exposing the truth behind it all was the key to resolving the situation. It was a challenging and tense time, and they needed to remain patient and thorough in their pursuit of justice.

Later that day, Daniel made his way to Tengku's family home. The once cheerful atmosphere was now overshadowed by worry and uncertainty. Alicia, who had always exuded grace and warmth, now wore a strained expression on her face. Her eyes, once filled with light, were now clouded with concern. The toll of Tengku's absence was visible on all their faces, and Daniel couldn't help but feel their pain.

As he walked in, Daniel's heart ached for the family. The once vibrant home now felt heavy with the weight of their worry. It was clear that their lives had been disrupted, and he was determined to offer whatever support he could. Seeing Alicia's distress, he understood that she needed reassurance and a kind presence. He made it a point to be there for them, ready to lend an ear or a helping hand.

Daniel's presence was a ray of hope for the family. They knew him well, and his genuine concern was a source of comfort. As he interacted with them, he could see how the uncertainty was taking a toll on their well-being. He extended his offer to help them stay connected with Detective Lam, allowing them to have updates on the investigation without adding more stress to their lives.

The family welcomed his assistance with open arms. Daniel's offer to stay in touch with Detective Lam eased their worries, giving them a lifeline to information and progress. He took care to ensure they were well-fed and rested, a small gesture to help them through the difficult days ahead. He had witnessed Tengku's dedication to his family and was determined to honour that commitment by offering his support in any way possible.

As the days rolled on, the intricate puzzle of events continued to unravel. The warehouse, the arms dealings, Tengku's disappearance—all these threads seemed to converge around Tristan. The pressure was building, but Tengku's family and Daniel found strength in their unity. They were prepared to weather the storm, fuelled by their determination to uncover the truth, and ensure justice prevailed.

Chapter 55

As the sun began to set, casting an orange and pink hue over the horizon, Tristan found solace in the anonymity of the coming night. He believed he had successfully diverted the police's attention toward Daniel, buying himself some time. With a bag of takeout in hand, he retreated to his apartment, a temporary sanctuary from the chaos that surrounded him. His calculated moves had kept him one step ahead, or so he thought.

Leaving his phone at the apartment, Tristan proceeded to the eerie construction site where he held Tengku captive. The air was thick with tension, a silent reminder of the danger that lurked within these bare and incomplete walls. The dim light cast elongated shadows, giving the place an ominous feel. Dust particles danced in the air, a testament to the forgotten state of the site.

Upon his arrival, Tristan's eyes fell upon Tengku, his captive. Tengku appeared worn down, a combination of exhaustion and hunger etching lines of defeat on his face. Tristan released the restraints, allowing Tengku to eat, his movements hesitant and cautious. A predator watching its prey, Tristan's cold gaze never wavered.

Words exchanged between captor and captive carried an air of menace. Tristan informed Tengku of the ongoing police search, his voice laced with a sinister confidence. He revelled in the belief that he had successfully concealed Tengku's whereabouts. His arrogance painted him as invincible, shielded from the law's grasp.

But beneath Tengku's facade, a storm of emotions raged. His identity remained concealed, the charade of being Tengku Beans a crucial survival strategy. He denied any knowledge of the arms deals, a truth that only he and Detective Lam were privy to. Tristan's anger and refusal to believe him only heightened Tengku's conviction to maintain the illusion. He couldn't afford to unravel the web of deception now.

Tristan's erratic behaviour unnerved Tengku. The captor's suggestions, veiled as ideas to secure his escape, were more akin to the musings of a deranged mind. The suggestion of demanding a ransom was ludicrous, bordering on macabre. Tengku sensed that Tristan's mental state was deteriorating, his obsession with power and control spiralling out of control.

Tengku's heart raced as he navigated the delicate dance of survival. He treaded carefully, attempting to pacify the unpredictable captor. He had no desire to provoke Tristan's fury further, recognizing the fine line between survival and a catastrophic end. Tristan's mind was a battlefield of rage and paranoia, a ticking time bomb that threatened to explode at any moment.

As the night deepened, the walls seemed to close in on them. The construction site, once a place of potential, now served as a makeshift prison. Tristan's desperation echoed through the empty corridors, a chilling reminder of the darkness that consumed him. Tengku maintained his facade, using it as armour against Tristan's mounting madness.

The moonlight cast eerie shadows, dancing along the rough surfaces of the walls. The air was fraught with tension, each breath a reminder of the perilous situation. Tengku's mind raced, searching for an opportunity, a weakness in Tristan's facade. The stakes were higher than ever, and Tengku's determination to survive burned brighter.

As the night wore on, Tengku clung to his identity, his family, and the hope that Detective Lam would find them. Tristan's grip tightened, his unravelling psyche pushing them both closer to the edge. In this suffocating game of cat and mouse, Tengku's strength and resourcefulness were his only allies, his unwavering determination to outlast the storm that Tristan had become.

Chapter 56

Detective Lam's determination burned as he stared at the gathered information, his mind racing to connect the dots. The pieces were coming together, aligning with Tengku's account of Tristan's movements. The Detective called Choi to verify if Tristan was indeed at home during the abduction. Choi notified the Detective that he was actually acting very suspicious, and he was only home for a few minutes at a time. This seemed to have made sense to the detective, but the detective needed evidence to confirm this. The idea of tracking Tristans phone came to the detective, and he managed to get a warrant for the phone signals as well as the GPS of the phone. This would put Tristan at the scene of the crime and will confirm that Tristan was the kidnapper. They headed to the service provider and showed them the warrant. This was enough for them to get all the information on Tristans phone. This took a couple of hours, but it was worth the wait. They managed to get everything they needed, and the detective took the evidence to the homestay to sift through it. As he studied the information given to him from Celcom, he began to see the timeline unfold before him. Tristan's movements were meticulously tracked, showing his visits to the warehouse and the waterfront on the day of the abduction.

They were well aware that the devil was in the details, and they couldn't afford to miss a single clue. The information provided a critical foundation for building the case against Tristan, but they needed something more concrete to tie him directly to Tengku's abduction.

Detective Lam decided to take the same route that Tengku took on the day of the abduction and checked if there was camera footage along the way. This would give them concrete proof that Tristan was there and following Tengku. The detective managed to get the footage from many random businesses that had cameras focused on the roads leading to the waterfront. They also managed to get the footage at the waterfront. With all the information that the detective retrieved, he knew it was going to be a long night so the detective managed to get some snacks and food for himself and Tengku. After getting everything together, he headed to their temporary home. From their home, the detective called Tengku's family so he would hear his family was well. He wanted to advise them that they were making progress and further information would be given to them soon. Daniel was with Tengku's family, so it put Tengku at ease to know his family were being taken care of.

They began sifting through the information with no interruptions. Hours turned into a blur as the detective and Tengku pored over the footage, their concentration unwavering. Snacks and food lay untouched as their determination grew. It was during one of these painstaking viewings that Detective Lam noticed a minor yet significant detail – a glimpse of a tattoo on Tristan's forearm. It was just a brief flash as Tristan adjusted his sleeve, but it was enough for the detective's trained eyes to catch.

The detective's heart quickened as he realized the potential significance of the tattoo. It could serve as a key identifier, a mark that linked Tristan to the crime scene. With renewed vigour, he continued scouring the footage for more instances of this tattoo, meticulously noting down timestamps and locations. If they could match this tattoo to Tristan, it would provide the crucial link they needed to tie him to the abduction.

As the night wore on, Detective Lam and Tengku became more confident that they were closing in on the truth. They had pieced together a comprehensive timeline of Tristan's movements, backed by the security camera footage. The tattoo seemed to be the linchpin, the final piece of evidence that could potentially seal Tristan's fate.

The detective took a moment to step outside, his mind racing as he considered his next move. He needed to have the tattoo verified, to ensure that it indeed belonged to Tristan. He also needed to gather enough evidence to warrant an arrest. With these thoughts in mind, he dialled his colleague's number, arranging for a forensic team to analyse the footage and match the tattoo to Tristan's identity.

Returning to the room, Detective Lam informed Tengku of their breakthrough, the excitement and tension palpable in the air. Tengku's eyes shone with a glimmer of hope, and the detective could see the gratitude in his gaze. They were in this together, a team united by the common goal of bringing Tristan to justice and rescuing Tengku's brother.

As dawn broke, the detective's phone buzzed with a call from his colleague. The forensic analysis had been completed, and the tattoo on Tristan's forearm was indeed a match. With this confirmation, they had the crucial evidence needed to secure an arrest warrant. The detective felt a surge of adrenaline as he thanked his colleague and hung up.

Turning to Tengku, he saw a mix of emotions on his face – relief, anticipation, and a lingering tension. It was time to act. The detective informed Tengku that they had enough evidence to move forward, to arrest Tristan and save his brother. Tengku's eyes glistened with gratitude, and his voice held a newfound strength as he expressed his trust in Detective Lam's abilities.

As they prepared to leave their temporary haven, Detective Lam felt a sense of determination like never before. The next steps were crucial, the arrest and the rescue of Tengku's brother hinged on their precision and coordination. With the tattoo as their evidence and the timeline as their guide, they were on the brink of a breakthrough that would unravel the web of deception Tristan had woven.

Chapter 57

Tengku sat in the dimly lit room, his heart pounding as he heard the footsteps approaching the door. The anticipation was almost unbearable, a mixture of hope and fear swirling within him. He recognized the sound of the doorknob turning, and as the door creaked open, it felt like the beginning of a nightmare. The room's atmosphere was heavy with tension, and the creaking seemed to echo ominously, like a prelude to danger.

Tristan's figure loomed in the doorway, his presence casting a dark shadow across the room. The subdued lighting seemed to enhance his menacing aura. Tengku's eyes locked onto Tristan, his heartbeat reverberating in his ears. The seconds ticked by in agonizing slowness, each moment stretching like an eternity.

Tristan's entrance was accompanied by the distinct scent of the food he carried – a stark contrast to the sinister situation at hand. Tengku's stomach churned with a mix of hunger and anxiety. He knew that this was another attempt by Tristan to break him, to force him into submission. The abductor's offer of food was a macabre gesture, a manipulation tactic meant to keep Tengku off balance.

As Tristan spoke, his voice laced with an unsettling calmness, Tengku felt a shiver run down his spine. He could sense the undercurrent of menace beneath the facade of composure. Tengku's mind raced as he weighed his words carefully, treading the fine line between defiance and compliance. Every word he uttered felt like a gamble, a move in a dangerous psychological game.

Tristan's attempts to coax information out of Tengku were met with resistance, his questions falling on deaf ears. Tengku knew that any slip, any admission of knowledge, would only lead to more manipulation and suffering. The room itself seemed to tighten around him, its walls closing in as he tried to maintain his composure. The ordeal had taken its toll, both physically and mentally, but Tengku clung to his resolve.

The passing hours felt like a slow descent into madness. Tengku watched as the shadows danced along the walls, each flicker mirroring his inner turmoil. He kept his gaze steady, his determination unwavering, even as Tristan's frustration grew palpable. The tension between them crackled like electricity, a silent battle of wills.

As the day wore on, Tengku felt the weight of exhaustion pressing down on him. He longed for reprieve, for an end to this nightmare. But he also knew that giving in wasn't an option. He couldn't risk betraying his family, his brother, and himself. The darkness outside the windows deepened, a stark reminder of the passage of time.

Meanwhile, Detective Lam and his team were working tirelessly, tracking Tristan's movements from a safe distance. The unmarked cars had blended seamlessly into the cityscape, their occupants hidden behind tinted windows. The detective's instincts were on high alert, his focus laser sharp as he followed the trail of the man responsible for the abductions.

The suspense of tailing Tristan added to the tension of the operation. The detective's mind was a whirlwind of calculations and possibilities, his experience guiding his decisions. Each turn of Tristan's car was noted, every stop meticulously observed. The detective's instincts told him that Tristan was leading them to something significant, but he also knew that caution was paramount.

As the cars followed Tristan, the detective's heart raced. He realized they were getting closer to a decisive moment, the potential breakthrough they had been waiting for. The dirt road leading to the abandoned construction site triggered a surge of adrenaline, the culmination of their efforts drawing near. They maintained their distance, shadows in pursuit, aware of the danger that lay ahead.

The detective's mind was focused on the task at hand, his years of experience guiding his approach. He knew that the rescue operation needed precision and coordination, that any misstep could jeopardize Tengku's safety. With the other car's driver apprehended, the detective's confidence in their plan grew stronger. They were ready for whatever awaited them at the construction site.

Tristan's arrival at the site was a pivotal moment, a culmination of their pursuit. He climbed the broken stairway, the sound of his footsteps reverberating like a countdown to confrontation. Inside the room, Tengku's heart raced, his senses on high alert. He knew that this encounter would determine his fate, that he needed to stay composed in the face of danger.

As the door creaked open, Tristan's presence filled the room, his aura one of authority and malevolence. Tengku's eyes met his captor's, a silent exchange of defiance and determination. The tension in the room was palpable, a clash of wills that resonated with every breath. The stakes had never been higher, the culmination of their confrontation inevitable.

Tristan's demands and Tengku's resistance created a charged atmosphere, a high-stakes negotiation between captor and captive. The darkness outside mirrored the uncertainty within, a stark reminder of the danger that surrounded them. Tengku's every word was a testament to his resilience, a refusal to bow to intimidation.

Amid the silence of the night, Tristan's departure marked a turning point. The unmarked cars followed his path, each manoeuvre calculated to avoid detection. The anticipation was electric, the stakes higher than ever. The winding dirt road led them to an abandoned construction site, a place of shadows and secrets.

The detective and his team watched, poised for action, as Tristan disappeared into the site. They knew that the moment had come, that their calculated pursuit was about to bear fruit. Their approach was deliberate, cautious footsteps leading them to the room where Tengku was held captive.

As the door burst open, the room was flooded with light, and Tengku's eyes met the familiar sight of law enforcement. The relief that washed over him was almost overwhelming, his emotions a whirlwind of gratitude and exhaustion. The weapons pointed at him were a stark reminder of the danger he had faced, but in that moment, they symbolized his rescue.

Tengku's rescue had come at the culmination of meticulous planning and unwavering determination. The operation had required patience, precision, and unwavering commitment.

The detective's instincts and Tengku's resilience had converged in a climactic moment that shattered the chains of captivity.

As Tengku stepped into the light, his ordeal finally behind him, he felt a sense of renewal. The dawn of a new day brought with it the promise of freedom and justice. The rescue mission had been a testament to the power of perseverance, the unyielding pursuit of truth, and the indomitable spirit of those who refused to be silenced by darkness.

Chapter 58

Tengku's heart swelled with relief as he embraced his brother. After the terrifying ordeal he had endured at the hands of Tristan, being in the presence of his sibling provided a sense of security that he had yearned for. Beans too was overwhelmed with emotions – seeing his brother safe and unharmed after the distressing days they had been through brought tears to his eyes.

Detective Lam offered a reassuring smile to Tengku Han, acknowledging the need for them to go through a debriefing and questioning. Beans, understanding the importance of their role in helping to close the case, requested if they could first head home and reunite with their family. The detective empathetically agreed, aware that the family needed this moment of solace and reconnection.

As they walked through the corridors towards Tengku Beans' home, a mixture of emotions washed over them. The sense of anticipation grew stronger with each step, their hearts racing in sync with their footfalls. The journey that had started with a dark cloud seemed to be leading them towards a much-needed ray of light.

Upon reaching the door of their family haven, Tengku carefully turned the handle and pushed it open. The family inside was consumed by a mixture of fear and hope – they had been anxiously waiting, unsure of who would be at the door. Stealthily, they moved forward, their breaths held in anticipation.

Then, their eyes locked onto the figures at the entrance, and time seemed to stand still. Alicia's heart pounded in her chest as she stared at her husband, almost unable to believe her own eyes. She had imagined this moment countless times, playing it over and over in her mind, but now that it was here, it felt surreal.

For a brief instant, her face lit up with an emotion that had been missing for days, a radiant smile that conveyed a mixture of disbelief, joy, and sheer relief. But then doubt crept in, and her smile wavered. Could it truly be him? Or was her longing playing tricks on her?

Kyrie and Akanji, their eyes wide with shock, were the first to break the stunned silence. "Dad!" they exclaimed in unison, their voices a mixture of disbelief and happiness. Their words echoed through the room, and suddenly, Alicia's hesitation melted away. She rushed forward, her steps quickening until she was in her husband's arms. The hug was a combination of relief, pent-up anxiety, and pure love. She held him tightly, as if she was afraid, he might disappear if she let go.

Detective Lam, standing by, watched the heartwarming scene unfold. The family's unity and the depth of their emotions were palpable, reminding him of the importance of his role in ensuring their safety. He gently interjected, letting them know that the two brothers were indeed safe and back home.

As the family embraced, the detective informed them of the ongoing situation. Though Tengku Han was home, Tristan was still at large, and the threat had not been fully eliminated. To ensure their safety, police officers would remain stationed there for protection. The family, though wanting to spend uninterrupted time together, understood the necessity and agreed wholeheartedly.

The apartment, once again filled with laughter, chatter, and the warmth of their shared love, was now also under the watchful eyes of vigilant officers. But amidst the presence of law enforcement, the Beans family found solace – knowing that they were not alone in facing this ordeal and that the protection of their loved ones was paramount.

The evening that had started with uncertainty had transformed into a night of togetherness and reconnection. With Tengku Han's safe return, the family's unity seemed even stronger, fortified by their shared experiences and the support of those who had stood by their side.

As the hours passed, laughter and stories filled the air, providing a sense of normalcy that had been missing for far too long. Detective Lam, satisfied to see the family finally at peace, quietly excused himself. Though the investigation continued, for now, this was a moment of respite and healing that he was glad to have been a part of.

Chapter 59

The family was finally safe, but Detective Lam's focus shifted immediately to the capture of Tristan. He briskly directed his fellow officers who weren't stationed at Tengku's house to rendezvous with him downstairs. The objective was clear: apprehend Tristan at his apartment. Armed with undeniable evidence of both the abduction and arms deals, they had enough to bring him down, but the whereabouts of Jack still eluded them.

The city's night was suddenly torn apart by the piercing wails of police sirens, the deafening cacophony echoing through the streets like a harbinger of chaos. Tristan's senses sharpened at the distant sound, his heart pounding in his chest. It was a symphony of impending danger, and he knew, instinctively, that they were closing in on him, like bloodhounds on a scent.

Without a moment's hesitation, he sprang into action. Tristan's pre-prepared bag, sitting patiently by the door like a loyal accomplice, was snatched up, its weight a reassuring reminder of his contingency plans. His keys were in his hand, and with a final glance around the apartment that had become both sanctuary and prison, he bolted out of the door.

The timing was impeccable, or perhaps it was fate itself guiding his steps. As the police vehicles screeched to a halt in front of his apartment building, the very building Tristan had just vacated, his car roared to life in the parking lot. Tires squealed in protest as he made his daring escape, leaving behind a trail of uncertainty and a befuddled team of law enforcement officers.

Tristan's flight through the city was a desperate race against time. The labyrinthine streets became his ally and his adversary, the flickering streetlights casting eerie shadows on the asphalt. Every twist and turn was a heartbeat skipped, every intersection a crossroads between freedom and capture.

His destination was remote, a hidden refuge that bore the alias "Adam." Here, Tristan had cultivated an underground network of allies, their loyalty shrouded in layers of secrecy. They were the unseen hands that could forge new identities, provide essentials, and erase traces. This hideout, a small, self-contained unit, was his sanctuary, a place to regroup, think, and strategize his next move.

Inside, essentials and provisions were stashed away with military precision. Every item was a tool in his arsenal, every resource a lifeline. Tristan intended to lay low, to become a ghost in the city he had once known so well. He would need to craft his next move carefully, outwit those who pursued him, and emerge from the shadows stronger than ever.

As he raced away from his old life, leaving the chaos and confusion in his wake, Tristan couldn't help but wonder about Choi. His loyal but unwitting companion had been caught off guard, still sleeping peacefully as the storm descended upon their lives.

Detective Lam and his team arrived at Tristan's apartment, believing they had him cornered. But the bird had flown the coop, leaving behind a startled Choi. The situation quickly escalated as Choi, rudely awoken, claimed ignorance about Tristan's whereabouts. One officer seized Choi, demanding answers. Suddenly alert, Choi insisted he genuinely had no knowledge of Tristan's escape. The forceful confrontation shook Choi, revealing the extent of Tristan's calculated evasion.

It was evident that Tristan had managed to evade their grasp this time, disappearing like smoke through their fingers. The apartment was cordoned off, waiting for the forensics team to comb through every inch, hoping for any lingering clue. The officers' determination was unshaken. With Tristan's trail still fresh, they believed they were getting closer to solving the case and finding Jack.

As they examined every detail of the apartment, Detective Lam's mind was racing. They had Tristan's tracks, and now they were determined to follow them to their conclusion. The anticipation among the officers was palpable; they were ravenous for Tristan's arrest, driven by the desire for justice and the safety of their community.

In the wake of Tristan's escape, a mix of frustration and renewed determination filled the air. Detective Lam knew that their task had become even more challenging, yet he was unyielding. They had uncovered so much evidence, and their net was tightening. As the forensics team worked meticulously, every fibre of the officers' beings was focused on the ongoing investigation.

The atmosphere was tense, but the team was resolute. They weren't about to let Tristan's escape deter them. The pursuit of justice was a relentless race, and Detective Lam was determined to see it through to the finish line, no matter how winding the road ahead might be.

Chapter 60

Tristan's heart raced as he scanned through the internet for any news about the recent events. The anxiety of being hunted was taking its toll on him. He was relieved to see that there were no immediate news articles, but his relief was short-lived when he stumbled upon a headline that made his blood run cold. The title read: "Abduction Victim Rescued, Kidnapper at Large."

His fingers trembled as he read the details of Tengku's rescue. He was hit by a wave of disbelief and horror when he learned that he had abducted the wrong Tengku. How could he have made such a colossal mistake? His meticulous planning and precision had crumbled because he wasn't aware of Tengku's almost identical twin brother.

The realization sunk in, making him furious at himself. He hadn't properly accounted for the possibility of mistaken identity. He punched the wall in frustration, anger coursing through his veins. Glass shattered, adding to the mess that surrounded him. His carefully crafted plan had fallen apart, and his world was spiralling out of control.

As if that weren't enough, his face was now plastered all over the internet. He was labeled as "Armed and Dangerous," a fugitive from justice. The image of his face, the manhunt intensifying, and the comments from people condemning his actions were overwhelming. He had anticipated the heat, but he hadn't prepared himself for the emotional toll it would take.

Tristan realized that lying low for a while was his best option. He needed to stay off the grid, evade the authorities, and rethink his strategy. He had resources, money stashed away for emergencies just like this. The coming days were critical; he would have to plan his escape meticulously and erase any trace that could lead the authorities to him.

But it wasn't just about disappearing. He needed a new identity, one that would erase all connections to his old life. He had contacts, people who could help him create a new persona, forge documents, and provide him with the means to leave the country unnoticed.

In the dingy apartment that had become his sanctuary, Tristan understood that time was not on his side. Detective Lam was relentless, a force that wouldn't rest until justice was served. The pursuit was unrelenting, a constant threat that loomed over him.

His escape plan would require careful execution. He had to leave no digital trail, no breadcrumbs for the authorities to follow. He couldn't trust anyone; even his closest allies might turn on him if the price was right.

Tristan stared out of the window, his mind racing through the options. He needed to choose his next moves wisely, consider every angle, and anticipate Detective Lam's moves. The detective was close, and the net was tightening. It was a battle of wits, and Tristan knew he couldn't afford any more mistakes.

As the sun dipped below the horizon, Tristan's resolve solidified. He would lay low, prepare for the ultimate escape, and disappear into the shadows. He couldn't change the past, but he could shape his future. Every decision he made now would determine whether he would fade away or face the consequences of his actions.

The hunt was far from over, and the stakes had never been higher. Tristan's escape was a countdown, a race against time, and only one question remained: would he elude justice or succumb to the relentless pursuit?

Chapter 61

In the wake of the failed capture and Tristan's escape, the old apartment where he had been staying became a hub of focused activity. The forensic team meticulously combed through every inch of the space, leaving no stone unturned. With gloves on and magnifying glasses in hand, they dissected every piece of evidence, from discarded takeout containers to crumpled paper and even the trash. The intensity of their search was palpable as they moved with a sense of purpose, aware that a single overlooked detail could be the key to cracking the case wide open.

Their investigation didn't stop within the confines of the apartment. Determined officers fanned out to the nearby food stalls, questioning every vendor and individual who might have interacted with Tristan. Faces were scrutinized, alibis examined, and stories cross-referenced. The atmosphere crackled with the urgency of their pursuit; each officer driven by the knowledge that Tristan was a dangerous man on the run.

The detectives returned to the cell phone service provider, demanding every shred of data associated with the number they had on record for Tristan. Text messages were dissected, calls analysed, patterns discerned. They sought that elusive breadcrumb that might lead them to Tristan's next move. However, even with all their efforts, there seemed to be no new lead to follow, leaving them frustrated but undeterred.

Meanwhile, Detective Lam was back at the police station, preparing for Tengku Han's debrief. The once-traumatized man had regained some composure after rest and a change of clothes, his willingness to assist growing stronger. Seated across from the detective, he recounted the harrowing events of his abduction. He remembered the darkness, the pain of the blow to his head, and the disorienting feeling of waking up in that grim room.

The detective probed further, seeking any inkling of information that could prove valuable. Tengku Han described Tristan's erratic behaviour, his volatile mood swings, and his apparent instability. But when pressed about any possible hints Tristan might have dropped about his whereabouts, Tengku Han's brow furrowed with frustration. He strained his memory, delving into every conversation they'd had, every seemingly inconsequential detail. Yet, at that moment, nothing stood out as a definitive clue.

Tengku Han couldn't shake the feeling of helplessness. He wanted to contribute more to the investigation, to help put an end to Tristan's reign of terror. The detective's reassurance was kind, reminding him that even the smallest, seemingly insignificant fragment of information could hold value. He urged Tengku Han to take his time and to call if anything resurfaced in his memory.

With that, Tengku Han left the police station, a mix of determination and frustration on his face. Yet, Tengku Beans remained, his gaze fixed on Detective Lam. He couldn't help but inquire about the progress of the investigation, his eyes holding a glimmer of hope. The detective's response was measured yet resolute, assuring Tengku Beans that the force was leaving no stone unturned.

As the day progressed, the intensity of the search never wavered. Every bit of evidence was analysed, every lead followed, and every resource mobilized. The pieces of the puzzle were slowly being gathered, ready to be assembled into a complete picture. Tristan's escape might have provided him with a momentary reprieve, but the forces of justice were closing in, and every detail, no matter how minute, was crucial in the pursuit of a man who was, for now, still one step ahead.

Chapter 62

Detective Lam's mind was a whirlwind of thoughts, considering every possible move Tristan could make. He knew that time was of the essence; Tristan was likely planning his escape, seeking refuge in the anonymity of neighbouring countries. The close proximity of Singapore and Thailand provided him with the perfect routes to disappear without a trace. And Detective Lam was determined not to let that happen. He immediately coordinated with his team to ensure border security and thorough checks, making it as difficult as possible for Tristan to cross.

The detective was well aware that Tristan's involvement in the illegal arms trade had likely fattened his bank account. Money was the lifeline for criminals looking to change their identities, start anew. Detective Lam was resolute in cutting off this escape route before it could even begin. While some of his officers were tasked with border control, he decided to delve deeper into Tristan's personal history.

The identity that Tristan had constructed under "Tok and Beans" was a facade, a mask that he had worn expertly. Now, with their access to his apartment, they meticulously collected every piece of evidence that could lead them to the truth. Fingerprints were lifted from surfaces; DNA swabs were taken from glasses. Every trace that Tristan had left behind was analysed, dissected, and scrutinized.

Sitting on Tristan's worn-out couch, Detective Lam looked around the apartment as if searching for invisible threads that could unravel the mystery. His gaze fell on a seemingly ordinary picture frame that had fallen and shattered. As they picked up the pieces, they realized that what they initially thought was part of the frame was actually a hidden picture of a boat. It was a small detail, but in this intricate puzzle, every piece counted. The frame, now in their possession, had the potential to reveal something crucial about Tristan's past, something that might lead them closer to unmasking his true identity.

Meanwhile, in the fishing village where Tristan had taken refuge, the salty breeze clung to his skin as he set out to sea. Fishing had become his refuge, his way of finding a semblance of peace amidst the chaos he had created. The boat, passed down from his father, held a special place in his heart. It was a connection to his past, a link to a simpler time when life hadn't spiralled into darkness.

Tristan's family had known hardship intimately. Their modest existence in Melaka was marked by poverty and illness. Fishing had been his father's legacy, a skill passed down to him. They had shared countless moments in that boat, father, and son bonding amidst the waves. But life's cruelty had taken both his parents prematurely, leaving him to navigate the rough waters alone.

Fate had not been kind to Tristan. His dreams of education and a brighter future had been dashed by circumstance. He possessed an innate intelligence that could have propelled him to great heights. However, destitution had driven him into the arms of darkness, where he learned to manipulate and deceive. The life he'd chosen had taken him far from the path he might have walked.

As Detective Lam pieced together the fragments of Tristan's life, the intricate mosaic of his motives began to form. Each detail uncovered was a brushstroke on the canvas of this enigmatic man's existence. The journey to apprehend Tristan was not just about justice; it was about unraveling the intricate threads of a life shaped by hardship, desperation, and choices made in the shadows.

Chapter 63

As Detective Lam and his team continued to piece together the puzzle of Tristan's identity, they delved deeper into his past. The discovery of the boat picture led them to explore Adam Wan's connections to the fishing village, hoping to uncover more about his upbringing and motivations.

The detective decided to visit the fishing village himself, accompanied by Tengku Beans. They wanted to speak with anyone who might remember Adam's family and shed light on his background. The village was a picturesque coastal settlement with colourful boats bobbing in the clear waters.

Upon their arrival, they found an old fisherman who had known Adam's family. As he shared his memories, a tale of hardship and tragedy emerged. Adam's parents had struggled to make ends meet, and his father's prized possession, the boat, had been their only source of income. The detective learned that Adam's father had passed away unexpectedly, leaving behind a grieving mother who battled illness.

Moved by the story, Tengku Beans saw a side of Adam he had never considered. He realized that desperation and a desire to change his circumstances might have driven Adam down a dark path. Despite feeling empathy, Tengku Beans and Detective Lam were resolute in their determination to bring Adam Wan to justice. They knew that his criminal activities were not a solution but an exacerbation of his troubles.

Back at the station, the forensic analysis yielded results. Fingerprints found on surfaces in Adam's apartment matched prints in the police database. The prints were a match for an individual named Adam Wan, a known associate of criminal networks. The revelation sent shockwaves through the investigation team as they realized that Adam's true identity was now within reach.

As they dug further, they discovered Adam Wan's history of involvement in illegal activities, from petty theft to more serious crimes. His connections stretched across the city, indicating a web of criminal affiliations that had helped him evade law enforcement for so long.

The team intensified their efforts to track down Adam Wan by employing a combination of technology and old-fashioned police work. They conducted stakeouts, monitored his known hangouts, and tapped into their network of informants. But the challenge was to determine where he had gone after leaving the fishing village.

Unfortunately, the people in Melaka knew that Adam had left and went with the boat, but they did not know where he would have gone to. This left Detective Lam and his team with threads to piece together but no clear destination.

Detective Lam shares the new developments with Tengku Beans. They discuss the challenge of tracking down Adam Wan's possible whereabouts and how they need to think like him to anticipate his next move. The determination to bring Adam to justice and rescue Jack remains strong, but the clock is ticking, and they know that every moment counts.

Even though the information they received captured the empathy of Tengku Beans and Detective Lam, they felt for Adam Wan's troubled past they knew that emphasizing their unwavering commitment to upholding the law and ensuring justice prevailed. The challenge of finding Adam's next location added suspense and urgency to the investigation.

Chapter 64

Now that Tengku Han was safely back and the family was attempting to regain a semblance of normalcy, the weight of the past few weeks had taken its toll on them all. Despite their efforts to carry on as usual, the lingering shadow of Tristan's escape cast a cloud of unease over their lives. The boys returned to school; their safety discreetly ensured by an unmarked police presence.

Tengku Han made his way back to Kuala Lumpur, determined to re-enter the routine of work. Detective Lam informed the KL station of the ongoing threat and emphasized the importance of keeping Tengku safe until Tristan was apprehended. Meanwhile, Alicia adapted to working from home, supported by an invisible shield of police protection that remained ever vigilant.

Beans, too, felt the pull of his professional responsibilities. Returning to the office, he aimed to assess the state of affairs and ensure the smooth functioning of the business during his absence. Settling at his desk, he delved into the tasks at hand. Just as he was immersing himself in his work, Amy, a supportive and concerned member of his team, arrived with a cup of coffee. The genuine relief on her face was palpable as she saw her boss safe and sound.

Seating herself across from him, Amy listened attentively as Tengku recounted the harrowing events that had transpired, including Tristan's flight from justice. Her expression shifted from shock to a deep concern, mirroring the tumultuous emotions that this news stirred within her. Amy had always admired Tengku's compassion and willingness to help those less fortunate, and now she could see the potential pitfalls of such empathy. After absorbing the gravity of the situation, she reassured Tengku of her unwavering support and willingness to assist in any way she could.

As Amy left his office to resume her own tasks, Tengku found himself alone with his thoughts. He couldn't help but reflect on the changes this ordeal had wrought in his outlook. The experience had taught him the value of caution and the importance of discernment when it came to opening up his business and his life to others.

A little later, a familiar face walked through his door. It was Daniel, his loyal friend, and ally. Their reunion was heartfelt, an embrace laden with gratitude and relief for the safety of loved ones. Amid the turmoil, Tengku had missed his friend's presence.

"Daniel, thank you for everything you did for my family. I can't express how grateful I am for your support," Tengku said, his voice tinged with deep appreciation.

Daniel grinned, his response filled with camaraderie. "We've always been brothers, Tengku. I couldn't stand by if you needed help. You've been there for me countless times, so this was the least I could do."

The conversation flowed, providing a cathartic release for both friends. Tengku updated Daniel on the ongoing situation, conveying that Tristan was still at large and the family was grappling with the aftermath. "We're all a bit shaken," Tengku admitted, "but we're trying to move forward and believe that things will improve."

With their hearts lightened by the camaraderie, the two friends parted ways. Daniel departed in his car, leaving Tengku to continue with his day. Tengku's next stop was the warehouse, a place that had recently become both a sanctuary and a source of distress.

Upon his arrival, he was greeted by Charles, who was overseeing the loading of goods onto a truck. The heightened security measures were evident, a testament to the apprehension that had taken root. However, Charles' face lit up at the sight of Tengku. He approached with a warm smile that held a mix of gratitude and relief.

"Mr. Beans, I'm so glad to see you safe and well," Charles exclaimed, his voice filled with genuine emotion. After a brief exchange of pleasantries, they proceeded to finalize paperwork related to the outgoing shipment.

As the day progressed, Tengku couldn't help but acknowledge the underlying tension that had seeped into every corner of his life. The balance between personal and professional, security and normalcy, was a delicate one. The turmoil brought on by Tristan's actions had cast a long shadow, but Tengku was determined not to let it consume him.

Chapter 65

As the day progressed, a palpable sense of curiosity and unease swept through the warehouse. The staff, buzzing with questions, gravitated towards Charles, their desire for answers almost overwhelming. News of Tristan's absence had ignited their curiosity like wildfire, and they sought an explanation for the sudden disruption in their midst. Whispers echoed across the warehouse floor as they shared their suspicions and speculations.

In response, Charles gathered his employees, their expectant faces reflecting a mix of concern and intrigue. He stood before them, a commanding figure amidst the sea of inquisitive eyes, and addressed their queries with a measured tone. "Ladies and gentlemen," he began, "as you are all aware, Tristan is no longer with us, and his absence has raised certain questions. I want to assure you that we are taking this situation seriously, as our primary concern is the safety and integrity of our operations."

A chorus of nods and murmurs rippled through the crowd, a collective acknowledgment of their shared commitment to the business's welfare. Some of the staff recalled the peculiar behaviour Tristan had exhibited during his time there. "He always seemed a bit off," one remarked, "had a temper, would snap without reason."

Charles, attentive to their observations, let out a sigh. "Indeed, we have reason to believe that Tristan may have been involved in activities that pose a risk to the company's reputation and our well-being. He is now a person of interest, and we need your cooperation to ensure that we can navigate this situation effectively."

The staff, united in their loyalty to Tok and Beans, readily agreed to assist in any way possible. Charles stressed the importance of notifying him immediately if anyone had recent contact with Tristan, a move intended to protect both the business and its people.

During the conversation, one of the staff members recalled a casual interaction with Tristan that had taken place before. He shared, "I remember he mentioned his love for fishing, even joked about taking us out sometime." A spark of recognition lit up Charles' eyes as he focused on this seemingly innocuous detail.

"Can you recall where he said he went fishing?" Charles inquired urgently, sensing a potential breakthrough. The staff member hesitated, his brow furrowing as he racked his memory. "It was a small fishing village," he began, "I think somewhere in Sepang."

Charles' heart raced as he absorbed the revelation. The name "Sepang" resonated, but the exact location remained just out of reach. He thanked the staff for their input and hastily departed, his steps quickening as he headed to the offices. The sense of urgency that pulsed through him was almost tangible.

Upon arrival, Charles burst through the door to Tengku's office, a whirlwind of excitement and determination. His breathless entrance startled both Tengku and Amy, their initial concern yielding to the charged energy that radiated from Charles.

In a rush of words, Charles blurted out, "Sepang!" The abruptness of his announcement startled Tengku and Amy, their initial confusion quickly giving way to curiosity and a shared sense of urgency. Charles' chest heaved as he attempted to catch his breath, his excitement almost tangible in the air.

Amy swiftly handed Charles a glass of water, concern etched onto her features. As he took a few sips to calm himself, Charles finally managed to string together coherent words. "Sepang," he repeated, this time with clarity. The significance of this word resonated deeply with Tengku, a surge of anticipation coursing through his veins.

Tengku leaned forward, his voice tinged with eagerness. "Charles, what are you saying? What about Sepang?" The suspense was palpable, a charged atmosphere that mirrored the urgency of the moment.

Charles, now composed, continued, "When Tristan joined us, he mentioned going fishing, particularly in a small village in Sepang." The connection was clear – if they could trace Tristan's whereabouts to this specific location, they might uncover a crucial lead in their pursuit of him.

With each passing second, the excitement in the room intensified. Tengku's heart pounded in his chest, the revelation igniting a spark of hope. The mention of Sepang was a clue, a beacon guiding them closer to the elusive fugitive. Charles' eyes met Tengku's, and the unspoken understanding between them was electric.

Breathing deeply, Tengku managed to control his racing thoughts. He looked at Charles with a mix of gratitude and determination. "Charles, you may have just given us a significant lead. I need to inform Detective Lam immediately." The words were laden with anticipation and urgency.

Charles nodded, a shared sense of purpose binding them. Tengku reached for his phone, swiftly dialling the detective's number. As the call connected, Detective Lam's voice resonated on the other end, his tone echoing the professional and personal stake he had in the case.

"Detective," Tengku began, "we might have a lead on Tristan's whereabouts. Charles just informed me that Tristan mentioned a small fishing village in Sepang. This could be the breakthrough we've been waiting for."

Detective Lam's excitement was evident, his voice quickening as he responded, "This is fantastic news, Tengku. If we can confirm the specific village, we might be one step closer to apprehending him. Keep me updated."

As the call ended, Tengku's gaze met Charles', their shared anticipation and determination palpable. With newfound hope, Tengku felt a renewed sense of purpose – the tantalizing prospect of finally cornering Tristan and ensuring justice was served.

The two men exchanged a knowing look, their hearts beating in tandem as they stood on the precipice of a crucial breakthrough. The journey ahead was uncertain, but with every step, they moved closer to uncovering the truth and bringing an end to the unsettling chapter that had gripped their lives.

Chapter 66

When all the pressing matters at Tok and Beans were neatly arranged and urgent tasks put to rest, Tengku found himself at a pivotal crossroad. A rendezvous with Detective Lam, his unwavering partner in this quest for justice, was in order. Tengku carefully stowed away the files that had occupied his attention, feeling a surge of satisfaction as he secured each one. The burden of uncertainty was gradually lifting, replaced by the hopeful determination to bring this chapter to a close.

Dialling the detective's number, Tengku's voice carried a note of readiness, "Detective, I am prepared to meet with you. Where shall we convene?" The familiar camaraderie they had developed amid adversity echoed in his words.

The detective responded in a manner that spoke of their shared experiences, "Let's gather at the homestay. It's your turn to bring the sustenance this time, my friend. I did my part when you were laying low." Their conversation resonated with a harmony born of trials endured together, laced with a touch of light-heartedness that only such companionship could foster.

Acknowledging the arrangement, Tengku chuckled, "Certainly, I can make it in an hour. What are your culinary cravings today?"

Detective Lam's thoughtful pause was followed by a decisive reply, "Thai noodles should hit the spot, and don't forget to add some spring rolls to the mix."

As they concluded their exchange, Tengku placed an order for their meal at his preferred eatery. This was a familiar ritual, a brief moment of respite before they embarked on yet another phase of their relentless pursuit of justice. He embarked on his journey to the makeshift office at the homestay, the scent of anticipation filling the air. The hour flew by, and soon they were seated in the familiar surroundings, armed with Thai delicacies and a shared determination.

A steaming bowl of Thai noodles adorned Tengku's table, accompanied by a plate of golden spring rolls, their crisp exteriors promising a savoury delight. As the two men savoured the flavours, they pondered their next move. Each bite was a small pause amidst the ongoing saga, a chance to fortify their spirits and regroup for the challenges that lay ahead.

With their appetites sated, the duo shifted their attention to the map sprawled before them. The map painted a mosaic of possibilities, offering up a tapestry of locations that held potential clues. Twelve sites peppered their canvas, each representing a point of interest along the route. These places were not the grand resorts and luxury hotels. No, their pursuit led them to the quieter pockets, the fishing enclaves, and coastal retreats that locals frequented.

Understanding Tristan's cautious nature, they deduced he would likely seek refuge within the proximity of villages, the nooks that offered anonymity while remaining within the embrace of civilization. The notion of an inconspicuous existence guided their plan; they would blend in as humble fishermen, unassuming and unobtrusive. The last thing they wanted was to trigger alarm bells, giving Tristan a chance to elude their grasp once more.

Dressed in the attire of local fisherman, their ensemble was a masterful disguise, a cloak that allowed them to inhabit the world they sought to penetrate. In their chosen vehicles, old pickup trucks that whispered stories of years gone by, they set forth on their quest. The engine's hum resonated with purpose, and the road stretched ahead like an uncharted river of opportunity.

The destination was known, the path was clear, and their resolve was unwavering. Armed with images of Tristan and the distinctive boat that had played a pivotal role, they prepared to uncover the threads that would lead them to their quarry. The plan was simple in its brilliance: engage the locals, inquire about boats, and gauge the familiarity with a face that had evaded capture.

As they embarked on this journey, the landscape changed around them. Scenes of rustic life and the serene waters painted an evocative backdrop. The people they encountered were the gatekeepers of the information they so desperately sought. Each conversation, each glance exchanged, held the promise of revelation. Their steps were purposeful, their minds focused, and their hearts resonated with the collective hope that this voyage would lead them closer to the truth.

In this moment, as they set forth on this new chapter of their investigation, a myriad of emotions stirred within them. The journey was not solely a physical one; it was a symbolic passage, a testament to their unwavering dedication. They were detectives, friends, and warriors of justice, bound by the common goal of righting wrongs and bringing closure to the afflicted. And as their vehicles traversed the roads less travelled, their shared destiny was forged in the crucible of adversity, ready to meet whatever challenges lay ahead.

Chapter 67

As Tengku and Detective Lam embarked on their mission to track down Tristan, a tense atmosphere enveloped their search. The urgency to find Tristan was palpable, with both men driven by a determination to bring him to justice. Their journey took them through winding roads and quaint villages, their old pickup trucks blending seamlessly with the scenery.

While the sun cast a warm glow on the landscape, the weight of their task cast a shadow over their minds. They discussed their approach, dissecting every detail of their plan. Detective Lam's experience in investigations and Tengku's familiarity with Tristan's history made them a formidable team. They shared anecdotes of their past experiences, forging a stronger bond between them.

As they drove along, they exchanged stories of their own lives. Tengku recounted childhood memories of fishing trips with his family, the gentle swaying of the boat, and the laughter that echoed across the water. Detective Lam shared snippets of his early days in law enforcement, the challenges he faced, and the victories he celebrated. Amidst their conversations, their resolve remained unshaken – Tristan had to be found and brought to justice.

Tristan, on the other hand, faced a different kind of challenge. The underground network he once relied upon had turned its back on him. The cryptic conversations over the phone only served to heighten his anxiety. Each conversation felt like a dangerous dance, where one wrong step could lead to his downfall. He realized that his past deeds had caught up with him, leaving him stranded in a world where trust was scarce.

As the days went by, Tengku and Detective Lam scoured the fishing villages one by one. They approached locals with genuine inquiries about fishing spots, casting their net wide to gather information. They displayed pictures of Tristan and the boat, hoping to trigger any memory that could lead them closer to their target. The response varied from nods of recognition to blank stares, but they persevered, understanding that patience was key in this pursuit.

The duo's presence drew the attention of curious villagers who were eager to share stories. Tengku and Detective Lam were introduced to a world of fishermen's tales, each story unveiling the soul of the village and its connection to the sea. They listened intently, absorbing the rich history and traditions that defined these communities. Amid their search for Tristan, they found themselves immersed in a world they hadn't known before.

Back in his hideout, Tristan's desperation grew. He had exhausted his options, leaving him with limited choices. The weight of his actions bore down on him, and he realized that he was now at the mercy of circumstances he could no longer control. The uncertainty of his fate gnawed at him, and he reflected on the choices that had led him down this treacherous path.

As Tengku and Detective Lam pressed on, their paths converged with the echoes of Tristan's choices. With every step, they uncovered the intricate tapestry of lives affected by his actions. Their determination was fueled not only by a desire for justice but by a sense of responsibility to those who had been harmed.

The search continued, each village revealing a piece of the puzzle. While they hadn't yet located Tristan, they were edging closer to him, one thread at a time. The journey was far from over, and the challenges ahead were formidable, but Tengku and Detective Lam were committed to seeing it through. Their resolve remained unshaken; their spirits undeterred by the vastness of the task before them.

Chapter 68

Tristan found himself at a pivotal juncture in his desperate bid to escape the clutches of the law. Armed with a lead to a man named Mark, who could provide him with forged documents and a new identity, Tristan knew that his chance for a clean getaway hinged on this risky meeting in Cyberjaya. Aware of the heightened risks, Tristan meticulously planned his route, meticulously avoiding major roads and tolls, opting for the labyrinthine network of smaller villages, a circuitous path that doubled the travel time but promised safety from prying eyes.

As he navigated the winding roads, Tristan's senses were on high alert, attuned to the possibility of any unwanted pursuit. Unbeknownst to him, he crossed paths with Detective Lam on the road, both figures unaware of the other's presence. For Tristan, each minute felt like an eternity, fraught with the tension of impending change.

Finally reaching his destination, Tristan met Mark, a seasoned operator in the shadowy world of forgery. Mark's history was riddled with narrow escapes from the law, an experienced hand in crafting new identities for those desperate enough to seek his services. Their meeting was far from casual; Mark made it clear that Tristan needed to display his commitment to this illicit venture. A down payment of RM2000 was demanded, a tangible demonstration of Tristan's earnestness.

Within the covert confines of Mark's workspace, a secretive operation was underway. Tristan's appearance had to be altered significantly to evade detection. New photographs were taken, bearing his altered visage. Silicone fingerprints were prepared to circumvent border crossings, a tool for seamless identity transitions. The intrigue deepened with fake retina scans, contact lenses that would further cement his new persona.

As the process unfolded, Tristan's desperation was palpable. His urgency was met with a stern caution from Mark, a reminder that hasty actions could lead to disastrous consequences. Despite the impending threat, Mark's meticulous approach was unwavering. He outlined a comprehensive package: a new identity, falsified passport, counterfeit driver's licenses, and the addition of travel stamps to mimic previous usage. Each element bore Mark's signature precision.

Tristan's impatience gnawed at him, a constant reminder that time was slipping through his fingers. He pressed Mark for expedited results, a demand that clashed with Mark's seasoned wisdom. The tension in the room escalated, a manifestation of Tristan's anxiety juxtaposed with Mark's measured pragmatism.

With the weight of his impending escape bearing down on him, Tristan confronted the reality of the cost. Mark did not cut corners; his meticulous work came with a price. The final bill amounted to RM40000, a steep figure that reflected the gravity of the situation and the intricacy of the task at hand.

As Tristan contemplated this newfound path, he grappled with the knowledge that every step he took was a gamble. The road ahead was fraught with risks and uncertainties, and his fate hung precariously in the balance. Mark's expertise offered a glimmer of hope, a slender thread of possibility that Tristan clung to as he ventured deeper into the abyss of his own desperation.

Little did he know that Detective Lam and Tengku were drawing closer to him, weaving a net of investigation that would soon converge with Tristan's tumultuous journey. The chase intensified, as two worlds hurtled toward an inevitable collision, each driven by their own motives and fueled by the inexorable pursuit of truth and justice.

Chapter 69

Tristan's meeting with Mark had left him feeling both relieved and anxious. The prospect of having the necessary documents to escape the country was a glimmer of hope in the darkness of his situation. As he drove along the winding road, the weight of his decisions bore down on him. The engine's hum seemed to match the rhythm of his racing thoughts.

His grip on the steering wheel tightened as he considered his next move. The road ahead paralleled his own journey – uncertain, winding, and shrouded in darkness. He knew that this week was his last in Malaysia, his final countdown in a place that had once been his home. His emotions were tangled, a blend of apprehension and a strange sense of liberation.

Lost in his contemplation, he suddenly realized how darkness had engulfed the surroundings, reflecting the shadow that had fallen over his life. Needing a respite, he pulled into a fuel station, the harsh fluorescent lights of the convenience store contrasting starkly with the dim night. He masked himself with a hoodie and a cap, a shield against recognition.

As he ordered some food, he observed couples and families sharing meals, their laughter cutting through the melancholic shroud that enveloped him. He felt isolated, the solitude of his decisions evident as he sat alone, a solitary figure amidst a world of connections. The food he consumed was a mere necessity to fuel his body, but it did nothing to satisfy the emptiness he felt.

Watching others living their seemingly simple lives intensified his awareness of his own complex situation. He acknowledged the stark contrast between his life and theirs, and a pang of regret coursed through him. The weight of his solitude and the choices he had made pressed down on his chest.

With an effort, he pushed away from those thoughts, allowing the determination that had driven him this far to resurface. The solitude of the road was a mirror to his current existence, and he needed to embrace it, if only for a while longer. He threw away the containers, symbolizing his intention to discard the negativity that had crept in.

Back home, his one-bedroom sanctuary offered a brief respite from the outside world. The familiarity of his surroundings mingled with the anxiety of the future he was about to embark upon. Collapsing onto his bed, he let fatigue carry him into a deep sleep. The dreams that visited him were a disjointed mix of memories and aspirations, a reflection of the blurred lines between his past and the unknown road ahead.

Tristan's life had become a delicate balance between surviving and striving. His thoughts and emotions churned as he navigated the intricacies of his circumstances. The journey ahead was uncharted, and he was both the traveller and the cartographer, shaping his path with each step.

Chapter 70

Detective Lam and Tengku found themselves navigating through a series of villages, each step bringing them closer to their elusive target, Tristan. They had already passed through three villages and were now approaching the fourth, a place that held the promise of potential answers. This village, like the others, was characterized by its close-knit community of locals who knew the intricacies of their fishing boats and the surrounding waters intimately.

As the night descended, both men sought respite in a humble meal. The fatigue from their days on the road was palpable, and they sought refuge in a modest homestay for a well-needed rest. Their minds were consumed by a mixture of exhaustion and anticipation, for the next day held the hope of significant breakthroughs.

During a moment of quiet reflection, Detective Lam realized that he hadn't contacted Jack's parents in days. The thought weighed on him heavily, and he recognized the urgency to reach out to them. However, he hesitated, mindful of the late hour, and not wanting to disturb them needlessly. He confided in Tengku, sharing the plight of Jack's family – how the money Jack had provided was not only for their well-being but had also sustained their lives. The absence of Jack left them struggling, compelled to curtail their basic necessities due to financial constraints.

Tengku's heart ached upon hearing this, his empathy for Jack's parents deepening. Though he had never met them, he felt a profound connection to their struggle. As someone who had experienced adversity, he understood the weight of their circumstances. In a gesture of remarkable compassion, Tengku expressed his desire to ease their burden. He committed to sending them financial assistance on a regular basis, recognizing that it was a small way to make their lives more manageable, even amidst the uncertainty surrounding Jack's whereabouts.

Detective Lam regarded Tengku with a mixture of admiration and respect. In a world often defined by self-interest, Tengku's selflessness stood out. It was a reminder that compassion and generosity could shine even in the darkest times. Determined to bring some semblance of good news to Jack's parents, the detective immediately placed the call. Their voices, laden with gratitude and emotion, resonated through the phone lines as the news of assistance reached them. Tears flowed freely, for this unexpected support was like a lifeline in their tumultuous journey to find their missing son.

With a new day dawning, the two men rallied themselves for the task ahead. Leaving the homestay, they ventured into the village once more, seeking interaction with the locals. They hoped that within these conversations lay the threads that could guide them closer to the enigmatic Tristan. The weight of the search, the web of uncertainty, and the glimmers of hope converged as they embarked on yet another day of determined investigation.

The village, awakening to the early light, offered a fresh start. The promise of answers lingered in the air; woven within the conversations they were about to have. Tengku and Detective Lam braced themselves for whatever lay ahead, united in their pursuit of the truth, and driven by the power of compassion that bound their hearts to this mission.

Chapter 71

Tristan awoke from his prolonged slumber, his body sluggish but his mind alert. The pressing need to orchestrate his escape jolted him into action. He rose swiftly, rushing to freshen up and chart his course of departure. Indonesia seemed like his only refuge now, a temporary sanctuary to elude the pursuing authorities. The sprawling urban hustle of Jakarta didn't appeal to him; he yearned for solace and seclusion. Amid contemplation, a fitting choice emerged – Bali. The island's vacation ambiance would grant him the perfect cover, blending in as just another tourist seeking relaxation.

Memories of his youth resurfaced – his friends' stories of the serene twin lakes in Bali, Lake Buyan, and Lake Tamblingan. These tranquil spots enticed travellers from across the globe, offering an escape from the mundane. Tristan envisioned himself disappearing into their soothing embrace, a phantom among nature's beauty. His search for a covert dwelling led him to Dajan Buyan, an idyllic apartment nestled in the heart of the forest. Here, he could find refuge from prying eyes, cloaked in secrecy. He was captivated by the notion of calling this haven his own for the upcoming weeks.

With his destination settled, Tristan shifted his focus to the logistics of his journey. He had to navigate the realm of transportation while remaining undetected. The prospect of a bus journey seemed too vulnerable – potential checkpoints could foil his plans. Airports, on the other hand, were rife with security measures, requiring a more covert approach. Trains and ferries seemed more plausible options. Tracing his route, he decided on a train ride to Johor Bahru, followed by a ferry from there.

A critical component of his stratagem was to create diversions and blind spots, confusing any potential pursuers. He decided to procure two train tickets – one in his true identity bound for Penang, the other under his new alias, destined for Johor Bahru. This clever gambit would cast doubt on his true intentions, obscuring his actual destination from prying eyes. It was an intricate plan designed to mislead and safeguard his newfound freedom.

As he mulled over his tactics, Tristan felt a surge of clarity. His intricate plans were aligning, a tapestry woven from his desperation and determination. With each detail meticulously plotted, he began to see a potential path forward, a chance at rebirth and escape from his suffocating past. He imagined the tranquil lakes, the lush forests, and the secluded abode awaiting him in Bali. It was a dream he could almost grasp, a beacon guiding him through the darkness that had engulfed his life.

With his preparations well underway, Tristan couldn't shake off the residual unease that clung to him. The journey ahead was treacherous, the challenges formidable. Yet, his pursuit of a new beginning held a glimmer of hope, a chance to rewrite his narrative and leave his past behind.

Chapter 72

Tristan found himself in a state of anxious waiting. He had set all the logistical aspects in motion, but everything hinged on obtaining his new alias. This made the passing of time feel excruciatingly slow. He needed this information to finalize his escape plan, but until then, he had nothing else to do but wait. The stillness of time was suffocating.

In an attempt to ease his restlessness, Tristan decided to seek solace on his boat. The open sea always had a way of bringing him a sense of calm and clarity. As he ventured into the vastness of the waters, the expanse seemed to reflect his internal state—unpredictable, yet tranquil. The gentle rocking of the boat beneath him, the rhythmic sounds of the waves, and the endless horizon ahead offered a momentary escape from the turmoil that swirled within him.

Meanwhile, Tengku and Detective Lam had set their sights on Wah Sempoh for their next lead. The intuition that this could be a pivotal location drew them closer. Upon arrival, they immediately noted the presence of numerous fishermen and locals. It felt like a place Tristan might gravitate towards—an ideal blend of anonymity within a modest community. This environment could easily swallow him without drawing undue attention. Their approach was to integrate themselves, to befriend the fishermen and glean any information that could inch them closer to Tristan's trail.

Engaging the local fishermen, Tengku and the detective tapped into their enthusiasm for their trade. Conversations flowed, and the men eagerly shared insights about the best fishing spots. While their initial inquiries seemed routine, the real purpose was to uncover any hints about Tristan's whereabouts. By inquiring about boat rentals and opportunities to join fishing expeditions, the duo skilfully maneuvered the discussions toward their target. The fishermen affirmed that while there were boats for hire, certain vessels were owned by individuals who preferred solitude and unpredictable schedules. One such boat caught their attention—the one that resembled Tristan's. The information painted a clearer picture, revealing that the boat's owner used it sporadically, usually later in the day.

Eager to make headway, Tengku and Detective Lam decided to spend the night in Wah Sempoh, continuing their quest the following morning. The tranquil atmosphere was a respite from their intense search, allowing them to momentarily detach from the urgency of their mission. As dawn approached, the two men found themselves standing on the fog-covered dock. The thick mist reduced visibility to mere meters, casting an eerie ambiance. The impending sunrise struggled to pierce through the dense fog, an apt metaphor for their journey—navigating through obscurity towards a breakthrough.

Among the sights and sounds emerging from the fog, a group of fishermen conversed while sipping coffee. A handful of boats bobbed on the water, ready to set sail. Despite their anticipation, the distinctive boat they sought was absent among the vessels. Engaging the fishermen, Tengku and Detective Lam learned that the boat they were looking for was indeed present in the village but rarely set sail until later in the day.

This information confirmed their suspicions—Tristan was indeed here. Fueled by this revelation, they hastened back to their lodging. In a flurry of excitement, they contacted their fellow officers who were also part of the operation. The culmination of their relentless pursuit was finally within grasp, and a renewed determination enveloped them. This moment marked the turning point in their investigation, a breakthrough forged through patience, keen observation, and strategic inquiries.

Chapter 73

The tension in the air was palpable as Detective Lam and Tengku finally closed in on Tristan. After days of patient surveillance and strategic planning, they were ready to make their move. The two additional officers arrived, adding to the intensity of the situation. The moment of reckoning was at hand, and they had to ensure that they played their cards right to catch Tristan off guard.

Their primary concern was to familiarize themselves with Tristan's daily routine and his hideout. They needed to know the layout of the place, the location of his boat, and any potential escape routes he might use. While the new officers took the lead, Detective Lam and Tengku decided to gather more information from the locals. The bustling seafood stalls provided the perfect backdrop for their inquiries. With each question, they hoped to gather more about the man known as "Adam."

As the sun began its descent, painting the sky with hues of orange and pink, they expanded their search to the lodging houses. They questioned the proprietors and visitors, asking if anyone had seen a man fitting Tristan's description. The name "Adam" seemed to be familiar, but no one knew the specifics of his whereabouts. They pressed on, determined to leave no stone unturned. Exhausted but undeterred, they finally struck gold when they met Nurin, a local woman who revealed that Tristan was indeed staying at a secluded lodging house. She discreetly shared his room number and promised to keep their presence a secret.

Empowered by this newfound information, the four officers headed toward Tristan's hideout with a sense of cautious anticipation. For Tengku's safety, Detective Lam insisted he remain in the car as a lookout. As the afternoon waned and shadows lengthened, they anticipated that Tristan might not be at his lodging house during this time. This provided them an opportunity to assess the surroundings and gather any evidence linking him to Jack's disappearance.

Entering Tristan's room with calculated silence, they methodically sifted through his belongings. Meanwhile, Tengku, stationed in the car, suddenly spotted a figure approaching the lodging house. Panic surged through him as he realized Tristan was returning. He attempted to reach Detective Lam, but the sound of his ringing phone was drowned out by the surroundings. Tristan's instincts kicked in; he noticed an unfamiliar car parked nearby. Slowly and deliberately, he investigated, his senses heightened. He noticed the irregularity, a car that had not been part of the scenery before. Wary of the potential threat, he approached the reception and inquired about an available room for his "friends." With the receptionist's confirmation, Tristan's suspicions deepened. He was sure the officers were close by, waiting for him to return.

Choosing not to enter his room, Tristan hastily left the lodging house, his heart pounding with adrenaline. He sprinted toward the dense tree line, his mind racing. Tengku, witnessing Tristan's actions, sprang into action, chasing after him. The pursuit had begun, the stakes higher than ever. Tengku's heart raced, his breath uneven, as he pushed himself to the limit. Tristan, driven by desperation, fired a shot in the direction of the noise behind him. Tengku miraculously dodged the bullet, pushing through the pain to keep running. Another shot rang out, this time finding its mark. The bullet struck Tengku's arm, causing him to stumble and fall.

Detective Lam, racing toward Tengku's location, witnessed the scene unfold. Urgently, he dialled for an ambulance while ensuring Tengku's wound was attended to. Tengku's pain was excruciating, his consciousness waning as shock and pain overwhelmed him. The ambulance arrived, rushing Tengku to the hospital as Detective Lam followed. The news reached Tengku's family, and they rushed to the hospital, their faces etched with concern.

Meanwhile, the other officers pursued Tristan, determined not to let him escape. However, Tristan's familiarity with the terrain gave him an edge, allowing him to elude them for the moment. The officers called Detective Lam, conceding that Tristan had slipped through their grasp, but vowing to continue the search.

Tengku was prepped for surgery, the bullet to be extracted. Detective Lam assured his family that the wound was not life-threatening, and his family exhaled a collective sigh of relief. Despite the chaos, the detective's unwavering support provided a sense of security. As Tengku was wheeled into the operating room, his family gathered in the waiting room, their thoughts dominated by anxiety and hope. The clock ticked slowly, each moment an eternity as they awaited news of Tengku's condition.

The hours in the waiting room were filled with tense anticipation. The detective continued to coordinate efforts with his fellow officers, ensuring that the pursuit of Tristan continued. Meanwhile, Tengku emerged from surgery, the bullet successfully removed. Detective Lam relayed the good news to his family, the collective sigh of relief echoing through the waiting room. As Tengku began his recovery, the detective had to break the news that Tengku's days as an active police officer were over. The priority now was Tengku's safety, his return to his family unscathed.

Tengku's family, grateful for the detective's commitment to his safety, shared their relief and happiness. The ordeal had highlighted the risks Tengku had been taking, and now, his well-being took precedence. The waiting room, once filled with worry, began to see glimpses of smiles and relief. As Tengku's recovery progressed, the determination to capture Tristan remained unwavering. The pursuit had taken an unexpected turn, but the focus on justice remained steadfast.

Chapter 74

With Tengku safe and under medical care, Detective Lam returned to Wah Sempoh, ready to continue the relentless search for Tristan. The officers on the ground had intensified their efforts, fanning out through the dense forest, leaving no corner unexplored. They were determined to locate the fugitive and put an end to his evasion.

The forensic team arrived at Tristan's lodging, greeted by the officers who had secured the scene. The room was a treasure trove of hidden items and secrets, revealing the complexity of Tristan's plans. They discovered a stash of money, clothes, and an emergency bag concealed beneath the floorboards. These findings indicated that Tristan had been prepared to escape, but something had thwarted his plans. The officers watched the room, waiting for any sign that he might return.

Their vigilance extended to Tristan's boat as well. Hidden eyes, expertly camouflaged, kept a watchful gaze on the vessel, ensuring that Tristan wouldn't slip away unnoticed if he attempted to retrieve it. The tense anticipation hung heavy in the air, as officers hoped for a breakthrough in the case.

Tristan, meanwhile, had sought refuge in a makeshift cave concealed by layers of branches and leaves. He had chosen a dip in the terrain that was known only to the locals, making it a nearly impenetrable hiding spot. The moist earth and dense vegetation camouflaged him effectively, and he remained quiet and still, trying to plot his next move. The setback had caught him off guard; his escape plan thwarted, and he was left without any resources.

Desperation and frustration were his constant companions as he wrestled with his predicament. His possessions, along with the evidence he needed to flee the country, were back in his room, waiting for retrieval. He knew that time was running out, and he needed to return to the scene of his lodgings when the officers were gone. He realized he had to be quick and clever if he was to evade capture and disappear once again.

As the forensic team combed through his room, their attention turned to a hidden laptop, cleverly stashed behind a closet. Tristan had carved out a portion of the wall, creating a concealed compartment where he had hidden the device. He had counted on his hiding place being overlooked, but the meticulous nature of the forensic team was proving formidable. The tech team was called in to crack the laptop's password, knowing that whatever was on it could hold crucial information about Tristan's actions and whereabouts.

Using sophisticated software, the tech team began the intricate process of breaking into the laptop. Hours ticked by, tension mounting with every passing minute. The laptop held the key to uncovering the extent of Tristan's plans, his contacts, and any traces of Jack's disappearance. The officers, led by Detective Lam, stood ready, knowing that the answers they sought could lie within the digital confines of the device.

As the sun dipped below the horizon, casting long shadows across the scene, the laptop finally yielded its secrets. The screen revealed a web of encrypted files, communications, and detailed plans. It became clear that Tristan had been meticulously plotting his escape for months, communicating with shadowy contacts who could help facilitate his journey.

The officers deciphered the encrypted messages, piecing together the puzzle of Tristan's intentions. They discovered that he had been planning to leave the country, using forged documents and contacts in various countries to ensure a seamless escape. He had been in touch with individuals involved in illegal activities, connections that likely played a role in Jack's disappearance.

With each revelation, the pieces of the puzzle began to fall into place. The officers now had a clearer picture of Tristan's motives and movements. The urgency to apprehend him grew stronger, knowing that he was armed with dangerous knowledge and connections that could lead to further harm.

As night settled over the scene, the laptop provided the breakthrough they had been hoping for. It was a race against time now. The officers had a newfound determination to locate Tristan and bring him to justice. With the intricate details of his plan unveiled, they were armed with information that could lead them directly to him.

In the heart of the forest, Tristan remained hidden in his makeshift cave, unaware of the progress the officers had made. He was still grappling with his options, his mind racing to find a way out of this dire situation. With the laptop's secrets now exposed, the net was closing in on him, and the officers' resolve to capture him was unwavering.

The pursuit continued, the tension mounting as both sides prepared for the final confrontation. The forest, once a place of quiet serenity, had transformed into a battleground of determination and strategy. The officers were on Tristan's trail, inching closer to his hiding place. The next chapter of this high-stakes chase was about to unfold, and the outcome hung in the balance.

Chapter 75

Detective Lam's mind buzzed with the revelation that Tristan had been in direct contact with Mark, the mastermind behind the forged documents. It was a breakthrough they had been desperately waiting for. They now possessed a treasure trove of insight into Tristan's escape plan, including the purchase of two tickets: one to Penang and the other to JB. Armed with this critical information, they knew the net was tightening around him.

The laptop they had seized contained a trove of evidence, meticulously outlining Tristan's elaborate plot. The detective and his team were now equipped with the names, dates, and details of arms deals, smuggling, and other illegal activities Tristan had been involved in. The laptop provided a clear picture of his intentions and connections, making it a powerful tool to bring him to justice.

Mark, the key to this unfolding operation, was contacted by officers. He was given a crucial task: to inform Tristan that the forged documents were ready for collection. Tristan had been assigned the alias Nathan, an identity he would need to rely on if he managed to slip away once more. The officers kept a close watch on Mark, as his cooperation was instrumental in finally closing in on their elusive target.

Detective Lam, however, was not leaving anything to chance. He devised a plan to ensure that if Tristan attempted to retrieve his hidden stash, they would be prepared. The money and belongings were placed back beneath the floorboards, but a hidden tracking device was carefully concealed within the cache. Every contingency was accounted for, knowing that Tristan's ability to evade capture was remarkable.

As darkness blanketed the area, Tristan ventured out of his makeshift hideout, his eyes scanning the surroundings for any sign of danger. The prospect of retrieving his money was tantalizingly close, and he was anxious to get his hands on the cash he needed to escape. The lodging, where his possessions lay hidden, beckoned to him, promising the means to continue his escape plan.

Unbeknownst to Tristan, the officers were lurking in the shadows, strategically placed to monitor the situation and seize their moment. They observed his movements, their heartbeat echoing the suspense that hung heavy in the night air. The lodging's door stood before him, offering access to his much-needed resources. However, a nagging intuition held him back. A sense of foreboding told him that this could be a trap, that walking through that door might lead him straight into the arms of the law.

Tristan's instincts were heightened by the realization that he was being watched. He weighed his options carefully, torn between the desperate need to retrieve his belongings and the fear of falling into a trap. With the night concealing both opportunities and dangers, he made a decision. Opting for caution, he retreated back to his hidden sanctuary, knowing that waiting for a safer moment might be his best chance.

The officers held their breath as Tristan's figure disappeared into the darkness, the opportunity slipping through their fingers for now. The tension was palpable, a blend of frustration and determination fuelling their efforts. They understood the complexities of this cat-and-mouse game, aware that Tristan's elusiveness was matched only by their determination to capture him.

As dawn approached, the forest was bathed in a soft glow, and the officers continued to maintain their vigilance. The laptop's revelations and the imminent exchange of documents had intensified their pursuit. Detective Lam knew that their patience would eventually pay off, that Tristan's options were dwindling, and the noose was tightening.

The next move, in this gripping pursuit, was hanging in the balance. The officers were prepared to wait, to outmanoeuvre and outlast their elusive target. With Tristan's every step carefully tracked and anticipated, the chase reached a fever pitch, and the outcome of this high-stakes game remained uncertain.

Chapter 76

The sun rose on a new day, casting its gentle light on the unfolding events. Tristan's heart raced as he embarked on a daring mission to retrieve his hidden bag from the lodging. With the cover of dawn, he maneuvered through the shadows, his every step calculated and deliberate. Under the house, he slinked into the crawl space, retracing his steps, and emerged into the room where his possessions lay hidden.

The suspense hung heavy in the air as he carefully retrieved his bag from its concealed spot beneath the floorboards. A victorious smile played on his lips as he realized that his cunning had paid off—the officers had missed this cache. The room bore witness to their thorough search, with the laptop gone, but he had managed to elude their grasp. The taste of minor triumph fueled his determination to escape their clutches once and for all.

With his bag secured, Tristan reversed his route, slipping back beneath the house and retracing his steps to safety. The officers stationed at the lodging grew restless, their vigil yielding no results. Detective Lam, however, was not ready to concede defeat. A signal from the tracking device flared to life, a beacon of hope amidst the tension. Urgently, he communicated with his team, urging them back to the room to investigate. Their frustration melted into swift action as they discovered the breach in the floor. The realization that Tristan had outsmarted their surveillance fueled their determination to apprehend him.

Back on the move, Tristan's heart pounded in his chest as he traversed the roads. The stolen car carried him closer to his final destination: Mark's place in Cyberjaya. The back roads stretched ahead like a lifeline, promising freedom. Yet, a sense of urgency underscored every mile he covered, the knowledge that this was his last chance at escape looming large.

The tension radiated through the air as the chase escalated. On one side, Tristan raced against time, his desire for freedom fanning the flames of his determination. On the other, Detective Lam and his team huddled in readiness, aware that this could be the pivotal moment they had been waiting for—the capture of their elusive prey.

Finally, the stolen car rolled to a stop in front of Mark's place. Tristan's heart pounded, the walls closing in around him as he stood on the brink of his escape. His anxious knock echoed through the doorway, and when Mark answered, their fates converged. The transaction was swift; money exchanged hands as the final pieces of Tristan's escape plan fell into place. With his bag packed and victory seemingly within reach, Tristan's breath quickened. He knew the stakes were high, the finish line in sight, yet the danger far from over.

Emerging from Mark's place, Tristan's senses were heightened. His every move was measured, his senses on high alert. As he stepped into the clearing, a sense of foreboding settled over him. The world seemed to contract as he glimpsed the law enforcement net closing in—a dozen officers, weapons drawn, encircling him. The air crackled with tension as their voices barked commands, demanding his surrender. In an instant, the tranquillity of the clearing transformed into a battlefield of urgency.

Tristan's heart pounded in his chest as he faced the officers' united front. The weight of his decisions, his choices, bore down on him. He was ensnared in their dragnet, his options dwindling as the confrontation escalated. The cacophony of shouted orders echoed in his ears, drowning out rational thought. He was trapped, caught between the desires for freedom and the reality of his actions.

The climax of the pursuit was here, the culmination of Tristan's choices and the relentless determination of Detective Lam and his team. The world seemed to stand still as the standoff played out, every second dripping with suspense. The officers' unwavering determination mirrored Tristan's desperation to escape, the two forces converging in a moment that would forever alter the trajectory of their lives.

And then, as abruptly as it had begun, the standoff reached its crescendo. Tristan's bag dropped to the ground; hands raised in surrender. The tension in the air shifted, the palpable energy dissipating in the face of his capitulation. The officers swiftly closed in, placing him in custody. The manhunt had come to an end, the game of evasion and pursuit reaching its climax.

With Tristan and Mark taken into custody, the dust settled on their tumultuous journey. The web of deception and intrigue that had woven their lives together now unraveled before them. The pursuit was over, but the echoes of their choices would reverberate through time, leaving a trail of consequences in their wake.

Chapter 77

The victory was palpable in the air as Detective Lam and his team basked in the triumph of finally apprehending Tristan. The tension that had gripped them for so long was released in a wave of exhilaration. Tristan was led into the holding cells of the police station, his face a mix of defiance and resignation. The detectives knew that now was the time to extract answers, to fill in the gaps and connect the dots that had eluded them for far too long.

Inside the station, the fluorescent lights cast a cold, sterile glow as the interrogation room awaited Tristan. Detective Lam, his expression a mixture of weariness and triumph, prepared to confront the man who had remained a step ahead for so long. He was determined to unearth the truth, to finally understand the intricate web of motives and actions that had led to this point.

The questions swirled in the detective's mind as he entered the interrogation room. He took a deep breath, his gaze fixed on Tristan. "You thought you could outwit us at every turn, didn't you?" he began, his voice laced with a mixture of challenge and curiosity. "But now you're here, and it's time to answer for your actions."

Tristan's eyes flickered, his mind racing as he grappled with his situation. He had thought he had accounted for every contingency, every possibility. But now, facing the relentless determination of Detective Lam, he realized that his calculations had fallen short.

The detective leaned forward; his eyes locked on Tristan's. "We have evidence of your arms deals, your smuggling operations. We know your plans to flee the country using forged documents." He paused, letting the weight of his words settle in the air. "But there's one thing we still don't know—Jack's whereabouts."

Tristan's face remained a mask of nonchalance, but his heart pounded in his chest. Jack was the one thread he hadn't been able to sever, the one loose end that still tied him to the consequences of his actions.

"We have proof that you were in contact with Mark," Detective Lam continued, his voice unwavering. "We know you were planning to leave, but what about Jack? What happened to him?"

Tristan's mind raced, his thoughts a whirlwind of calculations and potential stories. He had to navigate this interrogation with precision, to reveal as little as possible while maintaining a semblance of control. "Jack was an acquaintance," he replied coolly, his eyes fixed on a point beyond the detective. "I haven't seen him in a while. I have no idea where he is."

Detective Lam's gaze narrowed, his instincts homing in on the slight quiver in Tristan's voice. "An acquaintance? You were seen with him on multiple occasions, Tristan. Don't play games with us."

Tristan's façade wavered slightly, his mind working overtime to craft a convincing response. "We crossed paths a few times, that's all," he said dismissively. "I had no reason to be involved in whatever happened to him."

The detective's voice remained steady, a calm undercurrent beneath the surface. "Is that so? Because we have witness statements that place you in his company before he disappeared."

Tristan's pulse quickened, his grip on his self-assurance slipping. He had hoped to obfuscate, to redirect their focus away from Jack, but it seemed the walls were closing in. He had underestimated Detective Lam's resolve and the meticulousness of the investigation.

As the questioning continued, Tristan's mind raced through scenarios, a labyrinth of half-truths and diversions. He had to be cautious, to reveal just enough to satisfy their inquiries while keeping the truth hidden. The weight of his predicament pressed down on him, the awareness that his choices had brought him to this precipice.

Meanwhile, in the comfort of their home, Tengku and Alicia savoured a moment of respite. Alicia cared for her husband, their conversation a balm to their souls. Yet, even as they embraced the relief of being together, the phone call from Detective Lam jolted them back into reality.

Tengku's voice was a mix of astonishment and elation as he spoke to the detective. "Tristan is finally in custody?" he exclaimed. "How did you manage to catch him?"

Detective Lam's voice resonated with triumph. "We'll discuss the details later, Tengku. Just know that our hard work has paid off."

As the call ended, Tengku turned to Alicia, his eyes alight with a mixture of emotions. "They've got him," he said, a mixture of relief and anticipation in his voice. "Maybe now we can find out what really happened to Jack."

Alicia nodded, her expression a blend of hope and trepidation. The end of Tristan's evasion marked the beginning of a new chapter—one that held the answers they had been seeking for so long.

In the confines of the interrogation room, the conversation continued. Detective Lam persisted, each question a calculated step closer to unraveling the truth. And as Tristan's defences wavered, as the weight of his choices bore down on him, he knew that his game of deception was drawing to a close. The intricate dance of words and motivations reached its crescendo, the final act of a narrative that had spanned deception, pursuit, and reckoning.

Chapter 78

The interrogation room was a battlefield of words and tactics, as Detective Lam and his team pressed Tristan for answers. Hours passed, frustration mounting as Tristan stubbornly clung to his narrative—his insistence that he knew little about Jack beyond their shared time at the warehouse. Detective Lam's patience wavered, his determination to uncover Jack's whereabouts driving him forward.

Through the dimly lit room, the detective's gaze locked onto Tristan's, his voice an unwavering challenge. "You can't keep evading the truth forever," he asserted, his tone heavy with a mix of frustration and determination. "We know you were involved with Jack in more ways than you're admitting."

Tristan's expression remained a mask, his features revealing nothing of the thoughts racing through his mind. He had fortified himself against their questions, his defence unyielding as he navigated the complex terrain of half-truths and denial.

As the questioning continued, the room became a pressure cooker of tension. The detective probed, insinuated, and confronted, seeking a crack in Tristan's facade. But each attempt was met with a wall of obstinacy. The truth remained shrouded, elusive as ever.

Finally, Detective Lam called a temporary halt to the interrogation. With a sigh of exasperation, he watched as Tristan was led back to the cell, his face a mixture of defiance and exhaustion. The detective needed a respite from the mental and emotional intensity, a moment to gather his thoughts and refocus his strategy.

Outside the confines of the interrogation room, the station hummed with activity. Officers went about their duties, and the air was charged with a mixture of anticipation and weariness. Detective Lam knew that the key to closing this chapter lay in extracting the truth about Jack from Tristan. It was a puzzle piece that needed to fall into place.

The decision was made—Detective Lam sought a brief reprieve from the intensity of the station. He needed to clear his mind, to gain a fresh perspective before delving back into the fray. The journey to Tengku's house became a moment of solace, a chance to breathe amidst the chaos.

The streets of Port Klang unfurled before him, bathed in the soft glow of streetlights. The scent of flowers wafted through the air, mingling with the stillness of the night. Stars sparkled above, casting their gentle light upon the path. It was as though the universe itself acknowledged the weight of the detective's journey, offering a moment of tranquillity.

Arriving at Tengku's house, the detective was greeted by Kyrie, whose wary expression melted into relief as he realized the detective wasn't there on official business. The warmth of their camaraderie enveloped the detective, and he felt a sense of belonging in this moment of shared understanding.

As the detective and Tengku settled into conversation, their words flowed seamlessly—a blend of updates, camaraderie, and shared reflections. Alicia's presence added a touch of comfort, her hospitality extending through snacks and laughter. For a fleeting moment, the weight of their responsibilities lifted, replaced by the simple pleasure of human connection.

In the midst of their camaraderie, the detective relayed the details of Tristan's capture, offering Tengku a glimpse into the meticulous operation that had finally brought the elusive criminal to justice. The conversation flowed seamlessly, a testament to the bond they had forged through adversity.

Yet, even in the midst of their camaraderie, the shadow of Jack's disappearance loomed. The detective's words carried a quiet resolve—an acknowledgment that the case wasn't truly closed until Jack was found. The trio grappled with the uncertainty that still lingered, aware that their quest for closure was far from over.

As the night wore on, the detective's exhaustion became evident. With a grateful smile, he bid his hosts farewell, the promise of rest and renewed determination guiding his steps. The journey back to the station was a different one—marked by a renewed sense of purpose, the clarity that came from moments of respite.

Back at the station, the detective's steps were resolute as he entered the interrogation room once more. Tristan's face held the same cool façade, but there was a flicker of uncertainty in his eyes. The detective knew that persistence was their greatest weapon, that the truth would eventually emerge from the tangled web of deception.

And so, the dance of questions and answers resumed—a battle of wills, a tug-of-war for the truth. The detective's determination was unwavering, his resolve fortified by the support of those who stood behind him. In the heart of this storm, the answers they sought were closer than ever before, waiting to be unearthed from the depths of Tristan's guarded secrets.

Chapter 79

The following day dawned with a renewed sense of purpose for Detective Lam and his team. Leaving Tristan confined in the holding cell, they revisited the evidence and files related to Jack's disappearance. The weight of unresolved questions hung heavy in the air as they meticulously examined each piece of information anew.

The detective's mind was a whirlwind of possibilities as he reevaluated Jack's case. It was as though time had rewound, allowing them to look at the puzzle with fresh eyes. Old files and evidence seemed to take on new significance under the scrutiny of their determination. The detective's fingers traced over the evidence boards, connecting dots, and seeking patterns that might have eluded them before.

As they retraced Jack's movements through phone data, a map of his last known locations began to take shape. The warehouse stood out as a pivotal point, the place where his trail had seemingly gone cold. Detective Lam's decision to revisit the warehouse was born of intuition—the sense that there might be something they had missed, a piece of the puzzle waiting to be uncovered.

Arriving at the warehouse, the detective and his team were met with a change in atmosphere. Relief hung palpably in the air, as news of Tristan's capture had spread among the staff. The weight of impending closure and justice was felt by everyone, adding a renewed energy to the environment. Charles, ever helpful, assisted the detective, allowing him access to the warehouse to retrace Jack's steps.

Walking through the familiar spaces, Detective Lam's eyes scanned for any detail that might have been overlooked. He engaged in conversation with Charles, probing for insights into the last hours Jack had spent within these walls. Charles' uncertainty mirrored their own—none could fathom why Jack would have lingered in the warehouse beyond his shift.

In the midst of their exploration, a forgotten piece of potential evidence emerged—a phone, scratched and battered, abandoned in the lost and found. The detective's interest was piqued, the possibility that this could be a missing link sparking renewed hope. Could this be the answer they had been searching for?

Back at Charles' office, the scratched phone lay on the desk, a silent enigma waiting to be deciphered. Could this phone hold the key to understanding Jack's disappearance? The detective's mind whirred with possibilities as they contemplated the role this seemingly ordinary device might have played.

Detective Lam's decision to take the phone into custody for further investigation was swift. With it held as evidence, the tech department began their efforts to extract the information locked within the damaged device. Every moment counted as they worked to piece together the fragments of data that might shed light on Jack's final moments.

As they waited for the tech department's analysis, a strategy formed in Detective Lam's mind. Keeping Tristan in holding, they maintained an air of mystery, leaving him to speculate about their actions. It was a psychological tactic—

a means to keep their suspect off balance, to disrupt any semblance of control he might have hoped to retain.

Days stretched on, the anticipation mounting as the tech department worked diligently to restore functionality to the phone. Detective Lam's thoughts never strayed far from the case, the weight of responsibility driving him forward. Every passing moment felt like a step closer to resolution.

The phone, once a discarded relic, now held the promise of answers. The detective's gaze shifted between it and the evidence boards in the station. The pieces of the puzzle were coming together, and with each passing day, the truth felt within reach. All they needed was the key to unlock the secrets hidden within that scratched, damaged device—a key that might finally bring closure to Jack's case and provide solace to his family.

Chapter 80

Excitement buzzed in the air as Iris, the tech genius, worked tirelessly to unlock the secrets hidden within the damaged device. She hurried over to Detective Lam, laptop in hand, eager to unveil any crucial information that could lead them to Jack's whereabouts.

Detective Lam, momentarily occupied on a call, gestured for her to take a seat at his desk. Iris, a mix of anxiety and anticipation coursing through her, waited impatiently. As soon as the detective concluded his call, she eagerly informed him about the breakthrough: they had successfully gained access to the phone and were now sifting through its contents for any significant clues.

Starting their investigation, they scrutinized the call logs meticulously. Initial impressions were normal – calls to friends, family, and missed calls after Jack's disappearance. But there was a growing sense that something crucial lay just beyond their reach. Messages were next on their list, but again, nothing seemed to stand out. Frustration was mounting as they hit a dead end, yet they refused to relent.

The detective's instincts guided them towards the browser history. And there it was – a trail of searches related to nanny cams and methods of surveillance without detection. The realization struck like lightning. This was the lead they needed. Jack had been searching for something, something that led him to that warehouse and, potentially, his disappearance.

A check of his gallery yielded no alarms, but Iris decided to venture further by examining the recycle bin. A peculiar app caught her attention – the very app designed to monitor the feed of a nanny cam. Although it wasn't actively connected to a feed, Iris noticed a deleted video in the bin. Her heart raced as she opened it, revealing a scene of a man operating in a dimly lit warehouse. Boxes were being unpacked; weapons were being placed inside them – a chilling sight that sent shivers down their spines. The man was unmistakably Tristan.

Watching the video with rapt attention, Detective Lam and Iris absorbed every detail. This was the crucial piece they had been searching for. Tristan's involvement in the arms smuggling and the warehouse was now undeniable. But more importantly, it tied him directly to Jack's last known whereabouts. The video ended, leaving a profound silence in its wake.

Detective Lam knew they were onto something significant, yet he also understood the challenges ahead. The video, while damning, wasn't enough to definitively implicate Tristan in Jack's disappearance. They needed more, and that meant they had to break Tristan's silence.

Despite the mounting excitement over this newfound evidence, they were also aware of the delicate path they were treading. Interrogating Tristan would require finesse and strategy. The detective's mind raced, formulating a plan on how to approach the questioning. He knew that confronting Tristan directly might not yield results, given his steadfast refusal to talk.

As they wrapped up their initial analysis of the evidence, Detective Lam exchanged a knowing glance with Iris. The real battle was just beginning. Armed with this critical lead, they had to devise a way to make Tristan reveal the truth about Jack's fate. The road ahead was treacherous, filled with uncertainty, but the pursuit of justice burned brighter than ever.

Little did they know that this breakthrough was about to ignite a series of events that would unravel hidden truths and send shockwaves through their investigation, leading them closer to the heart of a mystery that had gripped them for so long.

Chapter 81

A pivotal breakthrough had led them back to the warehouse, the scene of Jack's last known presence. It was imperative to ascertain if Jack had left the nanny cam within the warehouse, possibly hidden away in his locker, or concealed in a way that only a thorough search could unveil.

Detective Lam, aware of the significance of this step, swiftly arranged for access to the warehouse after hours. A call to Tengku secured their entry, as he willingly extended his assistance once again. With dusk settling in and the warehouse staff departing for the day, Detective Lam, Iris, and the team were on site, ready for an intensive search that could potentially provide them with vital leads.

They methodically combed through every nook and cranny – lockers, storage boxes, and even the spaces that one might consider too inconspicuous to warrant attention. Their objective extended beyond locating the nanny cam; they sought to piece together Jack's last moments within the warehouse, his movements, and his intentions. As Detective Lam entered the maintenance room, he seemed to momentarily embody Jack's perspective, seeking to relive the circumstances that might have led to his disappearance.

Yet, despite their meticulous efforts, the search yielded no trace of the elusive nanny cam. The frustration mounted, the sense that a vital clue was lurking just beyond their grasp becoming almost palpable. The warehouse, usually a place of structured order, had transformed into a labyrinth of possibilities, each corner holding a potential revelation.

As Detective Lam leaned against a pallet, seemingly lost in thought, a realization dawned upon him. He imagined himself in Jack's shoes, contemplating the events that had unfolded that fateful day. His mind conjured an image of Tristan amidst the warehouse, weapons being concealed within crates – an ominous tableau that begged to be deciphered.

Clutching his phone in hand, Detective Lam stood at the entrance of the maintenance room, the phone's light casting a faint glow beneath the door. Iris, sharp and observant, approached him with an insight that added another layer to the puzzle. She proposed that Tristan might have spotted Jack's phone light beneath the closed door, inadvertently revealing his presence in the maintenance room. It was the missing link, the catalyst that prompted Tristan's knowledge of Jack's presence within the warehouse. The revelation sent a jolt of energy through the investigation team – they were onto something substantial.

The pieces were falling into place, aligning in a manner that illuminated the events of that night. The once-frustrating puzzle was now revealing its intricate design, and the focus was sharpening on Tristan's potential involvement. The spark of understanding ignited their determination anew, fuelling their commitment to close this chapter of uncertainty.

As they departed the warehouse that night, Detective Lam's mind was alive with theories and deductions. The breakthrough had propelled their investigation forward, yet the road ahead remained challenging. They still needed more tangible evidence to definitively tie Tristan to Jack's disappearance. However, the newfound clarity had infused the team with renewed vigour. They were prepared to pursue every lead, follow every angle, and unveil the truth that had remained shrouded for so long.

With the echoes of their footsteps fading within the vast warehouse, the investigation had gained momentum. It was a race against time, a quest for answers that had now taken an exhilarating turn.

Chapter 82

As the investigation team began to wrap up their search of the warehouse, Iris abruptly halted in her tracks, a sudden realization gripping her. Her eyes widened with a mix of excitement and urgency. Digging into her bag, she retrieved her laptop, the device that held the potential to unlock the final piece of the puzzle. With an urgency in her voice, she beckoned Detective Lam over, her words tumbling out in a rush.

"Wait! Detective, I have an idea! Before we leave, let's try one last thing," Iris exclaimed, her voice tinged with a newfound determination.

Curiosity piqued, Detective Lam leaned in, his attention captured by the spark of inspiration in Iris' eyes. She opened her laptop, fingers dancing across the keyboard as she swiftly accessed the footage recorded by the nanny cam. With a methodical focus, she meticulously reviewed the footage, her mind racing to connect the dots that had eluded them so far.

"I think I might have figured out a way to locate the nanny cam," Iris announced, her voice a mixture of hope and excitement.

She outlined her plan to Detective Lam – a reenactment of the footage using the officers. By recreating the scenario, they could pinpoint the exact angle from which the nanny cam had recorded. Iris believed that this could lead them to the hidden camera's location.

Enthusiasm ignited among the team members, and they quickly positioned themselves as Tristan and Jack had been in the footage. Iris directed their movements, scrutinizing each step to find the perfect perspective that matched the recording. Her eyes darted between the screen and the officers, her mind racing to reconcile the images before her.

Suddenly, as the officers mimicked the actions captured on the nanny cam, Iris' gaze locked onto a detail that had previously eluded them. A beam, suspended high near the ceiling of the warehouse, caught her attention. It was a significant find – a potential hiding spot that could house the missing nanny cam.

"Stop! Hold it right there!" Iris exclaimed, her voice trembling with excitement.

Pointing towards the beam on the laptop screen, she directed one of the officers to climb a ladder and access the position she believed the camera had been mounted. The atmosphere crackled with tension as they watched the officer ascend, anticipation hanging in the air like a charged current.

The officer reached the specified position, and a collective breath was held as he began to explore the beam. A gasp of astonishment echoed through the warehouse as he retrieved the hidden nanny cam – the crucial piece of evidence that had eluded them for so long.

Euphoria swept through the team, a triumphant surge of achievement that reverberated in the warehouse's expanse. The missing nanny cam, once thought lost to the shadows, was now in their possession. It was a pivotal moment – a discovery that could potentially unravel the mystery of Jack's disappearance and provide the clues they needed to connect the dots.

As the officer descended the ladder, the retrieved nanny cam cradled in his hands, Detective Lam couldn't help but marvel at the perseverance and ingenuity that had led them to this point. Iris' idea had proven instrumental, rekindling the fire of hope and determination that had propelled them throughout the investigation.

With the nanny cam finally in their possession, the team left the warehouse that night with a renewed sense of purpose. The journey ahead remained uncertain, yet the discovery had infused them with the certainty that they were closing in on the truth. The puzzle pieces were aligning, and each step brought them closer to untangling the web of secrets that had enveloped this case.

Amid the shadows of the warehouse, the missing nanny cam glinted like a beacon of hope. Its recording held the key to unlocking a mystery that had haunted them for so long. As they left the warehouse behind, the anticipation for what the retrieved footage might reveal hung in the air, promising a revelation that could change everything.

Chapter 83

Back at the police station, the atmosphere was tense with anticipation as Detective Lam, Iris, and the officers returned with the recovered nanny cam. The small device held the promise of answers – a glimpse into the events that had unfolded in the warehouse on that fateful day. Iris's heart raced with a mixture of hope and trepidation as she settled in front of her computer, ready to delve into the footage that had eluded them for so long.

With deft fingers, Iris examined the nanny cam, noting the slot for an SD card. She gently extracted the card, a wave of gratitude washing over her – the information they sought might be just a few clicks away, a record captured unknowingly by the camera.

The card found its place in her laptop, and her focus became laser sharp. The footage was neatly categorized by dates, a well-organized chronicle that Iris delved into with a sense of urgency. She navigated to the date that aligned with the original footage from Jack's phone, anticipation swelling in her chest as she pressed play.

As the footage played out on her screen, she quickly realized that the nanny cam had continued recording beyond the point where Jack's phone had stopped. Her excitement grew, recognizing that this might hold the key to unraveling the truth they so desperately sought.

Detective Lam positioned himself next to Iris, a mixture of apprehension and hope etched across his features. They watched as Tristan emerged on the screen, heading toward the maintenance room. The seconds ticked by, and then, in an eerie twist, Jack reappeared in the footage beside Tristan.

The detective's breath caught as the chilling realization dawned upon them – this was the moment that held the truth. Iris paused the footage, her voice laced with urgency as she beckoned the detective.

"Detective, you need to see this," she said, her tone grave yet determined.

He leaned in, their eyes locked on the screen as the events continued to unfold. The footage showed Tristan guiding towards the maintenance room, where Jack was hiding, an exchange that unfolded in silence, a sinister understanding passing between them. Then came the pivotal moment – Jack turning away to dispose of his phone, unaware of the impending danger.

With a sudden ferocity, Tristan attacked Jack, the visuals on the screen leaving no room for ambiguity. Horror twisted Detective Lam's features as he witnessed the shocking act, the brutality of it sending shivers down his spine.

As the seconds ticked away, Iris paused the footage once again, a heaviness settling in the room. The truth they had sought, the answers they had tirelessly pursued, lay before them in chilling clarity. Jack's last moments had been captured on that tiny screen, a haunting testament to the darkness that had consumed him.

Their hearts heavy, Detective Lam and Iris exchanged a solemn glance. The proof was undeniable – Jack was no longer among the living, and Tristan was responsible for his untimely demise. It was a heartbreaking realization, yet it was the evidence they needed to bring justice to Jack and his grieving family.

"We have to give the family closure," Detective Lam murmured, his voice laced with determination. "We need to find Jack's body and ensure that justice is served."

Iris nodded in agreement; her fingers poised above the keyboard. The path ahead was clear – they had the evidence, they had the truth, and now they had to bring Tristan to justice for his heinous act. The road would be fraught with challenges, but they were armed with the unassailable truth, a beacon of light amidst the shadows that had shrouded this case.

With a final look at the screen, Detective Lam stood up, his resolve unwavering. The journey was far from over, but they had taken a significant step forward. The horrifying footage, while haunting, had granted them the power to fight for justice, to uncover the truth that had remained elusive for so long.

Leaving the room, the detective and Iris carried with them the weight of their discovery, a newfound sense of purpose propelling them forward. The battle against darkness was far from won, but they were armed with the truth – a truth that would guide their steps as they pursued justice for Jack and his family.

Chapter 84

With the damning footage in hand, the detective and his team were ready to confront Tristan once more. As Tristan walked into the interrogation room, he couldn't help but notice the expressions of disdain and accusation on the faces of those present. The air in the room was heavy with tension, and he could feel the weight of their collective gaze upon him.

The detective's voice was steady but stern as he addressed Tristan, his eyes locked onto the suspect. The question was simple yet loaded with significance – "Where is Jack?"

Tristan, seemingly unfazed, repeated his denial, maintaining his stance that he had no knowledge of Jack's whereabouts. His confidence wavered, however, when Iris entered the room with her laptop. The room seemed to hold its breath as the footage began to play, casting an undeniable light on Tristan's dark secret.

As the footage unfolded, Tristan's complexion shifted from its usual hue to an ashen pallor. His bravado evaporated in the face of the irrefutable evidence that was displayed before him. Every detail of his confrontation with Jack, every sinister interaction, was laid bare for all to see. It was a mirror to his guilt, reflecting the truth he could no longer deny.

Tristan's eyes remained glued to the screen, his expression a mix of shock, fear, and desperation. The realization that he had been outsmarted by the very technology he thought he had eluded was a bitter pill to swallow. With a trembling voice, he demanded a lawyer, a feeble attempt to regain control over a situation spiralling out of his grasp.

The detective knew that Tristan's demand for a lawyer was an admission of his guilt, an acknowledgement that the walls were closing in. With evidence as compelling as the video footage, it was only a matter of time before they would unearth Jack's body. The detective's mind was already racing with the logistics of recovering the remains and giving Jack's family the closure, they desperately needed.

However, the immediate challenge before him was more personal and gut-wrenching – breaking the news to Jack's parents. The detective's heart weighed heavily in his chest as he contemplated the emotional burden of delivering such devastating news. He knew that words would never be enough to ease the pain, that the grief that awaited them was a chasm no words could bridge.

As he wrestled with his thoughts, his phone rang, Mueez's name flashing on the screen. Mueez was reaching out, concerned about Jack's absence. The detective's heart sank – he couldn't reveal the truth over the phone. He needed to face Mueez in person, to tell him and Jack's parents the painful reality that had been uncovered.

In a calm yet strained voice, the detective suggested they meet in Penang, where he was headed to speak with Jack's family. Mueez agreed, the gravity of the situation evident in his voice. The call ended, and the detective was left grappling with a multitude of emotions.

The night descended, a blanket of darkness that mirrored the weight on the detective's heart. He knew that the truth was a double-edged sword – it had brought them closer to justice, but it also carried a pain that would reverberate far beyond the confines of the interrogation room. With every step he took towards Jack's family, he knew that he was about to shatter their world.

The detective's resolve remained unflinching. He had to confront the truth head-on, to ensure justice for Jack and his grieving family. As he prepared to face the storm of emotions that awaited him, he carried with him the burden of responsibility – to deliver the truth with compassion and to offer support in the face of unimaginable loss. The road ahead was fraught with challenges, but the detective was committed to seeing it through, to seeking justice and closure for a life cut tragically short.

Chapter 85

Early the next morning, Detective Lam embarked on the emotionally charged journey to Penang. Each mile seemed to stretch infinitely before him, carrying the heavy burden of the heartbreaking news he was about to deliver to Jack's parents. The weight of the revelation bore down on him like an insurmountable force. Jack, a hero who had valiantly stood against the torrent of illicit trade, had left an indelible mark on the hearts of all who knew him.

Back at the warehouse, Tengku Beans had summoned the staff to share the devastating news. The atmosphere in the cavernous space grew dense with unspoken questions and sorrow. Jack, their colleague, and friend, was no longer with them. His absence created a void that seemed impossible to fill.

Finally, Detective Lam arrived at the remote village where Jack's parents resided, greeted by a modest stilted house that appeared to have been frozen in time. The cabin-like exterior, enveloped by lush tropical greenery, exuded an air of quietude. He parked his car on a grassy patch beside the house and, with a heavy heart, removed his shoes before ascending the wooden stairs leading to the entrance.

Jack's father, a stoic figure with world-weary eyes, and Mueez, his confidant and close friend, welcomed the detective inside. The living room, warm and humid due to the tropical climate, had curtains drawn to shield against the harsh sunlight. The windows, however, were left wide open, allowing a faint breeze to offer some respite. Jack's mother, a woman radiating maternal warmth, switched on the electric fans, their whirring providing a gentle backdrop to the somber atmosphere. She offered Detective Lam a glass of juice, a small yet heartfelt gesture of hospitality in the face of tragedy.

Seated in the compact living room, all eyes remained fixed on Detective Lam, their collective hope and fear hanging heavily in the air. They yearned to hear the news they had been waiting for, but they couldn't have anticipated the devastating blow that was about to be delivered.

Detective Lam lowered his gaze, his eyes carrying the weight of the world as he braced himself for the harrowing task ahead. He began by telling them that Jack would not be returning home, that he had fought valiantly against his assailant to protect the truth. His actions had exposed an international arms smuggling syndicate, leading to its dismantling. Jack was indeed a hero, but the cost of his heroism had been immeasurable.

Jack's mother could no longer hold back her tears. Her heart swelled with pride for her son, but the agony of his absence overwhelmed her. She wept openly, her tears serving as a testament to the depth of her grief and despair. Mueez knelt by her side, offering what little comfort he could, though her sorrow remained inconsolable.

Jack's father, a pillar of strength in their family, struggled to maintain his composure. His voice quivered as he spoke, a lump forming in his throat, making it agonizingly difficult to utter the next words. "Where is Jack's body?" he asked, the torment in his eyes reflecting the profound anguish of a parent's heart.

Detective Lam had dreaded this question, but he knew he had to be truthful. He informed them that they had the killer in custody, but the location of Jack's remains still eluded them. The words hung in the air, heavy and laden with sorrow. The parents were trapped in a nightmarish limbo, unable to find closure.

At the warehouse, Tengku Beans gathered the staff, his voice laced with sorrow. "Jack is no longer with us," he announced, his usually jovial tone now tinged with melancholy. Questions flooded the room, voices filled with disbelief and grief.

"Where is he?" Charles, a close friend, and colleague of Jack, demanded, his voice choked with emotion.

"We're working on finding that out," Tengku replied, his eyes reflecting the weight of their shared loss.

Back in the living room, Detective Lam asked, "Is there anyone I can contact for you, or anything you need?" The question hung in the air; their collective grief too heavy to allow for a response.

As he departed from their home, he left behind a family enveloped in a shroud of grief. The drive back to the police station felt long and arduous, much like the journey he had just taken to deliver the heart-wrenching news. His thoughts weighed heavily on the pain he had witnessed, and the knowledge that the hardest part was yet to come.

Mueez, who had accompanied Detective Lam on the drive back, looked at him with red-rimmed eyes, filled with a mix of sadness and anger. "Did he suffer?" he asked, his voice quivering.

Detective Lam met his gaze, his own eyes revealing the torment he had seen in the footage. "No," he replied gently, his voice steady with empathy. "He didn't suffer."

The two drove in silence as they were in their own thoughts. Detective Lam knew that he had to give this family closure; they had been through a lot, and this trip felt very heavy on the detective's heart. Mueez had hoped that he was there for his friend, but he did not know what Jack was up to. They were in the process of grief, and this was the bargaining point. As the miles passed, the weight of their silent contemplation bore witness to the profound impact of Jack's sacrifice and the long road to healing that lay ahead.

Chapter 86

The day after Detective Lam returned from Penang, he knew he had to get answers from Tristan. The energy surged within him, fueled by the urgent need to find out what happened to Jack. He couldn't allow a grieving family to linger in sorrow any longer. This time, he wouldn't play the "good cop." He needed to make Tristan understand that further delays would not be tolerated.

Walking into the police station, he ordered the officers to bring Tristan to the interrogation room. There was no room for games. Tristan was visibly drained and worried, his usually confident demeanor now replaced by the look of a cornered man who knew he was trapped. He tried to conjure ways to escape this predicament but found none. Detective Lam's arrival signaled a stark change in their dynamic.

Detective Lam, his patience waning, stared at Tristan with a cold, determined expression. Tristan, on the other hand, looked defeated, a far cry from his previous arrogance. It was the first time Detective Lam had seen him like this, and he intended to use it to his advantage.

He told Tristan that he needed to cooperate or face a life behind bars for his actions. With an unflinching gaze, he reminded Tristan that they had overwhelming proof and evidence. He urged Tristan to do the right thing, to grant the grieving family the closure they desperately needed. It was a plea to awaken any shred of humanity within Tristan. However, the response was nothing but a smirk and a dismissive shake of the head. Detective Lam felt a rising frustration; this man remained unyielding.

Later that day, Mueez arrived at the station, eager to contribute in any way he could. Detective Lam updated him on the situation, revealing their struggle to break Tristan's silence. Mueez, understanding the gravity of the situation, asked if he could attempt to speak with Tristan. Maybe, just maybe, he could find a way to connect with him emotionally and break down the barrier. It was an unorthodox approach, but they were willing to try anything to get answers.

With palpable nervousness, Mueez entered the interrogation room. Tristan sat across the table, his demeanor cold and unfriendly. The scraping of the chair against the floor seemed to pierce the tense silence. Tristan's gaze met Mueez's, sending a shiver down his spine. He hoped his fear didn't show on his face.

Mueez took a deep breath and pulled out the chair, trying to maintain his composure despite the sweat forming on his brow. "I was a friend, more like a brother, to Jack," he began, his voice laced with discomfort. "Please, could you tell us what you did to Jack? His parents are mourning, and they need to see him."

A smug expression twisted Tristan's face as he responded, "So, you came all this way to ask me that? Why should I help you? What's in it for me if I give you this information?" His laughter filled the room.

Mueez's patience began to crumble. He felt the anger welling up within him, and his heart raced. Despite his best efforts, his voice rose as he pleaded, "You must know what it feels like to lose someone you love! You must understand how his mother and father are feeling right now. Surely, you've loved and cared for someone!" Tears welled up in Mueez's eyes as he spoke.

Tristan's cold exterior began to crack. He looked down, his emotions no longer concealed. The detective seized this opening to appeal to Tristan's humanity. He mentioned Tristan's own loss, the death of his parents to cancer, and how he, too, knew what it felt like to grieve. Mueez added that Jack had a similar family dynamic, an only son like Tristan. The similarities seemed to pierce through Tristan's hardened shell.

Emotions swirled within Tristan, a tumultuous mix of anger, grief, and longing. He shouted out in frustration, the weight of their words pressing down on him. Tears welled in his eyes, and he could no longer contain the turmoil within. It was a rare moment of vulnerability for Tristan.

Still, he resisted, offering no words. But the detective and Mueez could see that their persistence was breaking through. Tristan, a man who had kept his emotions locked away for so long, was finally unraveling.

He began to speak of that fateful night, recounting how he had driven along a remote road with Jack's lifeless body concealed in the car, away from prying eyes. He explained that he had taken the body to Wah Sempoh and cast it into the water, intending for it to sink to the depths below. He couldn't provide the exact location, but he estimated it was approximately a mile from the shore.

The detective and Mueez rushed out of the interrogation room, knowing they needed divers and that the search needed to start immediately. Tristan was led back to his cell, and the detective and Mueez couldn't help but breathe a sigh of relief. They had finally broken through his defences.

The information they had long sought was now within their grasp, and they were determined to bring Jack home to his grieving family.

Chapter 87

Armed with the newfound evidence, Detective Lam orchestrated a meticulous operation. He assembled a team of highly skilled divers, forensic experts, and officers, all converging on the picturesque shores of Wah Sempoh. Their mission: to unveil the chilling truth concealed beneath the tranquil surface of the sea.

The morning sunbathed the scene in golden light, casting long, dancing shadows on the powdery sand. Wah Sempoh had always been a haven of peace and serenity, with local fishermen gently casting their lines into the pristine waters. The air carried the soothing scent of salt, and the distant cries of seagulls added to the coastal symphony.

But today, this peaceful haven was transformed into a hive of activity. Police cars, their sirens silent but their presence commanding, lined the shore. Trucks laden with boats, diving equipment, and a swarm of professionals followed suit. It was as if the very earth quivered in anticipation of what was to come.

Divers, like modern-day explorers, bustled with purpose. They donned sleek black wetsuits, adjusted their oxygen tanks with precision, and exchanged glances filled with unspoken determination. Each one was acutely aware of the harrowing task ahead, navigating the chilling depths to uncover Jack's final secret and expose Tristan's malevolent deeds.

Yellow police tape marked an invisible boundary, creating a barrier between the operation and the curious onlookers. It served as a reminder that this was no ordinary beach day but a pivotal moment in a harrowing investigation.

The radios clung to the officers' belts crackled to life, transmitting vital instructions with military precision. As the team prepared for the dive, the once-peaceful beach echoed with the bustling sounds of purposeful activity.

Local residents, drawn by the spectacle, watched with bated breath. The revelation of Tristan's malevolence sent shockwaves through the community. Whispers and murmurs rippled through the crowd as they grappled with the unsettling truth. Could their friendly acquaintance have harbored such dark secrets?

The stage was set, and the search for answers was about to plunge into the abyss of Wah Sempoh' s depths, where secrets and revelations lay hidden beneath the waves.

Chapter 88

The search was underway, the sun casting its brilliant rays upon the clear, inviting waters of Wah Sempoh. Tristan, under the vigilant watch of police officers, pointed out the area where he had left the shore that fateful night. The divers, an elite team of underwater investigators, boarded the waiting boats. Their eyes were steely with resolve as they prepared to delve into the depths that concealed the truth about Jack's fate.

The boats gently glided over the placid surface of the sea, traversing the same path Tristan had taken that haunting night. A sense of eerie anticipation hung in the air, as the divers donned their gear with meticulous precision. Each piece of equipment felt like a lifeline, a tether to the unknown secrets lurking beneath.

As they reached a designated spot, about a mile into the serene waters, the divers shared a fleeting, nervous glance. With a nod from their leader, they descended into the water, disappearing beneath the shimmering surface. The boats, now still, seemed to hold their collective breath, as if the ocean itself were a silent sentinel to the unfolding drama beneath its surface.

Back on the shore, a heavy silence enveloped the spectators. Their gaze was locked onto the boats, willing the divers to succeed. Time felt suspended, and the natural world seemed to hush, as if paying homage to the high-stakes mission taking place beneath the waves.

Minutes ticked by like hours, and the silence grew more profound with each passing second. The only sound was the gentle lapping of the waves against the boats, a rhythmic reminder of the tranquil seascape.

Then, almost imperceptibly, a disturbance broke the stillness. Bubbles, small at first, then growing in size, rose to the water's surface near one of the boats. The crowd onshore held its collective breath, their eyes widening with anticipation.

And then, with a triumphant surge, the divers emerged, their expressions a mix of exhaustion and hope. But as they gathered on the boats, it was clear they had found nothing in that location. The sense of disappointment was palpable, like a dark cloud casting a shadow over the eager hearts gathered on the shore.

The search team marked the unfruitful spot on their map, a stark reminder of the challenges that lay ahead. They knew the key to unlocking the truth still lay beneath the water, and they couldn't afford to relent.

Determined, they pressed on, orchestrating a well-coordinated relay of divers. This strategy ensured that no one became overly fatigued during the relentless underwater quest. With each new attempt, they descended into the abyss, hoping to unravel the mysteries that surrounded Jack's disappearance.

The relentless search continued, pushing well into the night. By sunset, visibility beneath the surface had become compromised, forcing the divers to halt their efforts. It was a frustrating pause, a cruel reminder that time was slipping away.

As the night descended upon Wah Sempoh, the search team reluctantly retreated to their accommodations. Exhaustion clung to them like a second skin, but they knew they couldn't rest for long. The weight of the investigation pressed heavily on their shoulders.

Meanwhile, Tristan, the centre of the storm, had been transported back to the police station. The detectives kept a watchful eye on him, knowing that their pursuit of justice hinged on his cooperation.

Back at Wah Sempoh, the unexpected had occurred. The news of the search had spread like wildfire, attracting an ever-growing crowd. Reporters, like vultures to a feast, had descended upon the scene, their cameras and microphones capturing every moment.

The sudden influx of attention added a layer of complexity to an already challenging operation. The police knew that to succeed, they had to quell the burgeoning circus of onlookers and media frenzy and refocus their efforts on the task at hand.

By the end of the second day, Wah Sempoh had transformed from a serene coastal village into a bustling hub of activity. Locals, though troubled by the circumstances, couldn't help but notice the silver lining. Their businesses flourished, as restaurants overflowed with patrons, and accommodations were fully booked. A sense of bitter irony hung in the air as they reeled in their most impressive catches of fish and prawns to meet the demands of the unexpected influx of visitors.

The stage was set for a pivotal chapter in the investigation, and the tranquil waters of Wah Sempoh concealed secrets that would soon demand to be brought into the unforgiving light of truth.

Chapter 89

Amid the ongoing search, Detective Lam and his team recognized the need for additional expertise to aid them in understanding the complex underwater currents and weather patterns. They enlisted experts to calculate the probable drift of a body in the water. The precision of their calculations was paramount; they couldn't afford to waste any more time.

The detective's unwavering dedication to the search had blinded him to the arrival of a familiar face - Tengku, his friend from the warehouse. Tengku, along with his family, had come to show their support. They brought food, a comforting gesture that touched the detective deeply. Amidst the chaos of the search operation, the warmth and presence of Tengku's family provided a much-needed respite. Detective Lam found himself sharing stories, laughter, and energy with his newfound friends. Their moral support rekindled his determination.

Days turned into nights, and the search pressed on, moving further from the initial search area. The lack of progress was demoralizing, and hope was beginning to wane.

The crowd that had gathered over the past few days showed no signs of dispersing. T-shirts in support of Jack were being sold, makeshift accommodations sprouted up, and the scent of various cuisines wafted through the air. The locals capitalized on the influx, creating new businesses and attractions. Wah Sempoh, once a quiet village, had inadvertently been thrust into the spotlight.

Detective Lam, however, remained unfazed by the distractions. His singular focus was finding Jack, a determination that had not wavered.

Then, on the fourth day, a breakthrough emerged. The plastic that had concealed Jack's body bobbed to the surface, released from its underwater confinement. Parts of it remained attached to heavy bricks. The divers, their anticipation palpable, cautiously approached the site. The more they moved the plastic, the muddier the water became due to the stirred-up sand. They needed a delicate touch to uncover the evidence without causing it to sink further into the murky depths.

A decision was made to deploy a remote camera, a tool that would allow for minimal disturbance. Slowly and steadily, they maneuvered the camera into position. What it captured sent shockwaves through the team - bricks and another, elongated weight, likely Jack's body.

The divers surfaced, urgently requesting ropes to secure the bricks and plastic bag. The delicate operation to retrieve the evidence had begun. News of the discovery spread rapidly through the camp, and everyone was on edge.

Detective Lam, alerted by the buzz on the radios, rushed to the scene. The tension was palpable as he joined his team at the shore. Binoculars were trained on the boats, which were now bustling with activity. Another boat departed from the shore, carrying essential supplies to aid in the recovery operation. All eyes were locked on the water, awaiting any sign of progress.

As the divers carefully secured the evidence with ropes, silence fell over the onlookers. The underwater world concealed its secrets, and the team moved with the utmost care to unveil them. The cameras of the press were also poised, ready to capture the momentous discovery that lay beneath the surface.

As the divers descended once more, the tension in the air reached its zenith. This was the moment they had all been waiting for - the moment that could finally bring closure to Jack's family and justice to those who had conspired against him. The waters of Wah Sempoh might have concealed their secrets for a time, but today, they would yield their grim truths to those who sought them.

Chapter 90

The discovery of Jack's body was an agonizing moment, one that reverberated through the hearts of everyone present. As the divers gently lifted the remains from the depths of the ocean, the heavy shroud of silence hung heavily over the boat.

Their meticulous efforts ensured that the body was treated with the utmost respect. It was encased in a somber black body bag, shielding it from prying eyes and the relentless clicking of cameras. The press had descended like vultures, their lenses hungry for a sensational shot, and the noise of their shutters filled the air. The shock and horror were palpable, not just among the journalists but also among the bystanders who had gathered to witness the grim discovery.

For the onlookers, the sight was a horrifying awakening. The tranquil waters they had visited daily concealed an unthinkable crime, a tragedy that had unfolded beneath their very feet. The fishermen, who had cast their nets and lines in these waters for years, were struck dumb by the revelation. The sea had given them their livelihoods, but it had also hidden a gruesome secret.

Once the body was secured, it was carefully transported to the shore, where an awaiting ambulance would take it to the mortuary. Every piece of evidence was collected, catalogued, and sealed in bags, preserving the crime scene's integrity.

Slowly, the boats that had played a pivotal role in this search were loaded back onto the waiting trucks. They departed the seaside village in quiet procession, retracing their earlier path. The police team, with their heavy burden of evidence, was on their way to the next phase of the investigation.

As hours passed, the commotion around the village dwindled. The reporters, eager to cover the story's latest developments, followed the police convoy. However, many others chose to remain. They had found unexpected solace in this coastal community, relishing the simple joys of the village even amidst the tragedy.

Meanwhile, Detective Lam waited in the mortuary's sterile waiting room, his mind filled with a tumult of emotions. The process of identifying the body was complex; the ravages of time had taken their toll. They would rely on dental records to confirm the identity.

Hours seemed to stretch into eternity as the mortuary staff worked diligently to prepare the body. They cleaned and prepared it as best they could, making it presentable for what would undoubtedly be a painful identification.

Mueez, with trembling hands and a heart heavy with grief, was called upon to perform the grim task of identification. He understood the immense weight of the moment; he was the bridge between his dear friend and Jack's grieving parents. As he entered the room where Jack lay, the gravity of the situation pressed upon him.

Beneath the cold, sterile cloth lay a body bloated and discoloured, a stark contrast to the vibrant Jack they had known. He appeared more like a character from a macabre movie than his cherished friend and brother. Mueez forced himself to look closer, seeking any familiar detail that would confirm this was Jack.

And then, he saw it—the scar on Jack's left arm, just near the elbow. It was a relic of their childhood, a reminder of a day when youthful curiosity had led Jack to a forbidden sweet jar hidden by his mother. Mueez had been there when Jack fell, his arm brushing against a door handle that left a distinctive mark. The memory of that fall had stayed with them both, and that scar now served as a bittersweet confirmation.

Tears welled in Mueez's eyes as he realized the irrevocable truth. This was Jack, his cherished friend, forever lost to the depths. He summoned the strength to lift the cloth, to say his final goodbye to the friend who had been like a brother.

Leaving the room, Mueez's composure shattered. He rushed to the nearest bathroom; overcome by a tumult of emotions that he could no longer contain. The retching sounds echoed his anguish as he expelled the pain and sorrow he had carried since Jack's disappearance. This was closure, but it was also an agonizing farewell to a dear friend.

Arrangements were made to return Jack's body to his grieving family in Penang. They needed this closure, this final opportunity to say goodbye to their beloved son. Detective Lam, Tengku, his family, and some of the warehouse staff who had become entangled in this tragedy all decided to accompany the body to its resting place.

When they arrived at Jack's family home, the sight that greeted them was overwhelming. A sea of mourners had gathered, a testament to the love and respect Jack had garnered in his too-short life. It was a poignant reminder that their efforts had not only uncovered a truth but also allowed a community to come together to grieve and find solace in each other's presence.

Chapter 91

The courtroom was packed, with every seat occupied, as Tristan's trial began. It was a somber occasion, and the air in the room was thick with tension. Detective Lam and the prosecution team had built a meticulous case against Tristan, one that was like a puzzle with each piece fitting perfectly to reveal a disturbing picture of his criminal activities.

The charges against Tristan were a litany of felonies that ranged from shocking to downright sinister. The prosecutor, an imposing figure with a reputation for securing convictions, rose to address the court.

"Ladies and gentlemen of the jury," he began, his voice resonating with authority, "Today, we shall peel back the layers of deceit to expose a criminal whose actions have sent shockwaves across borders. Tristan stands before you accused of kidnapping, arms trafficking, murder, illegal firearm possession, forgery, and a litany of other heinous offenses."

As each charge was enunciated, the jury members exchanged uneasy glances. They could sense the weight of responsibility on their shoulders.

The prosecution commenced by unveiling the video footage of Jack's murder. The courtroom fell into a stunned silence as the screen displayed the chilling act, recorded for eternity. Tristan, his eyes fixed on the screen, remained impassive, but his eyes betrayed a flicker of unease. The jury members, however, reacted with shock and horror, their faces contorted by the brutality they were witnessing.

The next witnesses to take the stand were the victims of Tristan's atrocities. Tengku Farhan, his composure remarkably steady, recounted his harrowing experience of being kidnapped. The tension in the courtroom was palpable as he detailed the fear and despair he had felt during those terrifying days in captivity.

Tengku Beans followed, his testimony revealing the physical and emotional scars he still bore from being shot by Tristan. As he spoke, the jury couldn't help but be moved by his resilience. The image of him, a survivor bearing witness against his tormentor, left a profound impression on all who listened.

The prosecution meticulously presented the extensive network Tristan had constructed for arms smuggling, calling forth accomplices from around the world to testify against him. Each witness painted a damning portrait of Tristan's role in the international criminal underworld.

Tristan's defence attorney, a wily and resourceful advocate, attempted to create doubt by arguing that Tristan had been coerced into these criminal activities by shadowy figures who held his life hostage. But it was like trying to douse a wildfire with a garden hose. The evidence was overwhelming, and the prosecutor systematically dismantled each of the defence's arguments.

Throughout the trial, Detective Lam, his eyes unwavering, watched Tristan. He had dedicated himself to this pursuit of justice, and now, as the culmination of his efforts unfolded before him, he couldn't help but feel a sense of grim satisfaction.

The families of the victims, including Tengku and his family, sat together in the courtroom. Their faces conveyed a spectrum of emotions, from seething anger to deep grief.

Each moment of the trial was an agonizing reminder of the pain Tristan had inflicted upon them.

As the days of the trial wore on, it became increasingly apparent that the justice system was resolute in its determination to hold Tristan accountable for his crimes. The weight of the evidence bore down upon him, and the jury's verdict loomed as an inescapable reckoning.

In the end, the trial was a testament to the unwavering pursuit of justice. Tristan, once a cunning criminal mastermind, now stood exposed and vulnerable before the might of the law.

Chapter 92

The culmination of Tristan's trial was a momentous event that cast a long shadow over the courtroom. After weeks of impassioned arguments, emotional testimonies, and unimpeachable evidence, the jury returned with their verdict: guilty on all counts.

As the judge pronounced the verdict, Tristan's expression remained unchanged, a mask of stoicism concealing the turmoil within. He had expected this outcome, but it was a blow, nonetheless.

The families of the victims, sitting in the gallery, could hardly contain their emotions. Tengku, his family, and Detective Lam exchanged glances, sharing a collective sigh of relief. Justice had prevailed, and the weight of their ordeal seemed to lift, if only slightly.

The sentencing phase of the trial commenced, with the prosecution pushing for the harshest penalties allowed by law. Tristan's defence attorney, now resigned to his client's guilt, attempted to appeal to the court's sense of leniency, citing Tristan's cooperation in revealing crucial details about his criminal network.

Choi, once an accomplice in Tristan's illicit dealings, had turned state's witness, offering crucial information that had aided in dismantling the arms smuggling operation. He had once been ensnared by Tristan's web of deceit, but his conscience had led him to change sides, cooperating with Detective Lam and the authorities.

Choi's testimony and cooperation played a pivotal role in ensuring Tristan's conviction. He stood before the court, his voice steady as he described his own involvement in the criminal activities and his eventual decision to break free from Tristan's influence.

Sam, an employee of the Port Authority who had been coerced into assisting Tristan, also testified. He revealed the threats and intimidation he had endured, painting a vivid picture of Tristan's ruthless methods. Sam's testimony corroborated many aspects of the case, strengthening the prosecution's argument.

As the sentencing hearing continued, the judge listened to impassioned pleas from the families of the victims. Tengku, his voice quivering with emotion, addressed the court, describing the pain and suffering his family had endured. He spoke of the loss of his dear employee, Jack, and the trauma his family had faced during his kidnapping.

Tengku's words resonated with the judge, who seemed deeply moved by the raw anguish in his voice. Detective Lam also stepped forward, highlighting the resilience of the victims and the tireless efforts of the investigators who had unraveled Tristan's criminal empire.

In the end, the judge handed down a sentence that left no room for doubt. Tristan would spend the rest of his life behind bars, with no possibility of parole. The courtroom erupted in a mix of relief, satisfaction, and applause from those who had worked tirelessly to ensure justice was served.

As Tristan was led away in handcuffs, the families of the victims, Detective Lam, Choi, and Sam shared a collective moment of closure. The courtroom doors closed behind them, sealing the fate of a man who had once wielded power and fear, now reduced to a mere convict.

Outside, a sense of catharsis washed over those who had been touched by Tristan's malevolence. The victims could finally breathe freely, knowing that the man responsible for their suffering would never again walk among them as a free man.

The sun cast a warm, hopeful glow over the courthouse, symbolizing the dawn of a new chapter for those who had endured so much. Tristan's reign of terror was over, and justice had been served.

Chapter 93

With Tristan behind bars, Detective Lam's life took an unexpected turn. His relentless pursuit of justice and unwavering dedication to the Beans family had not gone unnoticed by his superiors. Recognizing his exceptional leadership and investigative skills, they offered him a promotion to head a prestigious division in the bustling city of Kuala Lumpur.

The news of his promotion was met with mixed emotions. Tengku and his family, who had grown close to Detective Lam during the harrowing ordeal, were elated for their friend's success. They knew that the promotion was a testament to his commitment to bringing down Tristan and dismantling his criminal empire.

The day Detective Lam bid farewell to the serene town of Port Klang was bittersweet. He had come to Port Klang on a mission to solve a puzzling case, and in the process, he had forged deep connections with its people. Tengku, always the gracious host, held a small gathering to celebrate the detective's achievements and bid him a fond farewell.

As they sat by the sea, the gentle waves providing a soothing backdrop to their conversation, Tengku expressed his gratitude. "Detective Lam, you've become more than a friend to us. You're family. You brought justice for Jack, and you've helped us heal. We'll miss you, but we know you're destined for great things."

Detective Lam smiled, his eyes reflecting the warmth of the moment. "Tengku, it's been an honour to know you and your family. You've shown me the true meaning of resilience and strength. I'll carry your friendship with me always."

With a final toast to their shared journey, Detective Lam left Port Klang, headed for the bustling city lights of Kuala Lumpur, where a new chapter awaited him.

Chapter 94

In Port Klang, the bonds of friendship and trust had been reforged. Daniel, a cherished childhood friend of Tengku, had once faced a difficult crossroads. He remembered the days when anger and resentment had clouded their friendship, the result of a heated disagreement. Daniel had turned to Tengku for financial assistance in a time of need, but Tengku, mindful of his own reckless spending habits, had hesitated. It was a decision that had initially strained their friendship.

However, as time passed, the two friends sat down and engaged in a long, heartfelt conversation. Their words flowed freely, carrying with them the memories of their shared childhood, their dreams, and their aspirations. Tengku listened intently, realizing the depth of his friend's struggles and dreams. Understanding bloomed between them, erasing the anger that had once separated them.

With newfound clarity and a renewed sense of camaraderie, Tengku decided to support Daniel in his time of need. He became not just a friend but also a shareholder in Daniel's burgeoning real estate agency. Together, they ventured into a world of opportunities, their combined strengths propelling the agency to new heights.

As Daniel's real estate business flourished, so did his friendship with Tengku. Their bond was unbreakable, forged in the crucible of shared dreams and tested by the trials of life. Now, as Daniel stood on the threshold of a new chapter in his life, preparing to marry the love of his life, Zara, he knew that Tengku would be by his side, not just as a best man but as a lifelong friend and confidant.

The upcoming wedding was a celebration not just of love but also of enduring friendships and the promise of a bright future. Daniel had come a long way since the day he and Tengku had reconciled. Their journey had taken them through challenges and triumphs, but through it all, their friendship had grown stronger.

As the wedding preparations continued, with Tengku as Daniel's loyal best man and trusted friend, Port Klang witnessed a joyous union that reflected the power of reconciliation, the strength of friendship, and the beauty of new beginnings.

Chapter 95

In the wake of Jack's tragic passing, his parents embarked on a painful journey of healing and recovery. The loss of their beloved son had left a void that could never be completely filled. However, time had a way of mending even the deepest wounds, and with the support of their extended family and friends, the pain began to gradually subside.

Tengku, who had forged a strong bond with Jack's parents, became not only a pillar of emotional support but also a beacon of financial assistance. Recognizing the burden that the parents had shouldered due to their circumstances, he ensured that they had the resources they needed to rebuild their lives. From covering essential expenses to helping with various financial matters, Tengku played an invaluable role in alleviating their financial strain.

Mueez, Jack's close friend and confidant, visited the grieving parents regularly. He had become more than just a friend; he was like a son to them. Mueez's presence offered a sense of solace and continuity, a tangible connection to the son they had lost. His unwavering support and companionship were a source of immense comfort to the parents during their darkest hours.

Over time, the pain that had initially consumed Jack's parents began to ebb. While the wound of his absence remained, they learned to carry their grief with grace and resilience. Memories of Jack filled their home, and through stories and photographs, his spirit lived on.

Their healing was not a solitary journey. Support poured in from various sources, their community rallying around them in their time of need. Friends, neighbours, and even strangers offered condolences, assistance, and kind words. It was a testament to the power of empathy and compassion, the knowledge that in times of adversity, humanity had a remarkable capacity for collective strength.

As they navigated the complexities of grief, Jack's parents began to find moments of peace. They knew that their beloved son would forever hold a special place in their hearts. While his physical presence had departed, his love remained, an enduring source of strength and inspiration.

The pain they had experienced would never be forgotten, but it gradually transformed into a bittersweet reminder of the love they had shared with Jack. With each passing day, they took small steps toward embracing life once more, knowing that their son's spirit watched over them, a guardian angel guiding them through the challenges of their journey.

Chapter 96

With Tristan's malevolent influence permanently purged from Tok and Beans Sdn Bhd, the company began to flourish. News of the courtroom drama, the indictment of Tristan on multiple charges, and Tengku Beans's steadfast commitment to ethical business practices reverberated throughout the shipping industry. Clients who had been wary of the company's association with a criminal enterprise now flocked back, reassured by the new direction Tok and Beans had taken.

Tengku Beans was resolute in his determination to maintain the company's reputation and integrity. The pledge to adhere strictly to legal and ethical standards resonated with their clients, and business began to boom. Contracts rolled in, and the company's portfolio expanded. The trajectory of Tok and Beans was nothing short of remarkable.

As the business expanded, so did its positive impact on the local community. More jobs were created, offering employment opportunities to the residents of Port Klang and its surrounding areas. Tengku Beans had always believed in elevating others along with him, and he remained true to this principle. The prosperity of Tok and Beans was shared by all who contributed to its success.

Amy, the dedicated secretary who had stood by Tengku throughout the tumultuous journey, continued to play a vital role in the company. Her intimate knowledge of Tengku's preferences and the inner workings of the business made her an indispensable asset. She ensured that the company ran smoothly, her efficiency and dedication reflecting the core values of Tok and Beans.

Charles, the stalwart head of the warehouse, remained at the helm. In the wake of Tristan's downfall, he implemented stringent security measures to safeguard the company's operations. His leadership and commitment to excellence were essential in upholding the company's reputation for reliability and efficiency.

Tok and Beans Sdn Bhd stood as a testament to the triumph of integrity over deceit, resilience over adversity. It was a beacon of hope in an industry that often grappled with corruption and illicit dealings. The company's success was a testament to the unwavering principles of its founder, Tengku Beans, and the dedication of its employees.

The story of Tok and Beans was not just one of business acumen but of moral fortitude. It demonstrated that, even in the face of darkness, the light of righteousness could prevail, illuminating a path towards success and prosperity.

Chapter 97

Tengku Farhan, affectionately known as Tengku Han, had always been a man of ambition. He had carved a path in the bustling financial services sector, making his mark in the metropolis of the Tun Razak Exchange (TRX) in Kuala Lumpur. But life had a way of altering one's priorities, and Tengku Han had undergone a transformation, both in his professional and personal life.

The traumatic events of the past, especially the harrowing kidnapping experience, had left a profound impact on him. It was as if life had shaken him awake, urging him to reassess his priorities. The pursuit of success in the corporate world, while still important, no longer consumed him as it once did. Instead, Tengku Han found himself yearning for something more.

That something came in the form of a woman named Tasha. She had a presence that radiated warmth and a smile that could brighten the darkest of days. Tasha was a remarkable woman, full of life and passion, and Tengku Han was captivated by her spirit. Their connection was undeniable, and it didn't take long for their relationship to deepen.

Tasha brought a sense of balance to Tengku Han's life. She understood the demands of his career and the weight of his responsibilities, yet she also encouraged him to savour life's simpler pleasures. Together, they explored the vibrant city of Kuala Lumpur, discovering hidden gems and enjoying quiet moments amid the urban hustle and bustle.

As their love blossomed, Tengku Han's once meticulously structured life began to take on new dimensions. He found joy in sharing his aspirations and dreams with Tasha, envisioning a future where their lives intertwined harmoniously. The prospect of building a family together, of seeing their love grow and flourish, became a beacon of hope.

Tengku Han knew that the scars of the past would always be a part of him, a reminder of the challenges he had faced and overcome. But in Tasha's embrace, he found solace and healing. She was his confidante, his partner in crime, and his unwavering source of support.

The bustling metropolis of TRX continued to thrive, a testament to Tengku Han's dedication and expertise. But beyond the gleaming skyscrapers and financial transactions, he had discovered a different kind of wealth—the richness of love and companionship.

Tengku Han's life had undergone a profound transformation, one that had led him to Tasha and a newfound sense of happiness and fulfillment. As they embarked on this journey together, the future held endless possibilities, and Tengku Han was ready to embrace them with an open heart.

Chapter 98

In the heart of bustling Port Klang, within the walls of their luxurious penthouse apartment at Pier 8, Alicia sat in the quiet room, lost in her thoughts. She gazed out of the floor-to-ceiling windows, where the breathtaking view of the harbour unfolded before her. This was a place she had come to for solace, a retreat from the chaos of the world outside.

The past few months had been incredibly challenging for the Beans family. They had weathered the storm together, the trials and tribulations that had come their way. The toll it had taken on their family was undeniable. Alicia, as a wife and mother, felt every moment deeply. The stress, the fear, the uncertainty; it all had left its mark.

As she looked at the bustling port below, she couldn't help but think about how far they had come. The ordeal was finally over, Tristan was behind bars, and justice had been served. The family was safe, and her husband, Tengku, had proven to be their rock throughout.

Alicia's mind wandered to the idea of a break, a getaway from it all. Tengku had been working tirelessly to keep their business running smoothly during the tumultuous times. The entire family deserved a moment of respite, a chance to rejuvenate their spirits.

She turned to Tengku, who had joined her in the room. "Tengku," she began, "I've been thinking. After everything we've been through, maybe it's time for a break. A holiday, perhaps?"

Tengku looked at her, a small smile forming. "You know what, Alicia? I think that's a fantastic idea. We could all use some time away from the daily grind. And I know just the place."

The Cameron Highlands, a lush and picturesque hill station nestled amidst the Titiwangsa Mountains, awaited the Beans family. Tengku, Alicia, Tengku Han, and Tasha set off on their adventure. Here, amid the cool, crisp air and stunning natural beauty, they found peace and serenity.

Their first stop was the Berjaya Hills Resort, an enchanting French-themed village with charming architecture and vineyards. They explored the cobblestone streets, sampled exquisite fruit juices, and marvelled at the breathtaking views.

Next, they ventured to the tea plantations, where acres of emerald-green tea bushes stretched as far as the eye could see. The family learned about the tea-making process and enjoyed cups of freshly brewed tea in the midst of the serene plantations.

At the strawberry farm, they picked plump, juicy strawberries, their laughter filling the air as they enjoyed the simple pleasures of life. They indulged in delightful strawberry treats, from fresh fruit to jams and desserts.

The family embarked on exhilarating hikes through the mossy forests, enchanted by the mystical atmosphere reminiscent of scenes from "The Lord of the Rings." Towering trees, draped in moss and ferns, created a sense of wonder and adventure.

The Gunung Jasar mountain hike provided them with breathtaking panoramic views of the surrounding hills and valleys. At the summit, they felt on top of the world, a shared sense of accomplishment binding them closer together.

The Cameron Lavender Garden greeted them with a riot of colours and fragrances. They strolled through fields of lavender, their sweet scent filling the air, and reveled in the beauty of the blooming flowers.

Their journey led them to the colonial-style Lakehouse Hotel, where they savoured sumptuous meals and basked in the tranquillity of the surrounding gardens. Here, they discovered that time spent together was the greatest luxury of all.

And of course, there was the Cameron Lavender Garden, where vibrant flowers danced in the breeze, their brilliant hues a feast for the eyes. The family reveled in the simple joys of nature, their hearts lighter with every passing moment.

As they returned to Port Klang, their souls refreshed and bonds strengthened, the Beans family carried the memories of their Cameron Highlands getaway with them. It was a reminder that, no matter the challenges they faced, they could always find solace and joy in each other's company.

The Bean family's story was far from over, but for now, they had discovered the true meaning of family and the healing power of togetherness.

Chapter 99

Port Klang, the picturesque coastal town, had seemingly returned to its idyllic state. Its vibrant streets bustled with life, echoing the laughter of children playing by the shore. The daily routines of its people carried on, seemingly unaffected by the shadows that had recently loomed over the town.

With Tristan safely locked behind bars, the crimes that had once plagued the town remained hidden, as if swallowed by the depths of the sea. The illicit activities that had thrived in secrecy now seemed like distant memories, replaced by a sense of security that had long been absent.

As the sun dipped below the horizon, casting an amber glow across the harbour, Port Klang transformed. Its bustling streets gave way to a tranquil evening, the sky painted with hues of purple and gold. Families gathered for dinners at local eateries, sharing stories and laughter.

But beneath this façade of tranquillity, unbeknownst to the town's residents, a new plot was taking shape. Tristan, with his cunning and malevolence, was far from defeated. From the confines of his prison cell, he meticulously crafted the next phase of his dark agenda.

His thirst for revenge burned brighter than ever, fueled by the desire to settle scores with those who had brought about his downfall. Tengku Beans, Detective Lam, and all those who had thwarted him were now marked targets in his twisted game.

Tristan knew that he couldn't act openly; the authorities would be watching his every move. Instead, he began to weave a complex web of intrigue and deception, recruiting unsuspecting pawns to carry out his sinister plans. The very heart of Port Klang, a town that had just begun to heal, would become the stage for his malevolent designs.

As night settled over Port Klang, casting shadows over its tranquil streets, the townspeople remained blissfully unaware of the darkness that lurked beneath the surface. The quietude of the town belied the storm that was brewing, one that threatened to unleash chaos once more.

In the heart of this coastal haven, where sea breezes whispered secrets, the next chapter of Tristan's malevolent tale was being penned. And as the night deepened, so did the enigma that was Port Klang, a town teetering on the precipice of darkness, ready to face a new, sinister dawn.

Chapter 100

Inside the prison walls where Tristan was destined to spend the rest of his life, his sinister reputation had already preceded him. Tales of his malevolence and dangerous cunning had rippled through the prison's population like wildfire. Men who had faced hardened criminals now trembled in fear at the mere mention of Tristan's name.

In the cold, unforgiving world of the prison, Tristan found himself in an unfamiliar position. Here, he was not just another criminal, but a figure of both awe and dread. His reputation had granted him an unlikely yet terrible power. In the confined, shadowy corridors of his new existence, he became a ruler of sorts, an inmate who commanded respect through fear.

Tristan's manipulation skills, honed over years of criminal endeavors, now served a new purpose. He identified potential pawns among his fellow inmates, those who had grudges against the world and an appetite for destruction. With subtle persuasion, he began sowing the seeds of his dark agenda, convincing them to carry out his vengeful plans beyond the prison walls.

His masterstroke was to exploit the cracks within the prison's hierarchy. Tristan's machinations were so subtle that they often went unnoticed by the guards and wardens. He used every ounce of his persuasive charm to make the prison's lower ranks look the other way as his pawns prepared for their assigned tasks.

Tristan's emotional state was a whirlwind of hatred and vengeance. Each day that passed behind bars stoked the fires of his malevolence. He couldn't, and wouldn't, let go of the past. The faces of Tengku Beans, Detective Lam, and others who had been instrumental in his capture haunted his every waking moment.

His isolation had only sharpened his resolve. He was consumed by a singular desire – to see those who had wronged him suffer as he had. And he was willing to wait, to plot, and to scheme for as long as it took to see his wicked vision come to fruition.

As the prison's walls closed in around him, Tristan hatched his malevolent plans, day by day, step by step. He knew that patience was his greatest ally, and he used it to his advantage. The world outside had moved on, believing him contained and powerless. But the truth was far more sinister. Tristan's quest for revenge was just beginning, and he was determined to make his enemies pay, no matter the cost.

In the dark recesses of his prison cell, Tristan plotted and schemed, weaving a web of deceit that would soon ensnare those who had crossed him. The next chapter of his malevolent tale had begun, one that promised to bring pain, suffering, and chaos. And with each passing day, his resolve grew stronger, as did the shadows of his impending revenge.

Chapter 101

Tristan knew that in the world of organized crime, connections were everything. And now, within the cold, imposing walls of the prison, he had found an unexpected ally in Hakimi.

Hakimi, a lanky, bespectacled man in his twenties, might have appeared unassuming to most. His reputation, however, was far from it. He was known among the inmates for his cyber prowess – hacking into systems, accessing confidential information, and traversing the dark corners of the internet's underworld. His crimes, while not violent, had earned him respect among the digital underworld.

As Tristan's plans took shape, he recognized the potential in Hakimi. With his impending release, Hakimi would soon be back in the outside world, where he could use his hacking skills to navigate the intricate network of criminal connections that Tristan had nurtured over the years.

But Tristan needed more than just Hakimi's technical expertise. He needed unwavering loyalty and someone who would follow orders without question. Someone who, despite being free, would still cower in fear of Tristan, the formidable puppeteer pulling the strings from his prison cell.

It wasn't a difficult task to convince Hakimi to be his eyes and ears on the outside. After all, the allure of financial gain and the fear of what Tristan could do to him if he refused were potent motivators. Tristan knew how to play on Hakimi's vulnerabilities, skilfully exploiting his weaknesses.

Their interactions occurred mostly through coded letters and hushed conversations in the prison yard. Tristan outlined his grand design – a plan to strike back at those who had thwarted him. He knew that the threat of exposing Hakimi's hacking exploits to the authorities would keep him in line.

Hakimi, for his part, saw an opportunity for redemption. He believed that by following Tristan's directives, he could carve out a new life free from the digital mazes of cybercrime. He was captivated by the promise of a fresh start, one that he believed Tristan could provide.

As the days inched closer to Hakimi's release, Tristan's instructions grew more intricate. Hack this server, gather information on that individual, monitor their movements – each task was a piece of a larger puzzle, a puzzle that would pave the way for Tristan's vengeance.

Tristan, despite being confined to his prison cell, felt a renewed sense of power and purpose. He had found his emissary, a shadowy figure who would move in the darkness, unseen and unheard. And so, he continued to weave his web of deception and malevolence, biding his time until the moment of reckoning arrived.

Hakimi, the unwitting pawn in Tristan's grand scheme, was about to be set loose upon the world. As he walked through the prison gates to freedom, he carried with him a sinister agenda, a plan orchestrated by a man who refused to be forgotten, a man who would stop at nothing to exact his revenge.

Chapter 102

In the heart of Port Klang, a bustling coastal town that echoed with the rhythms of trade and the ebb and flow of tides, Akanji Beans stood at the crossroads of his life. His family had called this place home for generations, but now, the time had come for him to spread his wings and chase his dreams in a distant land.

Akanji had always harbored a deep passion for engineering. The dreams that had taken root within him during his childhood had blossomed into a fierce determination. The acceptance letter from a prestigious university in London had arrived like a harbinger of new beginnings, promising to take him on a journey of knowledge and discovery.

The prospect of studying in the heart of the United Kingdom filled him with a mix of excitement and nervousness. London, a city steeped in history and innovation, was calling his name. Its iconic landmarks, diverse culture, and vibrant atmosphere promised adventures beyond his wildest imagination.

As the day of his departure loomed closer, the Beans household buzzed with preparations and emotions. Akanji's family, who had been his unwavering support throughout his life, now had bittersweet feelings about his journey. Pride swelled within them as they watched their eldest son prepare for this life-altering adventure, yet the thought of his absence weighed heavy on their hearts.

Akanji's mother, a source of boundless love and strength, couldn't hold back her tears as she carefully packed his bags. She had always been his staunchest advocate, and now, her son was setting forth on a path that would take him thousands of miles from home. In the quiet moments, she whispered silent prayers for his safety and success, her heart heavy with the impending separation.

His father, a man of few words but profound wisdom, offered words of encouragement. He spoke of the opportunities awaiting Akanji and the importance of pursuing one's dreams. Akanji knew that his father's unwavering support would serve as a guiding light in the years to come.

Akanji's younger brother, Kyrie, stood by his side with a mixture of admiration and longing in his eyes. He looked up to his brother as a role model, and although he was excited about Akanji's journey, he would miss his brother's presence and the warmth of his laughter.

Finally, the day of departure arrived. The family gathered at Kuala Lumpur International Airport (KLIA), where towering cranes and container ships painted a backdrop of the town's maritime importance. The excitement was palpable, but a solemn note of farewell hung in the air. Akanji's heart swelled with gratitude for the love and support that enveloped him.

As he walked toward the departure gate, he turned for one last look at his family. His mother's eyes glistened with tears, and his father offered a silent nod of reassurance. Kyrie waved and called out his goodbyes. Akanji felt a rush of emotion that threatened to engulf him.

With one last heartfelt smile, Akanji passed through the gateway, leaving behind the familiarity of Port Klang for a future laden with endless possibilities. The plane's engines roared to life, carrying him away from the shores he had known all his life.

As the aircraft ascended into the skies, Akanji gazed out of the window, taking in the familiar sight of KLIA below. The airport's bustling activity grew smaller and smaller, while London's bright promise beckoned on the horizon. The journey ahead was shrouded in uncertainty, but Akanji embraced it with a heart brimming with hope and dreams as vast as the boundless sea.

And so, Akanji embarked on his adventure, ready to carve his path in the world and make his family proud. As the plane soared higher, the unbreakable bonds of love and support that connected him to his family remained steadfast, a wellspring of strength to sustain him through the challenges and victories that awaited him in distant lands.

Chapter 103

In the vibrant digital realm of online gaming, where alliances were forged and rivalries blazed like virtual wildfires, Kyrie found his sanctuary. Tengku's younger son, always overshadowed by his older brother's achievements, had discovered solace in the electrifying world of competitive gaming.

His room transformed into a command centre, adorned with posters of fantastical creatures, and adorned with neon-lit gaming gear. Kyrie had become obsessed with a particular online game – "Chronos Nexus," a sprawling virtual universe where players clashed in epic battles, unraveled intricate quests, and amassed digital treasures.

The allure of this game was more than pixels and code; it was a realm where Kyrie could be his own hero, where he was lauded for his quick reflexes, cunning strategies, and indomitable spirit. In "Chronos Nexus," he wasn't Tengku Beans' son; he was Zephyr, a force to be reckoned with.

And as in any competitive arena, there were legends whispered about certain players, whispers that spoke of a mysterious and immensely skilled gamer known as "Shadowfiend." Kyrie had heard tales of this enigmatic figure, a player who moved through the game's intricate dungeons like a ghost, vanquishing foes with unmatched precision.

What Kyrie didn't know was that "Shadowfiend" wasn't just a formidable gamer. It was Hakimi, Tristan's unwitting ally, navigating the digital landscape with the sole purpose of infiltrating Kyrie's life.

Hakimi, with his skills in hacking and deceit, had identified Kyrie as the perfect entry point into the Beans family. What better way to sow discord and confusion than from within? Kyrie, the gaming enthusiast, was the unsuspecting pawn in Tristan's twisted game of vengeance.

Their online interactions began innocently enough. Kyrie marvelled at "Shadowfiend's" prowess, unaware that the gamer on the other end of the screen was his father's nemesis. Hakimi, under the guise of friendship, started gifting Kyrie rare in-game items and weapons, earning his trust and admiration.

The unsuspecting teenager saw Hakimi as a mentor and a friend, not realizing that he was playing right into the hands of the man who sought to destroy his family. Tristan's plan was slowly taking shape, hidden beneath the pixels and avatars of "Chronos Nexus."

As Hakimi's influence grew within the virtual world, Kyrie found himself more and more entangled in the schemes of a man he knew nothing about. Little did he know that the digital realm he cherished would soon become the battleground for a very real and dangerous game.

With each click of the mouse and each keystroke, Tristan's plan edged closer to fruition. He had infiltrated the Beans family from the shadows, and Kyrie was his unwitting gateway. As the screen flickered with virtual battles and alliances, the stage was set for a battle that would extend far beyond the confines of the game, a battle where the players were unaware that their every move was being manipulated by a master puppeteer.

And so, in the world of "Chronos Nexus," a new chapter of intrigue and deception was born, with unsuspecting Kyrie at its epicentre. Tristan, imprisoned but far from defeated, had found a way to exact his revenge from within the very heart of the family he sought to destroy.

Chapter 104

Kuala Lumpur, the vibrant metropolis that stood as the beating heart of Malaysia, now held Detective Lam within its bustling embrace. Promoted to head a new division within the city's police force, he found himself navigating a complex labyrinth of crime and intrigue. The concrete jungle of towering skyscrapers and labyrinthine streets offered new challenges and adversaries, but Detective Lam was undeterred, ever resolute in his pursuit of justice.

As he settled into his role, Detective Lam became acquainted with the inner workings of the Kuala Lumpur Police Department. It was a different world from the close-knit community of Port Klang, where everyone knew one another's secrets. Here, the corridors echoed with the footsteps of countless officers, each harboring their own agendas and alliances.

Among the officers who crossed Detective Lam's path, one name stood out – Jun Wong. Detective Jun Wong, a charismatic and seemingly dedicated policeman, had an uncanny ability to forge connections. He was well-liked among his peers, known for his affable nature and unwavering commitment to the job.

At first, Detective Lam saw in Jun Wong a potential ally, someone who could help him navigate the intricate web of the city's criminal underworld. Their camaraderie grew as they worked together on various cases, and Detective Lam began to confide in his new colleague.

However, unbeknownst to Detective Lam, Jun Wong was not what he seemed. He was a wolf in sheep's clothing, a pawn in Tristan's elaborate game of vengeance. Underneath the façade of camaraderie, Jun had a hidden agenda – to infiltrate Detective Lam's life and extract information, all on behalf of the imprisoned criminal mastermind.

Tristan's reach extended far beyond prison walls, his network of influence penetrating even the highest echelons of law enforcement. He had carefully orchestrated this deception, anticipating that Detective Lam's transfer to Kuala Lumpur would present an opportunity.

As Detective Lam and Jun Wong delved deeper into the city's criminal underbelly, their partnership unknowingly served Tristan's sinister purposes. The detective was drawn into a complex web of corruption and conspiracy, with Jun Wong as his guide, all while believing he had found an invaluable ally.

The city's skyline, illuminated by the glow of countless lights, masked the darkness that lurked beneath the surface. Kuala Lumpur, with its gleaming towers and bustling streets, held secrets that Detective Lam was yet to uncover. Little did he know that the city's shadows concealed a perilous game, with Tristan pulling the strings from the shadows.

And so, as Detective Lam ventured deeper into this new chapter of his career, he remained oblivious to the peril that lay ahead. The stage was set for a confrontation that would test his resolve like never before. As the city's heartbeat pulsed with life, a clash of titans loomed on the horizon, and the final act of this gripping tale awaited its dramatic climax.

Chapter 105

In the heart of Kuala Lumpur's urban sprawl, Detective Lam's dedication to his work remained unshaken, even as he navigated the intricate dance of alliances and rivalries within the police force. He had earned a reputation for being a diligent and incorruptible officer, traits that garnered both respect and resentment from his colleagues.

As Detective Lam continued to dig into the city's criminal underworld, he became aware of the pervasive corruption that tainted the department. It was an open secret, whispered in hushed tones among the officers. Rogue police officers, operating in collusion with criminal organizations, seemed to be the norm rather than the exception.

One evening, as rain poured down over the city, Detective Lam received an anonymous tip. It was a simple message: "Meet me at midnight, at the abandoned warehouse on Jalan Ampang."

Intrigued and cautious, Detective Lam decided to investigate. He knew that following this lead could be a significant turning point in his quest to dismantle the criminal network that plagued Kuala Lumpur.

As the clock struck midnight, he arrived at the desolate warehouse, the rain's relentless drumming masking his footsteps. The only illumination came from the distant city lights, casting long shadows over the crumbling structure.

Detective Lam waited in silence, his senses alert. He was not alone. Moments later, a figure emerged from the darkness, cloaked in the anonymity of a hooded raincoat.

"Detective Lam," the figure spoke in a hushed voice. "You're treading in dangerous waters. There are those within the force who would see you silenced."

The detective's pulse quickened. He knew he was standing before a whistleblower, someone willing to risk everything to expose the corruption that festered within the police department.

"What do you have for me?" Detective Lam asked, his voice low and determined.

The informant handed over a file, containing a trove of evidence detailing the corrupt activities of several high-ranking officers. It was a Pandora's box of secrets, revealing the extent of the rot within the department.

"These names," the informant whispered, "they're the heart of the corruption. Bring them down, and you'll cleanse the force."

Detective Lam nodded; his resolve unwavering. He understood the danger he was facing, the treacherous path he was about to tread. But he also knew that he could not turn away. The city depended on officers like him, who would not be swayed by greed or intimidation.

The informant faded back into the shadows, leaving Detective Lam with the weight of the evidence in his hands. He knew that exposing the corrupt officers would be a perilous undertaking, one that could cost him dearly.

As he drove back through the rain-soaked streets of Kuala Lumpur, Detective Lam felt a renewed sense of purpose. The battle against crime and corruption was far from over. He was determined to see it through, no matter the cost.

With the damning evidence in his possession, Detective Lam knew that he was on the precipice of a new chapter in his relentless pursuit of justice. The darkness within the city's police force would soon be brought to light, but it would come at a price, a price he was willing to pay.

And so, as the rain continued to fall, washing the city's sins away, Detective Lam prepared to confront the very heart of darkness that had taken root within the police department. The city awaited its reckoning, and the final showdown was on the horizon.

Chapter 106

Within the sprawling metropolis of Kuala Lumpur, life appeared tranquil on the surface. The city's vibrant streets bustled with the hum of daily activities, its people going about their routines with little knowledge of the storm gathering in the shadows. However, beneath this façade of normality, unseen forces were converging, and a sinister plot was unfolding.

Tristan, orchestrating his vendetta from behind prison walls, knew that his time was limited. The various elements of his plan had been set in motion, but he needed something more, a final, devastating blow that would leave his enemies reeling.

In a remote corner of the prison library, Tristan hatched a scheme that would send shockwaves throughout the city. He began to correspond with an enigmatic figure known only as "The Maestro." The Maestro was a criminal mastermind, a puppeteer who orchestrated grand heists, political scandals, and corporate takedowns from the shadows. His reputation was built on anonymity, and his true identity remained a mystery even to those who worked for him.

Tristan's letters to The Maestro were cryptic, filled with coded messages and veiled threats. He proposed a partnership that would serve both their interests. The Maestro, intrigued by the audacity of Tristan's plan, agreed to meet him in person.

Their meeting took place in a dimly lit visitor's room at the prison. Tristan, clad in his orange jumpsuit, was led to the meeting area, where he found The Maestro waiting, concealed by a hooded cloak. Their conversation was tense, filled with veiled references to their shared objectives.

Tristan's proposal was simple yet audacious: The Maestro would unleash a wave of calculated chaos across Kuala Lumpur. He would target the city's financial institutions, erasing records, diverting funds, and plunging the economy into turmoil, using Tengku Farhan as the fall guy. Simultaneously, he would expose corrupt officials, business magnates, and even members of law enforcement, triggering a cascade of scandals that would undermine the city's foundations.

In return, Tristan offered The Maestro a vast network of resources and connections. He promised to use his criminal ties to provide The Maestro with safe havens, access to classified information, and protection from law enforcement. It was a mutually beneficial alliance forged in the crucible of revenge.

The Maestro accepted the proposal, and their partnership was sealed. Tristan, from within the prison, would act as The Maestro's eyes and ears, orchestrating schemes and providing insider information. In return, The Maestro would execute a series of meticulously planned attacks on Kuala Lumpur's institutions and elite.

As Tristan returned to his cell that night, he couldn't help but smile. His vendetta was evolving into something far more sinister and complex than he had initially imagined. The city was teetering on the brink of an unprecedented crisis, and Tristan reveled in the knowledge that he held the strings of this impending chaos.

In the heart of Kuala Lumpur, a storm was brewing, one that threatened to upend the lives of its unsuspecting inhabitants. Tristan's thirst for revenge had taken a malevolent turn, and the city would soon bear witness to the consequences of his wrath.

Chapter 107

Tristan sat alone in his cramped prison cell; his thoughts consumed by the intricate web of revenge he had woven. The time had come to reflect on the pieces of his grand scheme that were now in motion, each element carefully designed to exact vengeance on those who had crossed him.

He gazed at the sprawling map he had drawn on the cell walls, each line and symbol representing a different aspect of his plan. It was a labyrinthine diagram, a testament to his relentless determination. With a piece of chalk, he traced the connections, his fingers following the intricate lines as he contemplated the chaos he had set in motion.

Detective Lam: Jun Wong, the corrupt police officer Tristan had cultivated as his inside man, was working his insidious magic. The trusted detective, once celebrated for bringing down criminals, was now unknowingly entangled in Tristan's intricate web. The plan was to undermine Lam's reputation, tarnishing his legacy in law enforcement.

Tengku Beans: Hakimi, the computer genius and newfound ally, had wormed his way into the Beans family through young Kyrie's fascination with gaming. It was a devious gambit, using an innocent child as a pawn in a dangerous game. Tristan envisioned the chaos that would ensue once the Beans family discovered the truth about Hakimi's ulterior motives.

Tengku Farhan: The Maestro, the enigmatic puppeteer, was orchestrating the financial turmoil that would implicate Tengku Farhan in a web of deceit. The scion of the Beans family would be brought to his knees, his pristine reputation shattered.

Choi: Tristan's thoughts turned to Choi, the man who had betrayed him. He had not forgotten the disloyalty that led to his capture. Revenge for Choi would be personal, a punishment that would make him rue the day he chose to betray Tristan.

Sam: And then there was Sam, the Port Authority employee whose cooperation with the authorities had exposed Tristan's smuggling operation. He, too, would face retribution for his betrayal.

With a final, sinister stroke of the chalk, Tristan outlined the remaining threads of his intricate plan. The pieces were in motion, and the city of Kuala Lumpur was teetering on the precipice of chaos. Tristan reveled in the knowledge that he was the unseen architect of this impending catastrophe.

As he surveyed the sprawling diagram on his cell wall, Tristan couldn't help but smile. His thirst for revenge had led him down a treacherous path, but he was resolute in his pursuit. The city would soon bear witness to the devastating consequences of his wrath, and there was no turning back.

Tristan had meticulously crafted a symphony of destruction, and he intended to savour every discordant note.

Epilogue

Detective Lam sat in his office; his gaze fixed on the wall of evidence he had meticulously built against the corrupt officials. His mind was a whirlwind of strategies and plans to take down the rotten core of the system. The concern etched on his face was a testament to the battles he knew lay ahead. His unwavering commitment to justice burned brighter than ever.

Tengku Beans, seemingly unshaken by the recent turmoil, continued to manage Tok and Beans Sdn Bhd. The shipping company thrived under his vigilant eye, expanding its reach and influence. He was determined to ensure that the illicit trade that had once tainted his business remained a distant memory.

Tengku Farhan had found solace in his new life. The scars of the past had healed, and he embraced the future with open arms. His work in financial services at TRX in Kuala Lumpur brought him a sense of purpose, and he cherished the moments spent with Tasha, his newfound love. Life seemed to have taken a brighter turn.

Sam and Choi, who had once been entangled in Tristan's web, carried on with their lives, grateful for the second chance they had been given. They had distanced themselves from the criminal underbelly, determined not to let their past mistakes define them.

Kyrie, the unsuspecting pawn in Tristan's plot, reveled in the excitement of his new gaming partner. The virtual world provided an escape from the complexities of reality, and he relished the challenges it presented.

Amidst the facade of normalcy, Alicia, Tengku Beans' wife, couldn't shake the unsettling feeling that something ominous loomed on the horizon. Her intuition whispered of impending upheaval, far worse than anything they had previously endured. She kept her apprehension to herself, unwilling to alarm her family, but she knew that their lives were far from tranquil.

In the quietude of their penthouse apartment in Port Klang, Alicia pondered the uncertainty of the future. The battles they had fought had left scars, but they had emerged stronger. Little did they know that their world, which had once been torn asunder, was about to be shaken once more.

As the days turned to weeks and the weeks to months, the city of Kuala Lumpur carried on, its residents blissfully unaware of the storm that brewed just beneath the surface. Tristan's shadow still loomed, a malevolent specter orchestrating a new symphony of chaos. The game was far from over, and the pieces were set for a chilling encore.

In the twilight of this chapter, the curtains fell, leaving the stage empty but for the whispered promise of another act, should fate decree it so.

Title: *Veil of Suspicion*

Summary:

In the quiet coastal town of Port Klang, where calm seas mask a turbulent underbelly, a seemingly chance encounter between Tengku Beans, a family man with a thriving shipping business, and Tristan, a seemingly down-on-his-luck stranger, sets off a chain of events that will shatter the tranquillity of their lives. Little does Tengku Beans know that beneath Tristan's facade lies a sinister plot to turn Tok and Beans into a front for illicit arms deals.

When Jack, a loyal employee of Tengku Beans, mysteriously disappears, the search for answers falls to Detective Lam. What starts as a simple missing person's case soon unravels into a web of international intrigue: arms smuggling across borders, a shocking kidnapping, and a chilling murder that shakes the foundations of Port Klang.

As Detective Lam races against time to unravel the truth, he unwittingly becomes a pawn in Tristan's dangerous game. With each revelation, the stakes soar higher, and the once-quiet town becomes a battleground of deception and danger.

The pursuit takes them on a manhunt that spans borders, leading to a confrontation with Tristan, who will stop at nothing to secure the illegal documents he needs to escape the country. But even behind bars, Tristan's thirst for revenge knows no bounds, casting a long shadow over Port Klang and beyond.

Veil of Suspicion is a gripping and suspenseful journey into the heart of darkness, where loyalties are tested, friendships strained, and justice hangs by a thread. From the quiet streets of Port Klang to the bustling metropolis of Kuala Lumpur, the search for truth will unveil a conspiracy that threatens to consume all in its path.

In this riveting tale of intrigue, danger, and revenge, the line between right and wrong blurs, and the cost of redemption may be too high to pay. Join us on a pulse-pounding adventure that will leave you questioning everything you thought you knew.

Genre: Mystery, Thriller, Crime Drama

■

■